In Maggie Robinson's sparkling new series, the quaint village in Gloucestershire is where the wayward sons and daughters of Great Britain's finest families come for some R&R—and good old-fashioned "rehab." But sometimes they find much more . . .

No one at Puddling-on-the-Wold ever expected to see Sarah Marchmain enter through its doors. But after the legendary Lady's eleventh-hour rejection of the man she was slated to marry, she was sent here to restore her reputation . . . and change her mind. It amused Sadie that her father, a duke, would use the last of his funds to lock her up in this fancy facility—she couldn't be happier to be away from her loathsome family and have some time to herself. The last thing she needs is more romantic distraction . . .

As a local baronet's son, Tristan Sykes is all too familiar with the spoiled, socialite residents of the Puddling Rehabilitation Foundation—no matter how real their problems may be. But all that changes when he encounters Sadie, a brave and brazen beauty who wants nothing more than to escape the life that's been prescribed for her. If only Tristan could find a way to convince the Puddling powers-that-be that Sadie is unfit for release, he'd have a chance to explore the intense attraction that simmers between them—and prove himself fit to make her his bride . . .

Books by Maggie Robinson

Cotswold Confidential Series

Schooling the Viscount

Seducing Mr. Sykes

The London List Series

Lord Gray's List

Captain Durant's Countess

Lady Anne's Lover

The Courtesan Court Series

Mistress by Mistake

"Not Quite a Courtesan" in *Lords of Passion*

Mistress by Midnight

Mistress by Marriage

Master of Sin

Novellas

"To Match a Thief" in *Improper Gentleman*

Published by Kensington Publishing Corporation

Seducing Mr. Sykes

Cotswold Confidential

Maggie Robinson

LYRICAL PRESS
Kensington Publishing Corp.
www.kensingtonbooks.com

LYRICAL PRESS BOOKS are published by

Kensington Publishing Corp.
119 West 40th Street
New York, NY 10018

All Kensington titles, imprints, and distributed lines are available at special quantity discounts for bulk purchases for sales promotion, premiums, fund-raising, educational, or institutional use.

Special book excerpts or customized printings can also be created to fit specific needs. For details, write or phone the office of the Kensington Sales Manager: Kensington Publishing Corp., 119 West 40th Street, New York, NY 10018. Attn. Sales Department. Phone: 1-800-221-2647.

Lyrical Press and Lyrical Press logo Reg. U.S. Pat. & TM Off.

First Electronic Edition: June 2017
eISBN-13: 978-1-5161-0001-9
eISBN-10: 1-5161-0001-8

First Print Edition: June 2017
ISBN-13: 978-1-5161-0004-0
ISBN-10: 1-5161-0004-2

Printed in the United States of America

Chapter 1

"It's Lady Maribel all over again," the grocer Frank Stanchfield muttered to his wife, checking the lock to his back room. "How the girl discovered the telegraph machine is a mystery."

Except it wasn't such a mystery, really. Lady Sarah Marchmain— "Sadie" to her late mama and very few friends—had eyes, after all, and there it was behind an open alley window, gleaming on a worn oak desk. She had climbed in, her tartan trousers very convenient for hoisting oneself into the building. After being caught trying to send a message to who knows who, she was now unrepentantly inspecting the jars of candy on the shop counter.

She might try to steal some of it, if only the shopkeepers would stop hovering over her.

"Bite your tongue!" Mrs. Stanchfield whispered, looking over nervously at Sadie. Apparently no one wanted another Lady Maribel de Winter in Puddling. The first had been bad enough. Sadie had heard of her in snatches from the villagers, and the woman's portrait hung in the parish hall. Her wicked reputation had outlived her, even if her decades of good works once she married had mitigated some of it. She had been a wild young thing who would have made Napoleon quake in his boots.

Or take her to bed. Lady Maribel had been, according to gossip, irresistible to men. Fortunately her husband, a local baronet called Sir Colin Sykes, had taken her in hand as best he could once they were married.

Sadie was determined never to be taken in hand.

Puddling was known as a famous reputation-restorer, a place to rusticate and recalibrate. Prominent British families had sent their difficult relatives here for almost eighty years. Lady Maribel was among the first to be gently incarcerated within its limits in 1807, according to the elderly vicar's wife, who seemed to know everything about everyone dating back to William the Conqueror.

Now it was Sadie's turn to be gently incarcerated, and she didn't like it one bit.

The village had a spotless reputation. It was a last resort before a harsher hospital, or worse, killing one's own offspring. Or parent. Lady Sarah Marchmain had angered her father so thoroughly that they'd come to blows. When the Duke of Islesford dropped her off, he had been sporting a significant black eye.

Well-deserved, in her opinion.

Sadie's own eyes were unbruised and light green, the color of beryl, or so her numerous suitors had said. Occasionally they threw in jade or jasper—it was all so much nonsense. Right now she was examining the penny candy in a glass jar, lots of shiny, jewel-like drops that looked so very tempting. Sweet, edible rubies and citrine, emeralds and onyx. Frank Stanchfield hustled over to the counter and screwed the lid on tighter.

She licked her lips. Unfortunately, she didn't have a penny to her name. She was entirely dependent on her housekeeper Mrs. Grace to dole out a pitiful allowance every Friday, and Friday was millions of days away. Sadie had spent the last of her money on a cinnamon bun earlier and had reveled in every bite.

Her father's draconian restrictions were designed to sting. Or so he thought. Sadie didn't really mind being impoverished and hungry in Puddling-on-the-Wold. It meant she was not about to be auctioned off to Lord Roderick Charlton, or any other idiot her idiot father owed money to.

The Duke of Islesford's taste in men and luck at cards was, to put it bluntly, execrable.

So far Sadie had overstayed her visit by one week. Originally consigned to her cottage for twenty-eight days, she had somehow not managed to be "cured" in that time.

Rehabilitated.

Restored.

Brought to reason.

Knuckle under was more like it. She was *not* getting married.

In fact, she'd like to stay in Puddling forever. It was very restful. Quiet. The little lending library was surprisingly well stocked, and she'd gotten a lot of reading done between lectures from the prosy ancient vicar who instructed her daily. She also helped Mrs. Grace keep the cottage up to a ducal daughter's snuff.

Despite the fact that Sadie had no interest in becoming a wife, she was remarkably domestic. It came of hanging about the kitchens of Marchmain Castle, she supposed. The servants had been her only friends when she was a little girl and she'd been eager to help them.

All that had changed after she was presented to the queen at seventeen, wearing those ridiculous hoops and feathers that threatened to put out someone's eye. Suddenly, Sadie became a commodity, a bargaining chip to improve her father's ailing finances. A surprising number of gentlemen— if you could call them that, since most men were absolute, avaricious, thoughtless pigs—were interested in acquiring a tall, redheaded, blue-blooded, sharp-tongued and two-fisted duke's daughter as wife. For the past four years, she'd avoided them with alacrity, aplomb, and those aforementioned fists.

Needless to say, her reputation was cemented in ruination.

It amused Sadie that her father was using the last of his funds to lock her away here in this very expensive Puddling prison, hoping that she would change her mind, acquiesce and marry the one man who remained steadfastly interested.

Not bloody likely.

She touched the glass jar with longing.

"What may we help you with, Lady Sarah?"

The poor grocer sounded scared to death. His wife hid behind him.

Sadie batted her lashes. Sometimes this feminine trick worked, although these Puddling people seemed remarkably impervious to charm. They were hardened souls, harboring the odd, uncooperative, and unwanted scions of society for a hefty fee, believing that being cruel to be kind was the only way.

"Do forgive my transgression, Mr. Stanchfield. I so longed to communicate with my old governess, Miss Mackenzie. Miss Mac, as I so affectionately call her. I found a book on telegraphy in the library and wondered if I had any aptitude for it," she lied. Science in all its forms confounded her. In truth, she'd read nothing but Gothic romances since her arrival, very much enjoying the fraying sixty-year-old books written by an anonymous baroness.

Moreover, Sadie's old governess had been dead for six years and had been an absolute Tartar in life. There had been little affection on her part,

Sadie thought ruefully. The woman was at this moment no doubt giving the devil a lesson on evil and grading him harshly.

"You know that's forbidden, miss. No telegrams, no letters. Perhaps when you are r-r-released, you may visit with the lady. A r-reason for your good behavior, what?"

Goodness, she was causing the poor fellow to stutter. She stilled her lashes.

"Ah." Sadie gave a dramatic sigh. "But I just can't seem to get the hang of it. Being Puddling-perfect, that is. Every time I get close, something seems to happen."

Like stealing Ham Ross's wheelbarrow full of pumpkins. It had been very difficult to push her loot uphill, and so many of the bloody orange things chose to roll out and smash along the road.

Or turning up in church in her tartan trousers...her *stolen* tartan trousers. Some poor Puddlingite was foolish enough to hang them on a clothesline to tempt her. After some tailoring—Sadie was handy with a needle—they fit her slender waist and long legs as if they were made for her.

Her father had always wanted a son. Instead her horrible cousin George would be the next duke, and Sadie would lose the only home—well, castle—she'd ever known.

It wasn't fair. She sighed again.

"Here, now, Lady Sarah. I don't suppose I'll miss a few boiled sweets." Mr. Stanchfield relented and unscrewed the jar, his wife looking disapproving behind him. He filled a paper twist with not nearly enough, and passed them to her.

Sadie saw her opportunity for well-deserved drama. Any chance to appear happily unhinged must be seized with two hands, so she might stay here in Puddling just a little longer. Dropping to the floor on her tartan-covered knees, she howled.

She had been practicing howling at night once her housekeeper Mrs. Grace went home. Her neighbors were under the impression a stray dog was in heat in the village, perhaps even a pack of them.

"Oh! You are too good to me! I shall remember this always!" She snuffled and snorted, slipping a red candy into her mouth. Red always tasted best.

"A polite thank you would do just as well."

The voice was chilly. Sadie looked up from her self-inflicted chest-pounding and the candy fell from her open mouth.

Good heavens. She had never seen this man before in all the walking she was made to do up and down the hills for her daily exercise. Where had he been hiding? He was *beautiful.*

No, not beautiful exactly. His haughty expression was too harsh for beauty. Compelling, perhaps. Arresting.

But, she reminded herself, he was a man, and therefore wanting. Lacking. Probably annoying. Not probably—certainly. Lady Sarah Jane Marchmain was twenty-one years old and had more than enough experience with men in her short lifetime to know the truth.

The man reached a gloveless hand to her to help her up, but it didn't look quite clean. Something green was under his fingernails—paint? Plant material? Sadie made a leap of faith and gripped it anyway, crunching her candy underfoot when he lifted her to her full height.

He was still taller than she was.

Not lacking there. Not lacking physically anywhere that she could see.

His hair was brown, curly and unruly, his eyebrows darker and formidable. His nose was strong and straight, his lips full, his face bronzed from the sun. His eyes—oh, his eyes. Blue was an inadequate adjective. Cerulean? Sapphire? Aquamarine? She'd have to consult a thesaurus.

But they weren't kind.

She found herself curtseying, her hand still firmly in his.

"Thank you, sir, for coming to my rescue." She fluttered her eyelashes again.

"You were in no danger on the floor. Mrs. Stanchfield sweeps it thrice a day. One could eat off it, it's so immaculate." He dropped Sadie's hand and kicked the crushed candy aside.

The grocer's wife pinked. "Thank you, Mr. Sykes."

Sykes. That was the name of the family the infamous Lady Maribel married into. Interesting.

"I only speak the truth, madam."

Sadie considered whether she should fall to the floor again. It would be fun to gauge this Mr. Sykes's strength if she pretended to swoon. Would he pick her up and hold her to his manly chest? Whisper assurances in her ear? Smooth loose tendrils of hair behind her pins?

But perhaps he'd just leave her there to rot. He wasn't even looking at her anymore.

Sadie was used to being looked at. For one thing, she was hard to miss. At nearly six feet, she towered over most men. Her flaming hair was another beacon, her skin pearlescent, her ample bosom startling on such a slender frame.

She had been chased by men mercilessly, even after she had made it crystal clear she had no interest. These past years had tested her wits and firmed her resolve. She was mistress of her own heart, body, and mind, and determined to remain so.

Mr. Sykes probably knew that—apparently everyone in Puddling had received a dossier on her. She'd come across a grease-stained one at the bakeshop under a tray of Bakewell tarts, and had tucked it into her pocket for quiet perusal, along with one delicious raspberry pastry. Theft was apparently in her blood.

It had been most informative. The dossier, not the tart. Sadie had been gleeful reading an account of her past recalcitrance. She rather admired the clever ways she'd gone about subverting her father's plans for her—she'd forgotten half of them.

It had meant, however, that she had to exercise creativity in Puddling and not repeat her previous pranks. No sheep in the dining room. No bladder filled with beet juice tossed out the window. No punching fiancés or fathers.

There was only the one father, but Sadie had endured several fiancés. The latest, Lord Roderick Charlton, was getting impatient. He'd given her father quite a lot of money to secure her hand. To be fair, he'd tried to woo Sadie with credible effort.

There wasn't anything really wrong with Roderick, she supposed. But there wasn't anything right about him either.

If Sadie could just resist the pressure to marry, she'd come into a substantial fortune when she turned twenty-five. She wouldn't have to turn it over to some man, and her father wouldn't be able to touch it. She could live her life just as she liked. She might even buy herself a small castle, if one could be found. One that wouldn't fall down around her ears. One that had working fireplaces and no rats.

However—and this was a *huge* however—the Duke of Islesford was threatening to have her declared incompetent, seize her funds, and lock her away in a most unpleasant private hospital. Sadie did not think it was an idle threat, and to some, it might look as if she deserved to be there.

She was much too old now for the tricks she'd played, and four years was a very, very long time to stall. Sadie was beginning to realize she hadn't done herself any favors with the pumpkins or the trousers or the howling.

But she couldn't succumb—she just couldn't. No matter how many times Mr. Fitzmartin, the elderly vicar, reminded her of a proper woman's place—as helper to her husband, silent in church, subordinate, obedient—she felt her fingers close into a fist.

Chapter 2

Tristan Sykes had not encountered the madwoman before. After just a few minutes with her, he felt enormous relief.

She was nothing like the heiress Greta Hamilton-Holmes, who last year had been coerced into an unhappy marriage with the unwitting assistance of the Puddling Rehabilitation Foundation. The unfortunate circumstances of her stay here had alerted the entire village that perhaps the enrollment process and instructional methods needed some adjustment and modernization. Not everything was always as it seemed. The foundation's governors were wary now of believing everything that was reported about their Guests.

Poor Greta had been an innocent, a pawn in her ambitious mother's game to marry her child off to an earl. But Lady Sarah Marchmain was no innocent. Any man who married her would have to sleep with one eye open and a dagger under his pillow.

She was cunning. Devious. Sly. A consummate actress, even though she was so young. She probably *should* be shut away where she couldn't cause anyone harm. Her father the duke was at his wit's end, her fiancé the viscount bereft. She'd already been in Puddling beyond the usual amount of time, with no sign of progress.

She was headstrong. Spoilt. Wicked. But rather attractive all the same.

Those pants...well. If women were allowed to wear them on a regular basis, men would not be responsible for their actions. The world would go to hell in a handbasket.

Tristan clouted himself mentally. Now that he was in charge of the foundation in his father's absence, he *had* to be responsible. He owed it to the village. He was not about to fall for the lures of an unrepentant hoyden and her derriere.

Those flirtatious, foxy lashes, the tremulous pout, those enormous br—. He lifted his eyes to the shop ceiling where it was safe from feminine pulchritude.

No cobwebs were to be seen.

He knew all about dukes' daughters. His grandmother had been one. Triston had loved her, but one had to acknowledge that Granny Maribel had been headstrong, spoilt and wicked, too.

Her son and his father, Sir Bertram Sykes, trusted Tristan to repair the family's and foundation's reputation while he was away, and so far, Tristan had. The Guests this year had returned to society whole, healthy and ready to make something of their lives. The new vicar Tristan had hired, a man married to his wife for over fifty years, was not going to forget his vows and fall for a scarlet-haired vixen in his care. Mr. Fitzmartin was a steady, sober old fellow, and if his sermons were not riveting, neither were they revolutionary. Puddling was back to normal, even if Sir Bertram remained in Paris.

Tristan was content to be left alone at the Sykes estate. The grounds were coming along, particularly the memorial garden Tristan had planted for his younger brother Wallace. Poor Wallace had died before he'd had to shave regularly. It had been a wretched waste, and Tristan wasn't sure he'd ever forgive himself for not paying enough attention to the boy while he'd lived.

Wallace had worshipped him, which Tristan had found rather absurd. He was nothing special then and he was nothing special now. Apart from his green fingers, Tristan Sykes was a most ordinary man. The only distinctive things about him were his fierce eyebrows, and all the Sykes males share that familial trait. The females sometimes too, poor things.

Despite his time in London, he was a country man to his scuffed boots, and luckier than most. His family was rich and influential, and he had a substantial fortune of his own left to him by his imperious grandmother. If living year round in Puddling-on-the-Wold was not precisely thrilling, he at least felt useful taking his father's place at the foundation and on the school committee. If Sir Bertram never returned, Tristan was prepared to lead.

His next instance of leading meant he probably should take the madwoman home. The two Stanchfields were unequal to handling her—they'd already given her candy. They had no difficulty steaming envelopes open and destroying correspondence, but face-to-face dealings with the Guests had never been their forte.

He turned from the quivering couple. "Lady Sarah, allow me to escort you back to Stonecrop Cottage."

She blinked those unusual eyes. He'd surprised her. Had she been planning more caterwauling? Another flop to the floor? Her dramatics were tedious in the extreme, and he was most averse to dramatics.

And Tristan suspected they were deliberate. She'd made an effort to defy her treatment and remain in Puddling. She was probably no more deranged than he was.

But if you pretended to be deranged, didn't that actually make you deranged? It was a conundrum. Both the vicar and Dr. Oakley had advised she continue her course of rehabilitation. If today's behavior was any indication, she'd never be fit to go home.

"To Stonecrop Cottage?" She sounded like she'd never heard of the place.

"Yes. Your temporary home in Puddling." Tristan emphasized the "temporary." It was imperative they cycle Guests in and out of the three cottages that were available to them as quickly as possible. Puddling's fortune depended upon it, and the waiting list was long. There were many, many crackpots in the best families of the United Kingdom of Great Britain and Ireland who needed redirecting and restoration.

"Now? But I haven't finished my walk."

"Beggin' yer pardon, Mr. Sykes, but Lady Sarah climbed in the backroom window this morning. The other governors should be informed." Mr. Stanchfield tried to puff out his chest at peaching upon their troublesome Guest but failed. There simply wasn't much to puff.

Tristan noted the green fire that flashed from Lady Sarah's eyes, and the grocer's flinch. "I thought we were friends, Mr. Stanchfield. I expected better of you."

"Mr. Stanchfield is obligated to report on your activities, Lady Sarah. We all are. It's for your own protection."

"Protection! Hah. As if any of you really cared." Her lower lip thrust in mulishness. It was very...pink. Had anyone ever said no to her before? Likely not.

"I assure you we take our responsibility for your health very seriously. We have an obligation to your father."

"My father! You should be obligated to *me*! My father wouldn't care if I fell in a vat of boiling oil as long as he got his hands on some money."

Tristan lifted an eyebrow. "The duke is very concerned for you." The man had written nearly daily inquiring about Lady Sarah's progress, and had been bitterly disappointed to learn that she was enrolled in a second month of rehabilitation.

Tristan was aware of all the particulars—how Lady Sarah defied her father, eschewed marriage, and created scandal wherever she went. Tristan could sympathize with the first part—he had no interest in the institution himself. After Linnet, he was unwilling to find himself in a woman's coils again. But Lady Sarah should marry and have children—it was what women did, whether they were duke's daughters or grocer's girls.

Lady Sarah stomped off in the direction of the shop door, but not before knocking a basket of onions over. Without breaking stride, she apologized over her shoulder and pulled the door open.

Tristan was right behind her, watching her plaid bottom swing from side to side. He should have helped the Stanchfields pick up the produce but felt it was more important to get Lady Sarah back where she belonged. She appeared to be in a considerable temper, her cheeks very flushed. Who knew what she'd knock over next?

He had no trouble keeping up with her, but Puddling was an exceptionally hilly Cotswold village. By the time they got to the corner of New Street, they were both breathless. It was nearly as difficult to go down as up; one had to mind one's steps or one would barrel right down the road like a runaway hedgehog.

He took a breath and steadied them both, tucking her arm firmly in the crook of his elbow. The air was perfumed by smoke; someone must be burning leaves. The early fall day was very fine—he could almost imagine them out for a normal stroll if she wasn't struggling so against his control. She glared and descended even faster, nearly dragging him down Honeywell Lane.

And then she shrieked, tripped over the cobblestones and brought them both to their knees.

"What the devil are you trying to do now?" he barked, thoroughly annoyed. He cared nothing for his clothing, although she had managed to find the only patch of pumpkin pulp left for them to slip in. Tristan had paid for the road's clean-up crew out of his own pocket.

She pointed up, speechless, and Tristan's heart tripped.

Stonecrop Cottage was on fire.

Lady Sarah scrambled up before he had a chance to stop her. She dashed down the middle of the road, her hair unravelling from its mooring. It fell in sheets of copper and gold and rust past her waist, and it took Tristan a minute to forgo his metallic illusions and gather up his wits and follow her.

St. Jude's church bells were now sounding throughout the valley, their particular cadence a call for help. Villagers were coming out of their houses, sleeves rolled up, aprons tossed.

They knew where they were needed. The black plume of smoke was obvious now that he was looking at the sky rather than his unwilling companion.

Puddling had no organized fire department, or any real emergency plans. An oversight, Tristan realized, which he would correct once the current crisis was over.

It was imperative to get water up from Puddling Stream, and he shouted orders as he ran down the hill. Horses were hitched, wagons dispatched. There was the Honey Well, too, older than the village itself, and not quite so far. Every cottage had a rain barrel.

It would have to do.

Where was the bloody madwoman? He half-expected to see her on her knees in the little garden howling again, but there was no trace of her. Smoke was pouring out of open windows, and he heard the sharp crackle of flames at the rear of the house.

The blue-painted front door stood ajar, its pebbled glass shining in the sun. It had been a beautiful, cloudless day until that moment.

She couldn't have been stupid enough to enter a burning house, could she?

Tristan pulled his neckcloth up over his mouth and tore off his coat. Holding it over his head, he fanned the smoke away.

Tristan had been in this cottage dozens of times—he'd been on the committee when it was designed and built a few years ago. He was an architect, after all, even if the Foundation had not followed all his suggestions. He imagined Lady Sarah had to duck under the low lintels upstairs. One of Puddling's previous Guests had knocked himself unconscious on a regular basis.

The little hallway was empty, the conservatory at the left untouched aside from drifting smoke. A wall of heat came from the kitchen straight in front of him.

And *then* he heard the howling. The hair stood up on the back of his neck.

He dashed into the kitchen, where the wall behind the range seemed to be on fire. Lady Sarah was bent over an inert body, attempting to drag it out of harm's way.

Mrs. Grace, the housekeeper. The woman's white cap was singed, her face the color of the thick smoke in the room.

"Get out of here! I've got her." Tristan tossed his coat to the duke's daughter and gathered up Millie Grace. A few villagers entered the kitchen, sloshing buckets of water in the direction of the fire. Tristan elbowed his way out, pushing Lady Sarah in front of him.

He laid Mrs. Grace on the garden bench by the koi pond. The air outside wasn't much better than it had been in the cottage.

He turned to the madwoman. "What the hell were you thinking?"

Lady Sarah's pale face was streaked with soot, but she stood tall and met his eyes.

"I don't like her—in fact, she is the most hateful person I have ever met, and I've met a few. She's worse than my old governess, always spying on me and saying something spiteful. But I knew she was inside fixing me some sort of bland, boring lunch."

"She has your best interests at heart," Tristan snapped. The bland, boring Puddling diet calmed the blood—everyone knew it. Softening, he added, "Thank you for trying to save her. Millie Grace is an integral part of the Puddling Rehabilitation Foundation."

"You couldn't obtain Attila the Hun's services? No, I suppose not—he's dead, isn't he? *She's* an absolute witch." Lady Sarah looked down. "I'm going to loosen her collar. You should fetch Dr. Oakley."

Damn her, but she was right, not about the witch part, but the doctor. Millie Grace was firm because she had to be. She'd had years of experience dealing with difficult Guests, and it wouldn't help any of them if she was too soft-hearted.

Hell was paved with good intentions by weak-willed individuals, and it was Puddling's steely mission to divert as many of its Guests to Heaven eventually.

After a few quick words, Tristan left the villagers to fight the fire and ran up the hill to Oakley's house. He met the older man halfway; he'd heard the bells, too.

When they returned to Stonecrop Cottage, Mrs. Grace's head was in Lady Sarah's lap, and the duke's daughter was massaging the housekeeper's temples. Mrs. Grace's hair covering had fallen to the ground, and her silver strands were as loose as Lady Sarah's.

"There, there. They're here, Mrs. Grace. Everything will be all right," Lady Sarah said in a soothing voice. If Tristan didn't know better, he'd think she actually cared.

Chapter 3

Well, this was a fine kettle of fish. The stupid Puddling people had no place to put her. The other two Foundation cottages had Guests—an elderly gentleman who liked to remove his trousers at inconvenient times in inappropriate places, and the widow of an earl who had just come to get away from it all and think. She'd actually signed *herself* in to the Puddling Program—there were no disapproving family members who wanted to get rid of her.

Sadie thought the world was full of places she'd much rather think in, but to each his own. She imagined the widow was trying to escape from something, and Sadie could sympathize.

To make matters worse, trying to save Mrs. Grace's life—although Mr. Sykes had officially done so—had apparently earned Sadie credit toward her Service and she might actually be released ahead of schedule. Each Puddling Guest was required to do something for the community or the wider world before they left, and Sadie had ensured that other Guests would be under Mrs. Grace's gimlet eye in the future.

Lucky them.

Right now, however, the woman was recuperating at home, her burned hands bandaged. She would not be cooking anything disgusting for anyone for a while.

Stonecrop Cottage was not a total loss, but the kitchen would have to be rebuilt, and new fittings and fixtures installed throughout the house. The smoke and water had damaged even the bedrooms upstairs, and every item Sadie had brought with her was ruined.

Which left her in her tartan trousers and dirty white blouse.

She held a cup of tea in the vicarage sitting room. Mrs. Fitzmartin smiled vaguely at her, her teeth on the yellow side. But they were all there, no mean feat for anyone so elderly. The rumbling of voices came from Mr. Fitzmartin's study, where the seven Puddling Rehabilitation Foundation governors were trying to figure out what to do with the Duke of Islesford's daughter.

It must be awfully crowded in there.

"A biscuit, Lady Sarah? I made them myself." Mrs. Fitzmartin passed a shaking plate. The woman was ancient and wrinkled and sweet, the perfect clergyman's wife. She had gone out of her way to be hospitable to Sadie, giving her one of the few warm welcomes she'd received in Puddling. Everyone else just looked at her as if they feared she was about to punch them.

Her reputation had clearly preceded her.

Sadie took one and bit into it. Oh dear. Perfection didn't extend into the kitchen. Salt for the sugar? Very likely. Perhaps Sadie could give Mrs. Fitzmartin a foolproof biscuit recipe before she left. She was quite proud of her cooking, which was why Mrs. Grace's meals were such a disappointment.

"How long have you and Mr. Fitzmartin been married?" Sadie asked, after discreetly spitting the salty mouthful into her napkin.

"Fifty-eight years."

"Golly. That's a long time." Sadie couldn't imagine being married for fifty-eight minutes.

"It is. But we've been very happy. Virgil has been a good husband. He had retired, you know, but then this opportunity to serve Puddling came up. The village is lovely, isn't it?"

Sadie supposed it was. Charming gold-gray Cotswold stone cottages lined the narrow streets. The *five* narrow streets. One couldn't get lost here easily. The green hills in the distance were dotted with sheep and oozed tranquility.

Maybe the earl's widow had the right of it. It was a pretty place to get away from it all.

"The current church dates to the fourteenth century, you know. There is speculation it was built on a Norman foundation. That villain Cromwell did his best, but the tower still stands. Have you seen the cannon damage on the north side?"

Sadie had not looked up that high. It was tricky to maneuver in Puddling, the uneven surfaces a challenge for the most intrepid walker.

"I'm afraid I haven't. Do you fancy yourself an amateur historian, Mrs. Fitzmartin?"

"Churches are of special interest to me, naturally. But Anne Boleyn stayed near here on her ill-fated honeymoon...."

Mrs. Fitzmartin continued, and Sadie lent half an ear. Men didn't behead their wives anymore, but there were other ways to show their displeasure and deprive women of autonomy. Husbands, fathers—what really was the difference?

"Absolutely not!"

The bellow came from the study, causing Mrs. Fitzmartin to interrupt her local points of interest lecture.

"Another biscuit?" she asked gamely, as if there weren't shouting coming from the next room.

"No thank you." Sadie set her teacup down.

What if they decided to reward her heroism by sending her home?

That wouldn't do at all.

There was nothing for it. She slid to the floor and began to twitch and moan, being careful not to kick over the tea table. Sadie sincerely hoped Mrs. Fitzmartin would not follow suit.

"Virgil!" the woman shrieked. "Dr. Oakley!"

The thunder of footsteps alerted Sadie that it was show time.

"The smoke! The smoke! I cannot see!"

"You would if you opened your eyes, Lady Sarah."

Smug bastard. Even with her eyes closed, she knew who spoke.

"What is wrong with her?" a female voice asked.

"An excellent question, Miss Churchill. I would say *nothing.*"

Damn that Mr. Sykes. He was all too perspicacious.

"Sometimes individuals react to trauma after the fact. She has lost everything to the smoke and water damage, all her little bits and bobs, you know. Step aside, please." Sadie could hear Dr. Oakley kneel down next to her, his joints creaking. His warm hand rested on her forehead. "No fever. Lady Sarah, can you hear me?"

"Throw some water on her." Mr. Sykes again.

Ooh, if she ever got the opportunity, she'd throw some water on *him.*

"My puppy. Where is my puppy? We must save little Lancelot." Sadie was tired, and somewhat desperate. It was the best she could do.

"Lady Sarah, wake up. You are in Puddling, and you have been very brave."

Dr. Oakley was so nice. She hadn't really seen all that much of him this past month, being perfectly healthy, but wouldn't mind having her forehead rubbed with such tenderness a while longer.

Since her mother died, tenderness had been in short supply at Marchmain Castle.

She fluttered her lashes. "Who are you? Who am I?"

Mr. Sykes bent over her, his eyebrows ferocious. "All right, all right, I'll do it. Anyone who would act in this nonsensical fashion *must* be disturbed. I warn you, Lady Sarah, I will not be taken in by you and your antics. For the next three weeks, you shall behave yourself, avail yourself of counseling and accept your fate. Then *go home*. And don't ask who I am, because you damn well know."

"You'll do what?" Sadie asked, not caring for his tone.

Dr. Oakley patted her hand. "The governors have decided the best place for you is Sykes House. There really is no other suitable accommodation at the moment. And there is precedent here for using the property as a respite for our Guests. I'm sure you'll be very comfortable."

Sadie sat up and grabbed Dr. Oakley's soothing hand. "What? I can't live with him! It's—it's not proper! He is a man!" And a disagreeable one at that.

"How astute you are, Lady Sarah. I don't live in the house itself, but my father's staff will be at your disposal. Reverend Fitzmartin will be welcome to give you your daily instruction—I can send a carriage for him. But I warn you, I will not extend my family's hospitality beyond this next month, whether you are fit to rejoin society or not. I have my limits." He glared at her, then turned to glare at the other governors.

"I won't do it!" Sadie said.

He raised an eyebrow. "Oh? Then I assume you'll want to return to your father's house."

"No! I mean, I'm not ready!"

And then Sadie did something most uncharacteristic. She broke into genuine tears, sobbing quietly onto her plaid-clad lap. There were no wolflike wails or arm-flailing, just honest dismay to find herself in such a predicament.

She never cried. It wasn't worthwhile. Now to fight—to yell and shout—that was the way to express emotion. What was more pointless than a woman's tears? She took a shuddering breath.

Miss Churchill patted her head. "It will be all right. We haven't lost a Guest yet. I'm sure with a little more time, you'll know your duty."

Duty! Duty was for soldiers and mothers and prime ministers. She certainly owed no allegiance to her father, who had only realized her usefulness when he was strapped for cash.

Mr. Sykes tugged her elbow. "Come on. Up and at 'em. Miss Churchill, could you see about acquiring some proper clothing for our Guest? She cannot go about Puddling looking like *that*."

Not to mention that Sadie didn't have a fresh pair of knickers left. Or a hairbrush.

"Can't I go shopping?"

"Not allowed, and anyway you have no money." Mr. Sykes seemed to take extraordinary pleasure in that.

"But surely, this is an emergency. I realize I'm supposed to remain in Puddling for the foreseeable future, but there is no dressmaker's shop here."

"We'll contrive something, don't you worry, my dear."

Sadie looked at Miss Churchill, whom no one could admire for her fashion sense. The woman looked like a Quaker, all in gray with a very depressing bonnet on her white curls.

"I—I can sew, if I have suitable fabric," Sadie offered. So what if she'd never made an entire dress—she'd been resourceful all her life. She'd tailored these trousers, hadn't she? If she wound up resembling Miss Churchill during her stay here, she really *would* go mad.

Chapter 4

Of all the bedeviling nuisances. Tristan installed his charge at Sykes House, with orders for a hot bath for his unwanted company to get the grime off her. He didn't care what she put on afterward, as long as it wasn't those scandalous trousers.

But he wouldn't see her anyway. He wasn't about to dine with the madwoman every evening. He'd go mad himself.

Tristan stomped off to the garden folly that he'd turned into his own home. The ingeniousness of the Sykes's Rococo-style pleasure gardens had been known far and wide across the land since 1757, when they had received their first formal visitor. Even Farmer George, King George III, had come once to discuss heritage vegetables and roses with Tristan's great-grandfather before the monarch had gone cuckoo.

In fact, the late king was something of an inspiration to the villagers. His mysterious illness had given them the idea to open up as a rest spa without the filthy-tasting mineral water. Puddling was a calming sort of place—nothing to do, nowhere to go. A place of quiet and reflection and great natural beauty. The steepness of the hills was ideal for healthful exercise, the weather clement, the air fresh, unspoiled from the black belch of factories.

Several people were encouraged to open up their weavers' cottages to paying Guests, and the simplicity of the surroundings were a balm to the over-stimulated, over-fed and over-bred sons and daughters of the nobility. One could think here, and repent of youthful and embarrassing indiscretions.

Word of mouth spread quickly, and soon the village's coffers were full of insurance money from Britain's first families designed to reserve a spot, if necessary. Lunatics could turn up in any generation, and it was best to be prepared.

In 1807, Tristan's own paternal grandmother, Lady Maribel de Winter, the Duke of Huntington's youngest daughter, was consigned here. She had vociferously objected to being housed in a humble weaver's cottage, and wound up in Sykes House.

Where she promptly drove Tristan's grandfather to distraction, then marriage.

History would not repeat itself if Tristan could help it.

He forged up his path. It always cheered him to see the red Jacobean folly on the hill. When they were boys, Tristan and Wallace had thought it a great lark to take turns sleeping in the various quaint outbuildings scattered throughout the gardens, but the Red House had always been Tristan's favorite.

It had never been intended for full-time occupation—in fact, Tristan could remember his grandmother and mother taking tea there with their friends, a chamber pot tucked discreetly behind an Indian screen and servants running back and forth to the main house for extra lemon slices and cakes.

But when Tristan had returned to Puddling after the debacle with Linnet, he sought privacy. Sir Bertram had always been an interfering sort of father, and now he had even more reason. He'd lost one son, and wanted to make sure the surviving one upheld the Sykes banner, especially after Tristan's scandalous divorce.

But the man had meddled enough in Tristan's affairs. It had suited Tristan to use his design skills to expand the folly and make the little building a home. And to see Sykes House at the far, far end of the wide sweep of gardens. He was always welcome to use the house's amenities, but even now that his father was abroad, he rarely stopped in.

Tristan was rather grubby himself. After he'd gotten the women settled under Dr. Oakley's care earlier, he'd helped the villagers fight the fire. Tristan sniffed his sleeve. He was afraid his clothes were now fit for the burn pile.

He was greeted by his valet cum butler cum cook, Anstruther, whom Tristan had stolen—liberated, really—from the main house a few months prior. The two of them lived rather simply in their five rooms, which suited them both.

Sykes House's formal entrance was about a mile from Puddling proper, but most of the servants summoned by the bells of St. Jude had dashed down the shortcut through the estate's back gate. Anstruther had done his share, and had changed into a fresh set of clothing from the last time Tristan had seen him.

"I have a bath ready for you, Mr. Tristan. But it may have cooled. What took you so long to get home?"

"A meeting with the governors about the madwoman. Lady Sarah. I had to bring her here."

"*Here?*" Anstruther was plainly aghast.

"Not *here* here. She's at Sykes House. You needn't have any contact with her. I don't plan to."

Anstruther was, on the whole, not especially fond of women, including his own wife Mrs. Anstruther, the housekeeper-cook at Sykes House. He was much relieved to be away from her and happy to be in Tristan's bachelor quarters.

Tristan was sure there was a secret story somewhere, but as he had one of his own, didn't pry. Marriage was usually until death, and if one were ill-matched, death would be preferable. As far as he knew, the Anstruthers had not spoken in a couple of years, which had made things a touch awkward in the servants' hall. The old butler had jumped at the chance to defect to smaller quarters with fewer responsibilities.

"I'd like some tea. No, make that a whiskey," Tristan said, untying and unbuttoning as he went to the bathing chamber. A quick look in the mirror told him a bath was most definitely in order. His face was as black as a chimneysweep's. No wonder Miss Churchill had handed him her lace-edged handkerchief.

"If you have no further need of me, Mr. Tristan, I shall pick some fresh lettuce to go along with your supper."

Tristan waved him away. The vegetable garden was directly outside Sykes House's kitchen door. Maybe Anstruther wished to catch a glimpse of his estranged wife and stick his tongue out at her.

Tristan tossed his clothes in a corner and sank into the tub, not much minding that the temperature had cooled. There was a great deal to think about.

Perhaps three Guest cottages were not sufficient, especially given that an emergency might occur, like today. Stonecrop was the newest and most up-to-date, the most desirable; the others were eighteenth-century buildings with fewer amenities and reserved for less particular and exalted Guests.

The Puddling Rehabilitation Foundation prided itself on attentive, appropriate care, but there was no reason the governors couldn't monitor five Guests rather than three. The waiting list for Puddling's special services was extensive. Not that Tristan thought the village should be running a hospital—that would rather defeat the purpose of individual, tailor-made care. But surely a few more modern cottages would improve the quality of residency, and, more to the point, increase the villagers' income. It was share and share alike here—every Puddlingite received an annual bonus for simply living within Puddling's boundaries.

Sipping his drink, he cast his mind about for vacant lots and land close enough to the center of the village. Keeping an eye on the Guests was a group effort, and no cog was too small. Even the schoolchildren had their role to play.

Could Reverend Fitzmartin handle the additional responsibility? The man was almost eighty. For the first time, Tristan doubted his decision to hire him.

But if Fitzmartin wasn't up to it, the plain fact was the man wouldn't live forever, may God forgive Tristan for borrowing trouble. Or perhaps an assistant could be hired. A young curate who wanted to make his mark, who would see the opportunity for his career. Many a Puddling padre had advanced in the church, being silent repositories of society's juiciest scandals.

Tristan could draw up some plans. Not charge for his services, of course. Simplicity was best, but a few harmless flourishes—

He was getting ahead of himself. He'd have to run any proposal by the governors, and they might think he was being too ambitious.

He ducked his head under the tepid water, scrubbing his hair with the bar of soap and rinsing. When he popped back up, the soap slipped straight from his fingers with a splash.

"What the blazes are *you* doing here? Anstruther!"

"If you mean that cadaverous old man, I saw him clear across the lawn. He was carrying a basket, heading toward the main house." Lady Sarah was sitting on the towels that were placed on a wooden chair. His towels. The towels he most desperately needed just now.

She adjusted them beneath her bottom. At least she was no longer wearing a pair of gentleman's pants, but he couldn't say her dress was becoming. It was so...brown. "He left the front door wide open, you know."

Tristan counted to ten. He suspected it would only amuse her if he went off like a rocket. "Lady Sarah, my door is always open to you. But perhaps now is not the time for a little chat."

"I didn't know you lived here. I thought it was a garden folly."

"It used to be. How may I help you, Lady Sarah?"

She looked about. "It's rather charming."

"I find it so." Tristan counted to twenty. "It may have come to your attention that I am presently in my bathtub."

"Yes, I see that. Your housekeeper helped me with mine. She is much nicer than Mrs. Grace."

Tristan resolved to speak to the woman at the earliest opportunity to be nastier.

Once he had clothes on.

Lady Sarah frowned. "Her name is Anstruther too, I believe."

"That is correct." A wave of gooseflesh marched up his neck and into his scalp.

"Is she your man's wife? Or his sister?"

"Lady Sarah, I will be happy to discuss the relationship status and genealogy of every single member of my staff at another time. It cannot have entirely escaped your notice that I am naked. In my bath." His hands were now beneath the water where they needed to be.

"So you are. And right where I want you so you can't run away or fob me off. I thought we should get a few things ironed out."

"And what might they be?" Tristan ground out. He longed for a very hot iron to toss in her direction.

"My routine. Who is to monitor me?"

Even before Mrs. Grace set the kitchen on fire, she had fallen down on her job. Someone should have been with the madwoman at all times, accompanying her on her walks. Lady Sarah Marchmain was not to be trusted. Those tartan trousers were proof of that.

"I will inquire. It was more important to find you a place to stay. I trust Sykes House is suitable?" The Sykes family might not own a duchy, but no one could find fault with the comfort and decoration of the manor house.

"It's all right. Nice enough. The gardens are exquisite."

Ignoring her first two sentences, Tristan felt a surge of pride. The gardens were exquisite because of his efforts, but he wasn't going to claim credit. Nor did he wish to discuss gardening when he was bollocky bare-ass.

"If that is all then? I am sure you could use the time before dinner to become more settled. The library is at your disposal, of course."

"Will you be joining me? For dinner, I mean?"

Tristan heard a tiny bit of wistfulness in her voice, but he stuck to his guns. "I'm afraid not. I have other plans." He was eating fresh lettuce.

By himself.

"Just as well. I have nothing to wear."

"You've got something on now," Tristan pointed out.

"Mrs. Anstruther persuaded one of the maids to lend me a dress. I know it's probably her best. But look." She pointed to her feet. No, her ankles. Actually, her calves. The madwoman was showing quite a bit of leg. None of the Sykes servants were as tall as Lady Sarah, not even the men.

"You can hem it or something. Didn't you say you sewed?"

"Are you absolutely, positively sure you cannot take me shopping? I don't think my father would like to know I was in a servant's castoffs. They might depress me and cause me to do something I shouldn't."

Like invade a man's bathing chamber. Tristan wondered what her "depression" might lead her to do next.

"We'll see."

She leaped up, clapping her hands. "Oh, goody! You are not as horrible as I thought you were. I'll be ready at nine tomorrow morning. Unless that is too early for you. Stroud is the closest town, isn't it? And I expect the Puddling Rehabilitation Foundation will pick up the tab, as it was Mrs. Grace's negligence that caused me to lose all my beautiful things."

"If they were so beautiful, why have you been strutting around in men's trousers since Sunday?" Tristan asked.

Point, Sykes.

Chapter 5

Sadie sat back down, enjoying how his face went from smug to dismayed. This was far more enjoyable and educational than she'd expected. For one thing, she had not expected to find Mr. Sykes in such a compromising position, or find him at all. She'd simply wandered out of the house to inspect the gardens, which were quite the loveliest she'd ever seen.

Everything was visible from a terraced lookout behind the house. There was a Gothic exedra curving around a round pool below, and a Doric seat, a tunnel arbor, late-blooming roses of every description, and vast lawns crisscrossed by packed earth paths that led to a rectangular reflecting pool at the center of the garden. Cunning little outbuildings and statuary were scattered everywhere, and a low boxwood maze wound up a distant hill. There were groomed forests and wild woods, water features, a stream, and a dovecote. Ostensibly she was out to dry her hair in the September afternoon breeze, and she had skipped down the stairs for a closer look.

A wide swath of lawn led to a charming asymmetric Jacobean-style folly, rather like a large doll's house. It was a mellow, fading red, and red had ever been Sadie's favorite color. So it was inevitable that she headed to it like a homing pigeon.

Sadie had never seen a full-grown man in the nude before, despite numerous thwarted attempts. She'd even wondered a little about the other Guest who was prone to dropping his pants. But Mr. Sykes was not a mad elderly gentleman. In fact, he was an exceptionally fine specimen, with broad brown shoulders and intriguing fur that dusted his chest. It was unfortunate that the bathtub was so full of soapy water, and that he was so diligent in protecting his manhood from Sadie's prying eyes by rather capable-looking hands and a large sea sponge.

His hair was slicked back from a noble brow, and his blue eyes were piercing. If Sadie had been a different person, she might be intimidated.

"It was a social experiment, you see. I wanted to know how it would feel to move about without obstruction. Like a man. We woman are covered in all those heavy layers, you know. Wire cage bustles and yards of petticoats. It's a wonder we can stand up and put one foot in front of the other and not topple over. And then once I put the trousers on, I decided there was no need for my boned corset, either, so I went without. Altogether it was very freeing."

The tips of his ears turned red.

Interesting.

"I shall return the trousers, of course. If I can remember where I, um, found them," Sadie added.

"Found them! You stole them from Arthur Babbage's clothesline! He saw you at the fire and told me."

For a brief, hopeful moment, Sadie thought he might rise out of the tub like a vengeful Neptune. But alas.

"Well, you can thank him for his inadvertent assistance with my experiment. I'm very grateful, and I'm sure I can alter them back to their original condition. Although they do smell dreadfully of smoke."

"I'm sure he won't care. What were you thinking? Theft is serious. So is breaking and entering." He was glaring at her, his expressive eyebrows a little frightening.

"I didn't break anything. The Stanchfields' window was wide open."

"Trespassing then. I won't have that sort of behavior here at Sykes House."

Sadie flicked her lashes, then looked down at the floor in faux contrition. "No, sir."

"I don't believe a word you say," Mr. Sykes grumbled.

"I will try. I promise." Her fingers crossed in the capacious folds of her borrowed dress. What it lacked in length was more than made up in girth.

It might prove very stimulating to experiment with Mr. Sykes. Nothing too *outré*—Sadie had to tread carefully. She sensed he would use any excuse to send her back to her father whether she was cured or not.

She cleared her throat. "I was wondering. While I'm here, do you think I might help your gardening staff? I know from the Welcome Packet I'm supposed to perform a Service before I leave, and since I'm here—" She twirled a loose copper lock around her uncrossed finger. She'd found the Welcome Packet to be less than welcoming, all the Puddling Rehabilitation Rules spelled out in menacing capital letters. But Sadie liked gardens—

she didn't know much about them, but how hard could tending them be? She could deadhead flowers and water things. She probably shouldn't be trusted with a scythe, however. "Idle hands, etcetera."

Mr. Sykes opened his mouth but nothing came out.

"Have I surprised you? I used to help in the kitchens at the castle."

"My garden?"

"Well, I understand it's really your father's."

"A garden is not like a kitchen, Lady Sarah."

"Obviously. For one thing, it won't catch on fire."

"Hopefully. But with you in its vicinity, anything is possible."

"I had nothing to do with the fire in the cottage!" Sadie said, feeling the warmth flood her cheeks. "Mrs. Grace said herself she forgot all about the Bath buns. Not that she'd give *me* any."

Sugar or anything that might be construed as delicious was forbidden. She hadn't eaten such revolting pap since she'd been an infant in arms. It wasn't as if she needed to slim—Sadie was tall and lean, with the exception of her embarrassing breasts. She blamed her mother, who had been so well-endowed both physically and financially that her father had overlooked her common background and married her, much to their mutual regret.

"We have rules in place, even to the comestibles of our Guests," Mr. Sykes said. "There is nothing wrong with plain, nutritious fare."

Rules, rules, rules. Sadie was heartily sick of them. Sadie would bet Mr. Sykes wouldn't sit still for the swill that had been served to her over the past month. She was hopeful that Mrs. Anstruther's kitchen skills would be an improvement.

"You haven't eaten Mrs. Grace's cooking, have you?"

"I have not had that pleasure. Now, if that is all, perhaps you will leave me in peace. My bathwater is cold."

Sadie stretched her neck, but was unable to see the effect of the cold water on Mr. Sykes's person.

"That is all. *For today.* See you tomorrow at nine!" She hopped up, took one more lingering look at the scummy water, and let herself out the way she had come.

But not immediately. Sadie was curious about Mr. Sykes's unconventional little house, and poked her head into each room as she passed. He had excellent taste in his furnishings—gleaming Oriental carpets, distinctive artwork, and plush furniture. His bedroom was particularly impressive, his bed a great carved thing covered in fur throws.

For a second, she debated bouncing upon it, picturing his wrathful brows if he caught her at it.

Best not to stir up trouble. She needed to go shopping. The trouble could come after.

The small kitchen was scrubbed and well-equipped. The range looked to be of the very latest design, just as at the kitchen in the big house. Surely that would bode well for Mrs. Anstruther's cooking and Sadie's general comfort.

Sykes House was a vast improvement over Stonecrop Cottage, although that had been sweet in its way. She hoped someone would remember to feed the fish in the little pond—it was one of her duties as a Guest. The plants in the conservatory would need watering too.

She'd fibbed a little about the Gothic-style door of Mr. Sykes's cottage being ajar. It had simply been unlocked, which had suited her curiosity. Now Sadie turned the handle, and faced the thin old man she'd seen from a distance. His gray eyebrows rose to the fringe on his balding pate, and he dropped the basket of vegetables on her feet. A huge head of lettuce rolled into the bushes.

She was having an issue with vegetables in Puddling.

"I do beg your pardon," Sadie said, picking up an errant bunch of radishes.

"You!"

"Yes, I. Allow me to introduce myself." She stuck out a hand, which remained ungrasped. "I am Lady Sarah Marchmain."

"I know who you are."

Hmm. There was no "my lady," or any of the deference Sadie had been raised with, just a substantially evil glare. Not that she cared much—she'd never stood on ceremony. England's archaic social system was really anathema to her. Her gormless cousin George could inherit her home just because he was a male, for example, and there wasn't a damn thing she could do about it. She had begun to read Cafiero's *A Compendium of Das Kapital* in translation before her father discovered her at it and tossed the book into the fire.

Not that she wished to give up all her possessions and toil in some field or take up arms against perceived injustice. She just wished everyone else had as much as she had.

Which, in the end, wasn't very much. She had no home of her own. All her earthly possessions were either ruined by smoke or locked up at Marchmain Castle, quite far away.

"And you must be Mr. Anstruther." She didn't bother to bat her eyelashes. Here was a man who was not to be trifled with.

Poor Mrs. Anstruther.

"What are you doing here?"

"I was just taking a walk. The folly is so charming, and naturally, I looked in. I didn't dream it was occupied." All perfectly truthful, but he was looking at her as if she were an ax murderess.

"Well, go about your business. Mr. Tristan has enough to worry about without you invading his privacy."

Tristan. What a romantic name. Like Lancelot, her erstwhile imaginary puppy, or Gawain. She could picture Mr. Sykes in armor atop a trustworthy steed, a medieval hero brought low by the love of a woman.

But better yet, she could picture him naked without using much of her imagination at all.

Chapter 6

"Bloody hell." Tristan thrust a foot in the wrong boot and collapsed on his bed. The madwoman had unsettled him, making herself at ease in his bathing chamber on top of his towels. Blast it, they had been warmed by her bum! And somehow she had talked him into taking her to Stroud to replace her wardrobe so he wouldn't have to look at her ankles.

Or her hair, which had curled, mermaid-like, as she'd sat on the chair harassing him. Waves of red and gold sprang about her brow and long white neck, inviting touch.

Not his. Never his. He would buy her lots of hairpins and a hat. A dozen hats if he had to. The early church had the right of it—women should be covered from head to toe. There was nothing wrong with modesty, especially if one's hair was living flame.

There was a rap at the bedroom door. She couldn't be back, could she, the hussy? He'd have to start locking the house up.

"Who is it?" he barked.

"It's Anstruther, Mr. Tristan. May I come in?"

"Of course. Since when do you bother knocking?" Tristan had known the man since he was in nappies. It wasn't like Anstruther to suddenly remember the demarcation between servant and master. They were even friends of a sort, if friendship meant not discussing anything meaningful.

"It's *that woman*!"

Tristan wasn't sure which woman had unnerved Anstruther, although he had a fair idea.

"Yes?"

"I caught her leaving here, bold as brass, when I came up the path. I did check all the rooms, and nothing appears to be missing. Did she disturb you? I do apologize. I should have been here to turn her away."

Tristan doubted anyone could turn Lady Sarah Marchmain away if she were determined to enter. "It's all right, Anstruther."

"It is not! She thinks she's mistress of Sykes House already. She's even gone down to the kitchens!" Anstruther said, clearly horrified that a young woman of so-called gentle birth could enter such a den of iniquity. "One of the footmen was having a smoke at the back door and told me all about her arrival and demands. She's trouble."

"All women are trouble, aren't they?" At least the ones he'd known had been, excepting his poor mother. "Don't worry, I'll handle her."

Or get someone to shadow her every move.

Who on his staff might suit? Offhand, his father's servants were pleasant, ordinary people. Well-trained and congenial, which wouldn't help at all. No one that Tristan could think of was equipped to deal with someone as extraordinary as his unwanted Guest.

"Shall I help you dress?"

"Certainly not. It's not as if I'm getting into evening togs." The only reason Tristan wore a tie and jacket at dinner at all was to assuage Anstruther's sense of consequence. He said it wouldn't help his reputation amongst the servants any if Tristan was not turned out well.

Tristan knew he was bullied by his servant, but was too good-natured to do anything about it. The man looked after him as a father might, and had saved Tristan's bacon too many times to count over the years.

"Very well. Dinner will be served in an hour."

"Capital. You haven't laid the table in the dining room yet, have you?"

"No, sir. There hasn't been time what with the fire and all."

"Good. I'll dine in the garden if it's all right with you."

Tristan had set every brick into the low-walled patio himself. An iron table and a pair of chairs overlooked a small knot garden. Its formality was in distinct contrast to the whimsy of his house, and Tristan enjoyed the peace and privacy. Soon the nights would be too chilly to eat outdoors, and he would take advantage of the mild weather. Tristan was always much happier outside than in.

But not if the madwoman was roaming all over the property.

It was clear he would have to do something. Guests had relative autonomy—as long as they followed their prescribed routine, they weren't saddled with minders twenty-four hours a day. Barriers to escape were in place, and many of the Guests actually enjoyed the regimentation their lives had been lacking. It was well-known children functioned better with structure; why not adults? Tristan himself was a man of regular habits. He'd seen firsthand what came of too much freedom.

He finished dressing and stepped out onto the patio. Large tubs of chrysanthemums and dahlias were in vibrant bloom. Anstruther had set an open bottle of burgundy and a wineglass on the table. French wine of late had been an iffy proposition. Several devastating diseases had attacked the vines, and Tristan's cellar was suffering. He poured a glass, took a sip, and was satisfied.

One day all of his father's estate would be his, but right now he appreciated the vista from his own little corner of it. Beyond the formal flower beds was a dark, hushed wood. Tristan once placed hide-and-seek there with his little brother, never hiding too seriously so the boy could find him.

There was something about the depth of the almost-black green that spoke to him. Calmed him. He didn't like turmoil in his work or his personal life. His architectural commissions were all progressing, his leadership in his little community rewarding, and if his love life was lacking, it didn't matter.

He'd experienced quite enough of love.

Anstruther brought his supper and his book out into the twilight. A candle was lit, the simple courses consumed, the story advanced. Over his port, Tristan resolved to call another meeting of the governors tomorrow. There was much to be done.

And then he remembered Lady Sarah and Stroud.

Perhaps Miss Churchill could be pressed to accompany her. Or Mrs. Anstruther. Tristan didn't have time for fripperies when Stonecrop Cottage had to be restored and arrangements needed to be made. He shouldn't be alone with the girl—no, woman—anyway. It would cause talk.

He pushed the iron chair back and stretched his legs. Despite the unusual activity of the day, he wasn't tired. A few stars winked down at him from the slate-gray sky, and he stood. There was enough light to take a postprandial walk, as was his custom. The white garden he'd designed in memory of his brother still had plenty of plants that perfumed the air and would glow in the encroaching darkness.

Tristan used his supper table candle to light a rusty lantern that had been set outside near the French doors and called out his plans to Anstruther. It was moments like this that he missed his old retriever. Maybe it was time to get a new dog to keep him company on his rambles. A country gentleman and his dog—what was more natural?

He wasn't wearing his workboots, so he stuck to the paths that had been laid out in his great-grandfather's day. The lawn was so expansive it took him a full ten minutes to walk to the end of the clipped grass, passing follies and shrubbery and various garden "rooms" along the way. He glanced to his left. His father's house on the hill was lit up like Guy Fawkes Night. Lady Sarah's doing, no doubt.

The wind picked up, and Tristan turned up his collar. A trace of smoke was still in the air, despite the distance of Sykes House relative to the village. The white iron gate to the memorial garden squealed as he opened it, and he reminded himself to bring an oil can the next time he came.

"Good evening."

Tristan nearly stumbled over his own feet. In the center of the garden, on the mahogany bench he had built with his own hands, was Lady Sarah Marchmain.

Tristan lifted the lantern. "You again? Is there no escape?"

"I certainly didn't expect you either," she said. "I was restless after supper, and went for a walk. Nowhere *near* your place, I might add."

This was *all* his place, in the absence of his father. He almost wished the man would come home from France and deal with Lady Sarah himself.

If he could.

The girl matched the garden, clad in what Tristan could clearly see as a plain white cotton nightgown. A knitted cream-wool shawl was tossed over her shoulders, and all that wild red hair was still loose and on display.

"You wander about in the dark in a strange place wearing only your nightclothes?" Tristan asked, feeling annoyed and, regrettably, something else.

"It's not totally dark yet, and I have very good eyesight. There's plenty of light coming down from the house, too."

Tristan wondered how much it was costing his father in candles and lamp oil to house a duke's wayward daughter for however short a time.

"Look, Lady Sarah, as you said, we need to get a few things ironed out. You will not run wild all over creation at all hours of the day and night. It is not safe."

Her lips curved. "Not safe? Are there vicious animals on the property? Or are you referring to yourself?"

"You have nothing to fear from me," Tristan lied. He very much wanted to take her over his knee and spank her cotton-covered arse. Thoroughly. "But surely you know that you should be in bed." *Alone.*

"So early?"

"We keep country hours here in Puddling. You have had a curfew, as you are well aware." All Guests were to be in bed with the lights out by ten o'clock. Neighbors reported them if they weren't.

"I'm afraid I don't have a watch."

"I believe you'll find some clocks in my father's house, possibly even one in the guest room you're staying in. On the mantel? Ormolu? Quite a pretty piece, as I recall. I suggest you take note of the time in the future." Tristan knew it wasn't anywhere near ten yet, but she didn't, or claimed not to.

"Even if I tried to go to sleep, I don't think it would be a success. It was a very...trying day." She paused in the darkness. "Everything is gone."

Tristan wondered what she had lost in the fire. A diary? A favorite book? Usually Guests came with a bare minimum of clothing and possessions. If she thought she would be buying a ballgown tomorrow, she was mistaken.

"You should ask Mrs. Anstruther for a cup of hot cocoa. That should do the trick." Tristan marched over to the bench intending to drag her up by an elbow and escort her back.

The lantern caught a splash of silver on her cheek.

Good lord, was she crying?

"Are you well, Lady Sarah?"

"Of course I am! I'm perfectly fine. It's a lovely evening and I was enjoying it until you came along." He heard a muffled sniff.

A few hours ago she had sobbed like a child but only briefly. Thank heaven she had pulled herself together now. Tristan had never been much good with crying women, despite plenty of experience. His life with Linnet had left him quite cold to tears.

"You'll be rid of me as soon as I return you to Sykes House."

"I can find my way."

"No doubt. But allow me to be a gentleman. I also want to arrange for one of the maids to accompany you on your shopping expedition."

She rose from the bench. "You aren't coming?"

Did he detect a note of disappointment in her voice?

He sighed, defeated. "I suppose I must, if only to protect the Puddling Rehabilitation Foundation. Tomorrow is market day in Stroud, and I dread to think what you could do with all those vegetables."

Chapter 7

If one were a romantic, which Sadie most definitely was not, the stroll up the terraced hill to the house would have been lovely. Her arm was tucked once again in Mr. Sykes's—Tristan's—and his slow pace accommodated her soft-soled bedroom slippers.

She shouldn't have come out in her bedclothes. But when she'd opened her window and breathed the night air, she knew she had to get outside again. She'd spotted the white garden at once, a ghostly square lit by the lights from the house. The groundskeeper at Marchmain Castle would have died with envy, since all he was employed to do was trim the patchy grass. The gardens had gone to seed soon after Sadie's mother died and her income was held in an iron-bound trust for her daughter—the late duchess and her advisors had suspected her husband's tendencies even before they married. There was no money for extravagant gardens or gardeners to keep them that way. The duke had done everything he could to break the financial arrangements he'd agreed to as an impoverished young bridegroom to no avail.

A fence entwined with rustling ivy served as a buffer from the sloping land below. With her free hand, Sadie clutched at her borrowed shawl as the night air cooled. The Sykes estate was a very pretty prison, her jailer even more attractive.

But she mustn't let him think he had any influence on her whatsoever.

"Do you usually roam about at night?" she asked. She'd have to be more careful in the future if he did.

"Sometimes."

That told her nothing.

"That gated garden—it's very otherworldly, isn't it?"

He stopped their ascent and turned to her. "Do you think so? I planted it in honor of my younger brother. He died eight years ago."

"*You* planted it?" That explained his dirty fingernails.

"It's a hobby. I find gardening very restful." He resumed the climb.

"I'm sorry about your brother. Were you close?"

"Not in age. I was almost five years older. But yes. He was my shadow growing up."

His voice was level. Steady. But Sadie heard the hurt.

"I envy you, even if you lost him. I'm an only child." Her childhood had been lonely, even when her mother lived.

"And spoiled rotten, I expect."

What did he know? Everyone assumed, and everyone was wrong. She shrugged her arm away. "Almost here, Mr. Sykes. I can see myself in."

"Good evening, Lady Sarah. Pleasant dreams."

The shadows on his face disappeared in the bright rectangles of light from the windows. He looked down at her, a rare experience for an over-tall woman. There was assessment in his eyes. Wariness.

Good. He should want to be careful of her.

"And the same to you." Impulsively, she stood on tiptoe and brushed her lips over his cheek. She meant to give him a peck only, a saucy thank you for walking her back to the house. But somehow he startled and turned his face in such a way that the light sharp bristles she'd first encountered turned to soft, sculpted lips.

For a long second, neither of them did anything at all. They were mouth to mouth, held breath to held breath. Sadie could feel the warmth of his body, hear the silence of it. He was so still, his hands resolutely at his sides.

Clearly, she should step back and get her lips as far away from his as she could. Yet she was as still as he, suspended in the darkness, velvet skin to velvet skin. An owl hooted in the distance, but the spell refused to be broken.

Really, *someone* should do *something*.

And then his mouth twitched the tiniest bit under hers. Opened the tiniest bit. Sadie felt his broad hands on her shoulders—

And he pushed her away with such force she landed on her derriere in the dirt. The ground was exceptionally hard, and covered with tiny stones that did nothing to improve her comfort.

"Blast—Forgive me. I didn't intend for you to fall." He reached a hand out and pulled her up. "What the devil did you think you were doing?" His voice was as frozen as snow. He fished out a handkerchief and was blotting his lips as if she'd contaminated him, the rotter.

"I wasn't thinking. Obviously. And I certainly didn't mean to really kiss you."

"No? Then why did your mouth touch my face?"

"That's it—I only planned to kiss your cheek. A friendly gesture. As if you were my...grandfather."

He snorted. "I pity all the grandfathers you've tried to bamboozle. I know your sort, Lady Sarah. You are here on sufferance, and I'll not be tricked by your feminine wiles."

Feminine wiles? How absurd. She'd not made the least effort to extract them from her arsenal. In fact, her wiles were on the dusty side, virtually atrophied. Usually she tried to repel men rather than attract them.

"I assure you, your virtue is safe," Sadie said with all the haughtiness one could muster after being sprawled on the ground.

He had the grace to look embarrassed. It was too dark to see if his ears turned red again.

Sadie knew she shouldn't. She really, really shouldn't. She gave him a push back. Hard.

To no effect. Tristan Sykes remained standing. He was made of marble, obdurate and unyielding.

"As I said, Lady Sarah, your tricks will not work on me. Nor your tantrums or tears."

Sadie had spent a good deal of her day on her knees or worse. Granted, she'd put herself in those positions—she was usually fairly graceful. Something about Tristan Sykes made her feel awkward, however, and it took longer than it should have for her to meet his eyes, her spine as stiff as his.

"You will honor your promise, won't you?"

"What promise?" he asked.

"To take me shopping. I cannot continue to borrow clothes from your maids. It's unseemly."

"And you'd know all about unseemliness."

She gave him a shove again, and it felt marvelous. "You despise me, don't you? Well, you haven't the right! You know nothing about me. Nothing. I don't care what it said in that silly Foundation report."

His eyebrows lifted. "What do you know of that? The information about our Guests is classified. For the residents of Puddling only."

Sadie straightened her shoulders. "Well, that means me too, doesn't it? *I* live here."

Unfortunately.

"For the time being. Where did you find it?"

He was growling. Sadie felt some sympathy for the baker, who was really quite accomplished even if he left important papers lying around beneath the Bakewell tarts.

"I forget."

"Just as you forgot where you *found* those tartan trousers."

"I have a great many things to think about." Sadie shrugged. "There are the vicar's daily instructions. My responsibilities at the cottage."

"Feeding the fish and watering the ferns," he said with disgust. "You don't know what an honest day's work is. Or honesty, for that matter." He said the last words under his breath, but Sadie heard them all the same and chose to ignore them.

"How is that my fault? Women of my class don't go out to work."

"There are charities you could involve yourself with. You are a duke's daughter with rank and privilege, and yet you are squandering your education and rather diabolical mind on childish games. Pumpkins. Petty theft. Punch-ups. Your rebelliousness is ridiculous."

Sadie grew quiet. To his narrow way of thinking, he was right, and surprisingly alliterative. Society would agree—she should marry. Bear children. Be kind to her husband's tenants. Change her clothes five times a day and be ornamental.

"I don't wish to marry the man my father has picked for me," she said softly. "In my experience, men are pigs. I don't want to marry at all."

Mr. Sykes ran a hand through his curly hair, appearing harried. "Why not? You'd be cherished. Protected."

"Protected? What do you mean?"

"Shall you argue with nature? Females are the weaker sex. It's a man's duty to care for a woman. See to her, um, needs."

Sadie rolled her eyes. The man had obviously never read Mary Wollstonecraft's *A Vindication of the Rights of Woman.* The book was nearly one hundred years old, for heaven's sake!

"Neanderthal. I imagine I can forage for and even club my own food if need be. You might be physically stronger, but I wager my diabolical mind, as you call it, can run rings around yours."

"It's much too late to argue." He touched her elbow, and Sadie felt a rather pleasant zing through the rough cotton. "Time for bed."

Sadie pictured Mr. Sykes in a nightshirt and night cap, and immediately undressed him. It would be a shame to hide those broad brown shoulders beneath fabric of any kind. And his unruly curls were rather intriguing as well, standing up now every which way.

But, she reminded herself, he was a Neanderthal. And as such, would be a bloody nuisance as she enjoyed his grudging hospitality. In a scant three weeks she would have to go back to Marchmain Castle and face her father, as Mr. Sykes seemed disinclined to allow her further license to remain in Puddling.

Unless she ran away. There were distinct disadvantages to that, but her diabolical mind would deal with them tomorrow.

Chapter 8

Tristan had spent a near-sleepless night. Just knowing the madwoman was across the vast lawn in one of his father's spare bedrooms interrupted his peace. She haunted his dreams, her pink lips pursed, her amber-tipped lashes flicking with unlikely innocence, her virginal-white nightgown just a wispy trick.

He had kissed her on the hillside path, God help him. It hadn't been much of a kiss, but he'd been this close to sweeping his tongue over the seam of her lips and taking her in his arms. Touching her loose red curls. Pressing her against him.

Instead, he'd flung her away like the Neanderthal she'd accused him of being.

Her madness must be catching.

And now, God help him again, Lady Sarah Marchmain was keeping him waiting when he didn't want to see her to begin with.

Tristan paced the black-and-white-tiled entry hall of Sykes House. As a boy, he'd taught Wallace how to play chess and checkers on it with paper cutouts. The usual urn of artfully disarranged flowers from the gardens stood on the center table—even in his father's absence, the house's habits were kept in force.

Linnet had not cared for Sykes House or its gardens. She'd been a London girl, a social butterfly who wilted without artificial light.

Tristan had been a fool to marry her.

But he'd been awfully young, and thought he knew everything back then. What he'd learned in the intervening years was that married life with all its uncharming drama was not for him.

Ha. He and Lady Sarah had something in common after all.

Mrs. Anstruther hurried down the staircase, rubbing her hands nervously when she reached him. She bore the look of someone who'd spent time with Lady Sarah and was regretting every minute.

Rather like himself.

"She's almost ready, Mr. Tristan. There was a bit of bother about what she would wear into town that would be suitable, and I'm...afraid you may not l-like what she's chosen. She's a very tall young lady, isn't she?"

Yes, she was. Too tall. Like an exotic giraffe. And her pink mouth was too wide for fashion, wasn't it? Lady Sarah was definitely not the wayward angel of his dreams, all pink and white and supplicant.

"What's she wearing? The bedroom curtains?" He'd put nothing past her, swanning around like a Roman senator with a laurel wreath.

"Oh, it's not as b-bad as that."

But bad, Mrs. Anstruther left unsaid.

He resolved not to look at his Guest when she finally made her grand entrance. Everyone, even the horses, were being inconvenienced by her.

Spoiled brat.

He turned to the door. "Tell Lady Sarah I'll be in the carriage." A housemaid recruited into chaperone duty and his driver were already there. It was almost five miles to Stroud, and the day wasn't getting any younger.

Tristan would have to offer Lady Sarah lunch in one of the hotels, which meant he couldn't avoid her all day. He had no intention of accompanying her to the dressmaker, watching her agonize over lace and buttons. He planned to poke around the market to see what late-season garden plants were available for sale. He'd visit the bookshop as well, not that he would have much time to read. He'd be busy in the coming weeks overseeing the refurbishment of Stonecrop Cottage and expanding plans for the Foundation. Tristan had already met with his father's estate manager this morning to get a work crew assembled to begin repairs. *Some* people started their day on time, early even.

He ignored the clumping of feet down the stairs behind him.

"Hey!"

"And good morning to you too," Tristan said, not turning. "Although it's closer to afternoon than I'd like."

"Sorry."

She didn't sound it. Tristan imagined she never truly apologized for anything. Like a duke, a duke's daughter was above ordinary mortals and their concerns.

He continued down the steps to the drive, but one look at his coachman's astonished face made him pivot.

What the bloody hell?

If Tristan wasn't very much mistaken, Lady Sarah Marchmain was wearing one of his outgrown Eton suits—striped trousers, tails and all.

And his old shoes, polished to a spit shine! Her hair was bound up and stuffed under his battered top hat.

"I know black isn't my color," she said, hopping into the landau without assistance, and giving Tristan a very fine view of her bottom as she swept the tailcoat out of the way. "And there is a lingering aroma of camphor. But this was the only thing we could find that fit me without alteration. There are a great many women's clothes in the attic, but I'm afraid your mother and grandmother were much shorter than I am. And of course, the fashions are completely out-of-date. I find men's clothing stands the test of time, don't you?"

She was doing this on purpose, out to make him a laughingstock. Pushing him beyond endurance.

Tristan remained rooted to the drive. "No."

"I beg your pardon?"

"I am not going anywhere with you dressed in such an outlandish manner. Get out."

"My ankles are covered," Lady Sarah objected.

"The curtains would have been better," Tristan grumbled. "I know what you're doing, and I will not be a party to it."

"What do you mean?" She batted her lashes as he'd seen her do to poor Frank Stanchfield.

He was made of much sterner stuff.

"Oh, cut line, Lady Sarah. I'll get Miss Churchill to assemble some clothes for you. Our shopping trip is canceled. I have more important things to do anyway."

"What is wrong with what I'm wearing? It was good enough for you twenty years ago."

Fifteen. Tristan felt like an ancient thirty and could practically feel his hair turning gray in Lady Sarah's presence.

Or falling out.

He took her ungloved hand and pulled her from the carriage. "We're done here."

"Unhand me! You are not behaving like a gentleman!"

"How would you know how a gentleman behaves when you refuse to act like a lady?"

Lady Sarah paled. Tristan was rather proud of his direct hit.

"You—you pompous, insufferable prig! It's not my fault I have nothing proper to wear!"

"Anything would be better than that, and you know it. This is just one more petty, childish ploy to try to stay here and not get married."

She looked as if she wanted to strike him. Well, let her try. He was light on his feet, and could duck any blow she thought to deliver.

But then her lower lip—lush and rosy—started to tremble. Those beryl-colored eyes filled with tears.

Damn, damn, damn.

"You don't know what it's like," she whispered. "You're a man."

And she was very much a woman. Tristan hardened his heart. "It can't be as bad as all that. The chap you're engaged to isn't such a bad fellow. I know of him," he said, pulling his handkerchief out.

"He's not a good fellow either. He's just—a fellow." To Tristan's dismay, she honked into his handkerchief in a most alarming way.

"Don't tell me you believe in romantic love." He had once, and where had that gotten him?

Her eyes flashed. "Of course I don't! Love is for"—she nodded toward the maid and the driver and spoke softly—"the lower orders. Lucky them—I don't know why people don't recognize they live far superior lives, even if they have to work hard. They can choose their life mates. Everything is much simpler when you're not uniting estates and dynasties or trying to get votes in Parliament. Or money."

Tristan shrugged. "It's the way of our world, Lady Sarah. Surely you've had enough time to prepare yourself for it." According to her report, she'd been out in society for four, very long, eventful years. Her hijinks had been legendary and reported in all the newspapers.

"I'll never be prepared to toss my life away." She tucked his despoiled handkerchief into her sleeve and fiddled with it.

"You don't want children?"

"I don't know much about them." She looked up. "Mr. Fitzmartin is always going on about being fruitful and multiplying, but I'm always reminded of maths. You think I'm unnatural, don't you."

"What *I* think means nothing, Lady Sarah. I'm not in charge of your release."

"You're head of the governors."

"Only in my father's absence." The last letter he'd received from his father had been vague in the extreme about a return date, so Tristan was stuck in his temporary position of control. "Let's go inside, shall we? There's a nip in the air."

"If I had a new coat, I wouldn't be cold."

She was incorrigible. "I'll add it to Miss Churchill's list."

She pulled out the crumpled handkerchief and wiped her nose. "You really won't take me shopping? *Ever?*"

"You'll remain here for less than four weeks. I'm sure we can find suitable clothing for that short a time." Tristan should have refused to take her to Stroud at the outset. It went against all the Puddling Rehabilitation Rules to allow a Guest to leave the village. And if he'd been seen dining with her in public, all sorts of tongues would wag.

His stomach rumbled. Breakfast was half a day ago. "Come, let's see if we can rustle up some lunch from Mrs. Anstruther. You set her into a pelter, you know. I can't have you upsetting my staff."

"I didn't do anything," Lady Sarah said mulishly.

Tristan's eyes swept from the tip of the top hat to his old black shoes. "Indeed. As fetching as you look, your ensemble is a shock to the average person. Sykes House is chock-full of average people. They aren't trained to deal with Guests as Mrs. Grace and the other keep—um, attendants are. I shall have a word with them."

"Keepers. Jailers. Let's not mince words."

"Well, yes, I suppose. Would you prefer to be in a hospital?"

Lady Sarah flushed. "I would prefer to be in my own accommodations, with my own clothes! I wouldn't try to be so difficult if only I could have my own way."

Tristan couldn't help it—he laughed. "The world would turn to chaos if we all had just what we *think* we wanted." He'd gotten what he wanted once, and the result had been tragedy.

Chapter 9

Sadie knew she'd gone a step too far—hell, several steps, and it's not as if these cumbersome leather shoes were comfortable. Poor Mrs. Anstruther had tried to talk her out of wearing Tristan Sykes's school uniform, going so far as to offer the clothes off her own back. As the housekeeper was half a foot shorter and twice as wide as Sadie, she would have looked ridiculous.

She would soon rival the woman's girth if she kept eating. The impromptu lunch Mrs. Anstruther put together was impressive—cream of tomato soup, cold chicken pie, a green salad, yeast rolls, seeded bread, thick slices of ham, three kinds of cheese, chutney, pickled vegetables, lemon curd, and strawberry jam tarts. Sadie had avoided the pickled onions but had wolfed down the rest.

Chewing kept her busy. She'd given up admiring the yellow rose-patterned wallpaper and family portraits. Small talk did not seem to be Mr. Sykes's forte, and if he began to lecture her again on her womanly duties, he might get the breadbasket hurled at his head. The servants were very deferential toward him, so at some point he might have shown them more charm than he was presently showing her.

Sadie still sported the Etonian suit. She'd have to go back to the attic after lunch and see what she could salvage from the trunks of women's clothing. Mr. Sykes seemed disinclined to reconsider his position on taking her shopping, and she could only imagine the dreadfully dull dresses Miss Churchill would select.

But the inconvenience, Sadie reminded herself, was for a few short weeks. Unless she figured out how to demonstrate that she was insane enough to stay in Puddling, but not insane enough to be institutionalized. Or…

It would require all of her mental reserves to formulate a plan to run away. She'd spent much of last night plotting before she finally fell asleep. The first obvious impediment was lack of money. It wouldn't be cricket to steal from Sykes House's servants, but Sadie could reimburse them once she was safely settled somewhere and found employment. And that was the second impediment. Where could she go? She'd worn the patience of her few friends, who in any event would be reluctant to cross a duke, even an impoverished one.

It wasn't as if she could blend into a small town—as a nearly six-foot redhead, it would be hard to hide. But if she could book passage to America—

Pipe dreams. Servants wouldn't have the necessary sort of money lying around, and Sadie was reluctant to start hiding candlesticks and silverware in the pockets of her nonexistent dresses.

Blast. She was usually so good at solving dilemmas, but perhaps she'd finally run out of ideas.

Tristan Sykes wiped his mouth on an embroidered linen napkin and rose. "I'll send a carriage for Reverend Fitzmartin." He rang for the footmen.

Sadie stood too. "I don't want to see anyone. I have nothing to wear." The vicar would expire from heart failure if he found her in trousers two days in a row.

He walked her out to the entry hall and picked up his hat from a chair, where it had sat next the battered top hat. "You missed yesterday's session."

"And I had a perfectly good excuse!"

"Well, nothing's on fire today. Except, perhaps, for your temper."

"I suppose a lady in your world would be sanguine about wearing servants' castoffs."

"I believe a lady knows which battles to pick. One's character is confirmed as to how one responds to adversity."

"Oh, bollocks."

When she was fifteen, she'd spent a great deal of her time in the stables at Marchmain Castle, and had picked up a colorful vocabulary. Tristan Sykes's distinctive eyebrows raised, but he said nothing.

She forged ahead. "I'd like to see how well *you'd* deal if your father picked out your wife."

"As a matter of fact, he did."

It was Sadie's turn to raise her eyebrows. He went around almost kissing women who were not his wife, did he? The—the rogue! "You're *married*?"

He looked down at the hat between his hands. "I was."

Two words, but they still didn't tell Sadie what she wanted to know. "What happened?"

"Not that it's any of your business, but my wife and I did not suit. We divorced some years ago."

Well! What a scandal! The prim and oh-so-proper Mr. Sykes had an actual past. Divorce was still extremely irregular, even if the laws had softened some.

"Where is she now?"

"I'm afraid she died shortly afterward. I could have spared myself the effort, expense and disgrace if I'd waited a little longer."

His voice showed no inflection, but he must be bitter. That explained why he was so...whatever the correct word was. Standoffish? Critical? Disapproving?

He hated women.

Well, except for Mrs. Anstruther. And the Sykes House maids, who blushed when he was spoken of. And Miss Churchill, and the elderly vicar's wife. Mrs. Stanchfield, too. They were safe from his opprobrium, and they seemed to beam in his presence.

Maybe he just hated *her*.

"I'm sorry."

"Nothing to do with you," he said curtly.

"But it is, in a way. You must know how awful it is to be forced into doing something you do not want."

He shook his head. "You misunderstand, Lady Sarah. I was anxious to marry my wife. I fancied myself fortunate in my father's choice."

Ah. So he'd been *in love*. Just this morning he'd scoffed at the whole idea of romance. His marriage had evidently cured him of such juvenile notions.

"How old were you when you married?"

"Twenty. As fascinating as this conversation is, I do have responsibilities, Lady Sarah. If you'll excuse me?" He angled the hat on his head. A footman appeared quickly from a corridor and opened the front door.

"Good day, Lady Sarah. You may expect Mr. Fitzmartin within the hour."

Bollocks again, but she kept the word inside her head. Twenty! Younger than she was right now. She couldn't imagine Tristan Sykes young and in love—he was so prim and grumpy now. She watched him stride around the corner of the house, heading for his own tiny patch of Eden.

And so she faced another insipid afternoon. At least the food here at Sykes House was much better than the swill that Mrs. Grace gave her.

She wondered how long it would take the governors to realize she was enjoying her dinners too much. It seemed part of their design was to flatten Guests' appetites for anything pleasurable completely.

Bored into submission. Sadie had no intention of submitting to anything. But how long could she hold out?

She'd better change into something less shocking. Mr. Fitzmartin was frail enough as it was. Sadie didn't wish to be responsible for his demise, although his wife's dreadful cooking might play a part eventually.

She took the stairs to the attic two at a time. Boxes and trunks were still thrown open from her earlier marauding. If she were a little girl with her heart set on playing dress-up, she had come to the ideal location. At least a century's worth of court and day and evening dresses were peeking out of folded tissue paper—a kaleidoscope of color.

It seemed a shame to cut into any of the lux fabrics. It wasn't as if she'd be going to parties, and the clothes were not part of her family's history to alter. Marchmain Castle's attics boasted nothing but mouse droppings and broken furniture. There wasn't a trace of Sadie's mother or her belongings anywhere.

Sadie stripped off the suit and reluctantly put it back from whence it came. At least the silky underthings she wore were serviceable. In fact, the flower-embellished corset and short lacy shift she'd found earlier were of the finest quality.

She dragged over a tuft-sprouting chair, sat down and bent over a canvas trunk. This one was layered with sprigs of lavender, much nicer than camphor. She pulled out a fringed Norwich silk shawl and draped it over her shoulders. It was stuffy and warm in the attic, but now she wasn't quite so exposed in case one of the maids or Mrs. Anstruther tracked her down. Sadie planned to try on a few things before she bothered to bring them downstairs.

Heavens, women had worn stupid things in the past. She bypassed garishly bright dresses with enormous barrel sleeves, the skirts so full it was a wonder one could walk without tripping. The artificial dyes used on the material were rather awful. Sadie had never been a slave to fashion, but she did like pretty things. There was nothing in this trunk that wouldn't require major alterations or a pair of dark spectacles.

She slid her chair to the next trunk and moved back in time several decades to the Regency. Spotted muslins, striped cambrics—now here were simple day dresses she might add temporary length to without spoiling them. They would require no cage crinolines or bustles to keep their classical lines.

She unfastened a row of tiny hooks and dropped a pale yellow dress over her head. Unfortunately, the bodice was so narrow she couldn't fit her arms into the sleeves, and she sat mummified in lavender-scented muslin for a few panicky seconds before she struggled out of it.

It was hopeless. She'd just have to receive the vicar in her dressing gown—well, one of the maids' dressing gowns. If Tristan Sykes weren't so pigheaded and woman-hating, he'd surely see that she needed proper clothes that fit her.

Sadie rose from her injured chair. She couldn't very well walk downstairs in her current state of undress. Perhaps there was a spare sheet she could sling around herself like a ghost.

The attic door squeaked open behind her before she had a chance to find a sheet, blanket or even a curtain. Clutching the shawl, she expected to see a servant when she turned. Instead, she met the ice-blue eyes of Tristan Sykes.

Chapter 10

The words died on Tristan's lips. He could do nothing but stare.

At first he thought she was covered only by a scarf, but the edge of an embroidered corset peeked out from under the paisley and straps as pale as her shoulders revealed she was wearing a shift as well. But not much of one. Lady Sarah Marchmain stood in a swirl of golden dust motes, strands of her coppery hair tumbling from its pins, her white legs mostly bare and endless.

He had come to tell her that Mr. Fitzmartin was indisposed, that she was saved from another lecture. Instead, he was mute, his eyes blinking when he really needed to avert them, his cock behaving as if he were a schoolboy looking at naughty pictures.

She stared right back at him, frozen.

He should excuse himself and dash back down the attic stairs.

His feet refused to move.

One of them should say something. Hell, she should be shrieking her head off. She was practically naked. To be discovered like this was the most compromising of positions. A normal woman wouldn't just stand there.

She was as brazen as her legs were long. Lady Sarah Marchmain had invaded his privacy in the bath, tried to kiss him, and was now tempting him, making him forget why—

This is what Tristan had feared all along—that something would happen between them that was inescapable. If they were in some foolish novel, he'd find himself in parson's mousetrap before the week was out.

Was that her plan? No, she claimed she didn't want marriage, at least to Lord Roderick Charlton. Or any of the other men who'd sought her hand—and the rest of her luscious self—since her debut. And besides,

Tristan was at fault this time, coming upon her without notice. Why hadn't he sent Mrs. Anstruther or another servant to the attic?

The truth was, he'd wanted to see her face light up when she learned her afternoon was free of the vicar's intervention. He'd been only minimally polite at lunch, trying to control the unwanted storm she created inside him—trousers, again!—and felt a trifle guilty. As a form of apology, he had planned to invite her to walk with him in the garden.

Right now, she'd give the marble statuary outside some competition. She was utterly still, pale and beautiful.

Let's see. To speak, one opened one's mouth. Arranged teeth and tongue in familiar combinations. Pressed one's vocal chords into service. Breathed too, somehow. All of that was quite beyond him at the moment.

And her as well. Her eyes were locked on his, her usually pink cheeks devoid of color.

He threw a hand over his eyes, because they didn't seem to want to look anywhere else but in her direction. "I—I beg your pardon."

"What do you want?" Her voice was thin, higher pitched than usual.

By God, his hand was shaking like an old man's. "I came to tell you Mr. Fitzmartin cannot come today."

"Good."

There. That was sufficient information, wasn't it? Time to turn around and go down the stairs.

But no. Here he was, rooted to the floorboards. Tristan peeked through his fingers.

"He is indisposed. Mr. Fitzmartin, that is."

Her knuckles were white from clutching the fringed scarf, but her lips curved slightly. "He probably ate too many biscuits."

Biscuits? This encounter was proving more absurd by the minute.

He cleared his throat. "Well, then, I'll be leaving."

"Yes, that's a very good idea."

From somewhere below, Tristan heard loud voices and doors slamming. Lady Sarah was standing quite near the window, but there was no hope for it—he had to go near her in all her half-naked glory. He edged around the boxes and baskets and cast-off furniture trying to keep his distance and looked down onto the curved drive of Sykes House. A dusty crested carriage was heading toward the stables, and the footmen were racing to bring in the baggage that was tumbled about on the cobblestones.

Tristan was not expecting any visitors. What the devil? Had his father decided Paris was *de trop*? His last letter had been filled with cheerful descriptions of various amusements, so very different from preternaturally quiet Puddling-on-the-Wold. The old man seemed to be having a splendid time, probably for the first time in his life. Growing up, Sir Bertram Sykes had suffered over his mother's wild reputation, and had consequently turned into quite a prig as a sort of revolt. Tristan loved his father, but the man's prudery and self-consequence could raise anyone's hackles.

He heard rapid thumping up the stairs. Without thinking, Tristan scooped up Lady Sarah, which wasn't precisely easy in her current slippery-scarf state, and dropped her into a largish open trunk.

"Not one word." He tossed what looked to be the old blue dining room curtains over her.

She pawed through the fabric like she was in the ocean coming up for air, her green eyes daggers. "How dare you?"

"Really, are you deaf? If you continue to talk, I won't be responsible for the consequences. Someone is coming. Do you wish to be discovered in *dishabille*? Fancy being Mrs. Sykes, do you?"

Her mouth dropped open in what Tristan perceived as horror.

"That's right. I see I've gotten through to you. Good. Now, be quiet." With one firm flip, he closed the trunk, fairly certain he heard a muffled yelp.

One of the footmen appeared at the attic door. "Mr. Tristan, sir, you have a v-visitor." The man looked scared to death.

"I heard the commotion. Who is it?"

"It's a bloody—I mean it's a blooming duke, sir! Lady Sarah's father. I've never met a duke before. He's not happy. And he's come with *luggage*. Tons of it, all with fancy crests and a snooty valet and everything."

Bloody, blooming hell. It was expressly forbidden for family to interfere with a Guest's course of treatment. Occasionally exceptions were made—the Marquess of Harland had even stayed in this house for a few days while his son was sequestered in Puddling last year.

"Islesford won't eat you. I don't think. What does he want?"

"To see Lady Sarah. They told him down in the village she's here. But we can't find her anywhere. He's in—he's in somewhat of a state, Mr. Tristan."

"I think I know where she is. Be a good fellow and go downstairs. Offer the duke refreshment. Tell Mrs. Anstruther to get his belongings settled in the best room."

"That's where the l-lady is, sir."

"The second-best room then. She'll know what to do. Hurry up, don't just stand there gawking." Lady Sarah might be suffocating even as he spoke.

The footman took off and Tristan opened the trunk. Lady Sarah rose out of the curtains like a disheveled Venus.

"You heard?" Tristan asked, trying not to notice that the shawl had slipped off completely and all of her throat and chest was exposed.

Pillowy white breasts were barely contained under an embroidered ruffle. The corset tapered to her slender waist, and a few inches of shift skimmed her milky thighs.

Milky thighs. Oh, Christ.

"Damn it! I don't want to see my father! Tell him to go away!" Her voice was not quite steady.

"You'll have to get downstairs to your room somehow," Tristan said, ignoring her.

"And then what? Wrap myself up in the coverlet? I have nothing to wear, Mr. Sykes. That's why I was up here."

"Put on that sack you were wearing yesterday. Perhaps your father will see to a new wardrobe for you while he's here." Tristan rummaged through boxes, spilling unfamiliar female garments to the dusty attic floor. Surely in all this there must be something the madwoman could put on before he was turned into a madman. He seized a wrinkled pink striped dress and thrust it at her.

Her nose twitched. "Pink? With my coloring?"

"Heaven help me. Now is not the time to worry over fashion. Just get the damn thing on so you can go down the servants' stairs to your room. I'll keep your father busy until you're decent."

Unable to help himself, he watched as she tossed the garment over her head. She was perfection, and even more perfect now that something was covering her muttering mouth. Her head appeared, and the mutters became clear.

She stuck an arm through a sleeve with an ominous ripping sound. "This doesn't fit. I'm strangling."

"It doesn't have to fit," Tristan said with impatience. "It only has to cover you."

The other arm followed suit, and she tugged the skirt three-quarters of the way down over her long legs, much to Tristan's regret. "My hair is caught in the hooks."

Her hair was a complete tangle. Tristan had some experience undressing women—though not lately—but dressing them back up was not his area of expertise. He wished he had a hairbrush to smooth through Lady Sarah's truly extraordinary hair.

"Hold still." The hooks were devilishly tiny, and even after he removed the long strands of her hair, there was no chance of doing them up. Lady Sarah, while slender, was too broad at the shoulders and the fabric gapped in the back.

He could smell her perfume. Roses. He wondered if he could cultivate a rose that would match the color of her hair. "This will have to do."

"I'd be better off in your Eton suit."

Seeing her in it again would be the death of him. "You look fine. I'm sure you won't encounter so much as a tweenie on the back stairs. Hurry up."

And for some reason, Tristan patted her bottom. By God, it was soft, so he did it again. And that act was how the ninth Duke of Islesford discovered his difficult daughter and her apparent lover.

Chapter 11

Her father was in a towering rage, but when wasn't he? Sadie had locked herself in her room, but she could still hear him shouting at Tristan outside in the hallway.

She looked at herself in the mirror. It was not difficult to see why her father thought she'd been compromised. Her hair was a Medusa's nest, and the silly pink dress didn't begin to cover her. She took it off with some difficulty and tossed it into a corner.

Back into the brown dress she had been given by the housekeeper yesterday. The rough material made her itch. Damn it, why hadn't they just gone shopping this morning as he'd agreed? Then she wouldn't have been forced to forage for clothes in the attic, and Tristan wouldn't have found her half naked.

And he wouldn't have *looked* at her the way he did. Sadie shivered. His gaze had been so direct before he threw a hand over his face. His entire body had straightened, practically vibrating with interest, when hers wanted to sink onto the floor. He'd reminded her of a hound on point. Obviously, she was the fox.

It was one thing for her to see him in the altogether, not that she'd seen much under the soapy bathwater, damn it all. But she had been barely clothed, her every freckle exposed. She was most fortunate there were only a few on her nose which she covered with powder, but her body was dusted with little golden spots that were the bane of her existence. Despite her horrible governess's every horrible remedy, they had remained.

And now—well, goodness knows how this was all going to end, although she had a fair idea. Her father had blustered about Roderick and money and lawsuits as she'd fled barefoot down the servants' stairs, her parent and Tristan Sykes in hot pursuit. She could still catch snatches of the conversation, not that she wanted to hear a word.

She was doomed. Tristan had patted her derriere. Twice. That was certainly grounds in her father's eyes for...something.

Sadie wanted to scream, but on the whole she'd shown enough unbridled emotion since she'd been stashed away in Puddling. It was time to be calm. Rational. Mature.

She wondered if she remembered how.

The pounding on her door only solidified her determination. Taking a deep breath, Sadie opened it, standing as proud and tall as her hideous brown dress would allow.

"You cannot escape me and the consequences of your hoydenish behavior this time."

Her father's face was brick red, his gray hair askew as he pushed in to the room. Tristan stood behind him, his face betraying nothing.

"Come in, Papa, why don't you. You as well, I suppose, Mr. Sykes." She hastened to pick up the offensive pink dress and stuffed it into the empty wardrobe. "Please take a seat."

The room she had been given at Sykes House was quite lovely. There was a sitting area before a bank of windows which overlooked the terraced gardens. Her father tossed aside some fringed pillows and collapsed onto the plush cream-colored sofa. After a moment's hesitation, she and Tristan sat opposite each other on the needlepoint chairs.

Her father looked around the well-appointed room. "I might have expected as much. I suppose you burned down your cottage so you could make yourself comfortable here in all this finery. This is not at all what I had in mind for you when I enrolled you into the Puddling Rehabilitation Program."

No. Her father had wanted her to suffer in very modest conditions. Starve to death. Be so deprived of fun and food and company that she would be grateful to marry *anyone.*

"Your daughter did not burn down Stonecrop Cottage. In fact, she was heroic, rescuing her housekeeper. I have explained this to you," Tristan said, his voice wooden.

"So you say. Perhaps *you* set it on fire, so you could put her under your roof and get your hands on her fortune as well as her bottom."

Sadie felt her face grow warm. "Papa! Don't be absurd. There's a perfectly good explanation—"

"Don't waste your breath. It's not as if I'll ever believe anything you'd tell me after your past history of prevaricating. Charlton has lost all patience with you as well."

"Good," Sadie muttered.

"Is it? He intends to sue me for breach of promise, you ungrateful chit! He loaned me money on his expectations."

"*My* dowry, you mean. *Mama*'s money. I don't care if you both wind up in bankruptcy. Serves you right! I am not some prize cow to be traded between farmers!"

Sadie saw Tristan's lip quirk for just an instant. To be sure, she felt plenty cow-like in this dirt-brown bag of a dress.

Her father appeared on the verge of apoplexy. "You should be married by now! I promised him!"

"Well, *I* didn't. I told you and told you I never wanted to marry any of the men you picked out for me."

He gave her an unsettling smile. "This was your last chance, my girl. This program. This godforsaken village. So much for their reputation for working miracles. You'll go to Bedlam where you belong and I'll get my money back for the treatment, which has certainly not worked. The Chancery Court will have no choice but to agree that you are insane once presented with years of evidence and your funds be released to me."

"Now, see here, Duke." Tristan's cheekbones as well as his ears were streaked with red. "Your daughter is no more mad than you. You cannot force her—"

"Who are you to tell me what I may do with my own daughter? Some back-of-beyond baronet's son? You've had your fun with her. I should horsewhip you!"

"I have done nothing—" He broke off his denial. Tristan's lips thinned.

Oh, dear. He must be remembering the very naked encounter in his bath. That mistaken almost-kiss under the stars. Those recent playful pats. The sparks that had flown between them ever since they'd met in the Stanchfields' store, hotter than the fire at Stonecrop Cottage.

Tristan stood abruptly, looming over her father. "How much money do you need?"

"I doubt you have enough," her father sneered.

"You might be surprised. I may be only a baronet's son, but I am the grandson of a duke's daughter and her principal heir. Grandmamma was very fond of me. I will pay you to go as far away as possible and settle your business with Charlton."

Sadie felt alarm course through her body. "Tristan! You can't—"

Her father's mouth twisted. "*Tristan.* Just as I thought." He pushed himself up from the sofa and glared into Tristan's eyes. "You have compromised my only child and no amount of money will make up for *that*."

As if she meant anything to him beyond being a source of undeserved income. "Papa, don't be ridiculous. I only met Mr. Sykes yesterday."

Gracious, it *was* only yesterday. Such a very lot had happened, none of it particularly good.

"He's a fast worker I see. You'll marry her then." Sadie watched in disbelief as her father poked Tristan's broad chest with a stubby finger. "I'm sure we can come to favorable terms regarding her dowry and any other amount you may wish to settle upon me for my trouble. She'll be your problem now."

"I am not a problem, and I don't want to marry anyone. I certainly cannot marry Mr. Sykes. I—I barely know him, and absolutely nothing untoward has happened!" Sadie said wildly, lying only a little, rushing between them. "This is all a terrible misunderstanding."

"He'll marry you if he knows what's best for this little scam they're running here. Who would send their vulnerable loved ones to be cured where they'll only be debauched by one of the governors? My poor Sarah is probably just one of many young women you've ruined."

"He didn't debauch anyone—and I'm not ruined, more's the pity. Oh, damn it, Papa! You don't even care anything about me." Sadie felt her eyes fill with tears of frustration. She could not let her father win. Not like this. She *would* be ruined, married to a man who didn't love her—who didn't even like her except on the odd occasion when she was undressed in an attic. Her fists clenched, as they so often did when dealing with her disappointing father and men in general.

Tristan Sykes touched her arm. "Be still, Lady Sarah, and don't worry. I'll have Mrs. Anstruther send up a pot of tea for you to settle your nerves. Your Grace, let's go below to my father's study. I'm sure we can work out the details like gentlemen."

Sadie dashed her arm away. "Tea? I don't want any bloody tea! You can't both decide what's to become of me while I'm locked up here like a, like a—"

Tristan raised a wooly eyebrow. "Like a lunatic?" His voice held warning.

Sadie had no doubt her father was desperate. That he would indeed incarcerate her somewhere, use his ducal influence to get his hands on her inheritance. It was a wonder he hadn't tried before now. She opened her mouth, but nothing came out.

"I'll take care of this. I'll take care of *you*," Tristan said with quiet resolve. "The jig is, I believe, up."

Chapter 12

Tristan had known Lady Sarah Marchmain was trouble from the first moment he'd clapped eyes on her on as she howled on the Stanchfields' floor.

But he could never have anticipated precisely how much trouble, even after committing her dossier to memory, as all good Puddlingites did for every Guest.

Tristan had a newfound appreciation for the Duke of Islesford. The man was impervious to reason, facts, and emotion. The duke wanted his pound of flesh and his money, and so would he get it, no matter the effect on his only child.

And Tristan had no reason to doubt that the duke would do everything in his power to throw a spoke into Puddling-on-the-Wold's wheel if he didn't cooperate. Tristan was supposed to be restoring the village's reputation as a place of sanctuary from everyday sin—instead, he found himself at the center of a potential scandal. He would deserve the uproar. He was a governor of the Puddling Rehabilitation Foundation, and had taken advantage of a Guest.

Though who had taken advantage of whom was a sore point.

He would have to marry Lady Sarah, damn it. He'd seen her long naked legs and touched her soft bottom, and had been caught at it.

The duke was busy writing letters to his solicitor and the Archbishop of Canterbury in his room. Tristan was staring into the bottom of a brandy snifter.

His father might be pleased. One didn't get a higher-placed daughter-in-law unless Tristan were to wed one of the royal princesses. Linnet had been a mere viscount's girl.

At least there would be no legal impediment to marrying again in the church. Linnet was long dead.

Tristan had thought himself dead to the idea of becoming a husband again. He had no interest in trying to soothe the histrionics of a high-strung woman once more. It seemed the gods were having a bit of fun with him. His life was about to become a living hell.

He'd have to lay down the law. He could only imagine how receptive Lady Sarah Marchmain would be to *that*.

They wouldn't have to cohabitate. He was perfectly happy in his bachelor quarters across the wide expanse of lawn. Sarah could have reign over the house, at least until his father came home from Paris. *If* he came home.

Tristan would have to write to him, but there was no rush. He wasn't anxious to explain how things had advanced this far and he had put the entire operation of the village in jeopardy.

He poured himself another finger of brandy. It was early in the day for him to drink, but he didn't usually sign his future away so soon after lunch.

There was a rattle of doorknob. Tristan had locked himself into his father's study to sulk.

"Go away."

"I will not! You've just left me to rot upstairs. What is going on?"

It was his damned fiancée. Delightful.

With great reluctance, Tristan put his brandy aside and strode across the ancient carpet. Lady Sarah—or someone—had brushed her hair and braided it in a neat crown around her head.

It seemed a pity to bind such beauty.

She entered the room in a blur of brown homespun and flash of white ankle. "Well? Is my father still here?"

"Oh, yes. He's arranging for our wedding the day after tomorrow."

Lady Sarah rolled her eyes. "For heaven's sake. Have you no backbone? We can't get married."

"We must. I cannot allow our foolishness to hurt the Foundation's mission. The entire village's fortune depends upon our good name. Your father's influence could ruin everything we've worked for since 1806."

"Poppycock. My father hasn't a feather to fly with."

"It doesn't matter. He is still a duke, and people will listen to whatever he has to say. You know what the ton is like. I cannot risk it."

She stalked over to his desk and picked up the decanter of brandy. "Have you another glass?"

Ladies did not drink brandy. Why was Tristan even surprised at her request? He went to the cupboard and selected a glass. He knew better than to offer to pour.

She filled half the snifter and downed it in one gulp. Was the prospect of becoming Mrs. Sykes really so ghastly?

Apparently so. She set the glass down with a clunk. "You don't have to do this. If you help me run away, my father won't find me. I'll need some of your grandmother's money, though. I have nothing. Not even clothes, as you know."

Run away? How on earth could she survive? She was for all intents and purposes practically certifiably crazy, and didn't even have a maid.

"Out of the question."

Her bronze brows scrunched in irritation. "Why? Because I thought of it?"

"It's a ridiculous idea no matter who thought of it."

"More ridiculous than attaching oneself for life to someone who is completely unsuitable?"

"My birth may not be as high as yours—"

"Oh, for God's sake. I am not talking about our standing in society. It's all rubbish anyway. My father doesn't deserve his exalted status—it's an accident of birth. He's made a hash of everything he's touched. If it wasn't for what's left of my mother's fortune—who was the daughter of a woolen mill owner, by the way—he would be living in a hovel on the Continent to avoid his creditors."

Ah. Tristan felt somewhat mollified. But she was right—he wasn't suited to be anyone's husband. His marriage to Linnet had proved that.

And the thought of Lady Sarah as a docile, compliant wife was risible.

He shook his head. "I will not help you run away. I'm sure we'll muddle along somehow."

"I don't want to muddle along! You don't want to marry me—you think I'm a disgrace."

"You can't deny you've gone out of your way to develop a difficult reputation," Tristan reminded her. Certifiable, yes indeed.

"Yes! So no one would want to marry me!" She threw herself down on a leather chair and clenched the fabric of the ugly dress between her fists. "Really, I won't need much money to escape. I can disguise myself as a man and wear your old clothes. Cut my hair."

Tristan could do nothing but laugh. Anyone less masculine was hard to imagine.

"Lady Sarah, I'm afraid we'll have to accept our fate. I cannot allow you to go racketing through the countryside in trousers. That's how we got into this fix, if you recall."

"*Allow* me? If you hadn't been such a prig we would be in Stroud shopping right now."

"Do not blame this predicament on me," Tristan said, annoyed. "You've dug your own grave."

"And I'll wish I were dead, being married to a man like you! So, so judgmental. So officious. So *mean*!"

Unfair and untrue. Tristan knew himself to be a perfectly ordinary gentleman. He was not prone to fits or flights of fancy. He was steady. Solid. A great catch.

If he had wanted to be caught.

"There is no point to us arguing. The arrangements are being made. I have a responsibility to Puddling, and now a responsibility to you."

She picked up the empty snifter. "I don't want to be some sort of duty. An albatross." She wound up her arm and smashed the glass into the fireplace.

Tristan should make her clean the mess up herself. The servants would have enough to do organizing a wedding. "Don't be childish. Destroying things will not change our circumstances. Your father is set on this marriage, and I cannot blame him. You know we have overstepped the bounds of propriety." *You especially*, he wanted to add.

"I don't care," she said, stubborn as usual.

"Well, I do. Though you needn't worry I'll expect to exert my husbandly rights. We'll have a marriage of convenience." Inconvenience was more like it. "You'll have your independence—within reason."

Her mouth opened, then snapped shut. Good. He had finally robbed her of speech. Tristan had a feeling that didn't happen very often.

Chapter 13

Insufferable. Insupportable. Insolent. And all the other "in" words she couldn't think of at the moment. If anyone was going to make the rules about their relationship, it should be she. It was her life that was officially ruined.

A white marriage. Devoid of all physical contact and comfort. Sadie supposed she should be happy that Tristan Sykes wouldn't be pawing at her night after night, but for some reason she wasn't.

Did he find her so unattractive? She didn't believe it. At twenty-one, she'd been the recipient of men's speculative looks for too many years. She recognized lust when she saw it, and Tristan was just loaded with it—when he wasn't being disparaging and oh-so-chilly toward her. If she was going to marry him, she'd have to find out more about his first wife. No doubt the woman was responsible for Tristan's grumpy reserve.

Oh, hell. What was she thinking? She wasn't going to marry him, and she didn't care anything about his divorced-then-dead wife. Sadie was going to run away, with or without his help.

She plastered a smile on her face. "Excellent news. As if you ever had a choice."

His lips twitched. "I should think you'd be grateful for my sacrifice."

"Oh, please. Let's not out-martyr one another. Can I go shopping *now*? I cannot get married the day after tomorrow in your maid's best dress."

Sadie's mind was whirling like the inside of a well-made watch. There was a train station in Stroud. If she could somehow get away during a shopping expedition, she could escape this insanity. The only one who deserved to be institutionalized was her father. She was being forced into a marriage just because she had been caught half-undressed and her bum patted! Surely grounds for a lifetime of misery had to be more substantial than that.

She knew the real reason. Her father had come to financial terms with Tristan. He would get sufficient funds "to give his blessing," and would no doubt be bleeding his unwilling son-in-law dry for the rest of his life. No matter how much money Tristan had inherited from his grandmother, it would never be enough to assuage Sadie's father. The duke was a very expensive man.

That was another reason to run away. Tristan might be a little grim, but he didn't deserve to be saddled with the Duke of Islesford for a father-in-law.

"I cannot take you shopping. There is the matter of the special license which must be obtained in London. I leave tomorrow."

If Tristan was going to London, she'd have to go in the other direction.

"Very well. What about Mrs. Anstruther? Or Miss Churchill?" She clapped her hands. "I have it! Mrs. Fitzmartin! You surely cannot object if I am chaperoned by the vicar's wife."

Tristan's eyes narrowed. "The woman is a million years old. I don't trust you not to try and trick her."

"I would never do such a thing!" Sadie lied.

"Let me give it some thought. I will see you at dinner."

The last thing on earth she wanted was to sit across a table from her sputtering father. "I'll have a tray in my room."

"No, you won't, you coward. We will face your father together."

Sadie was *not* a coward. She had done any number of courageous things in her life, things that had required intestinal fortitude and her celebrated cunning. Hadn't she just tried to send a message to the outside world just yesterday? She supposed she could face her parent, but it would be nice to do so in proper clothing.

She'd go back to the attic and see what could be found for tonight. Also, she would sneak Tristan's old suit and other disguising items down for her next adventure. While she couldn't leave for Stroud with a suitcase, there was no reason why she couldn't layer some clothes underneath this hideous baggy dress.

"Why are you smiling like that all of a sudden?" Tristan asked, suspicious.

Sadie schooled her face. It wouldn't do to reveal her plan. Tristan seemed fiercely intelligent even if he couldn't figure out how to wiggle out of an unnecessary betrothal.

But then, her father could be most persuasive. Dukes did seem to get their way more often than not, as did their daughters. "Tell me about your grandmother."

"What?"

"Your grandmother. The one who left you the pots of money you tried to bribe my father with."

Tristan sighed and poured himself more brandy. "She was a scandal. Like you."

"Thank you very much," Sadie said sweetly. "What were her crimes?"

"She refused to marry the man her father picked out for her. See, I told you she was just like you."

"And the poor girl was sent to Puddling. What else?"

"Isn't that enough? Disobedient daughters are the very devil. Thank God we will have none."

Sadie bit her tongue. It was far too soon to tell about that sort of thing. One day she might quite like to be a mother, although the thought of crusted nappies and spit-up was less than appealing at the moment.

"Is that her portrait over the fireplace? I saw one like it at the parish hall." She'd asked some questions then and had gotten an earful from Mrs. Fitzmartin. Tristan's grandmother was a byword of bad behavior.

Tristan looked up. "Yes. One of the proper ones. I believe there are some nudes in the attic."

Sadie clapped a hand over her mouth. She had never dreamed of posing without clothes, but then again she didn't know any artists who might have helped immortalize her.

"How did she come to marry your grandfather?"

"Oh, the usual way. They were caught in a compromising position, and Bob's your uncle. It was a fait accompli, and entirely engineered by my grandmother. Evidently my grandfather never seriously objected."

No wonder he seemed sanguine about their sudden marriage. He was repeating family history. But it still was ridiculous.

"They had a love match, although Granny Maribel never really settled down. Ran my grandfather ragged." He took a sip of his drink. "You would have liked her."

"She sounds fascinating." Lady Maribel had welcomed her wedding and never thought to run away.

Sadie was no Lady Maribel.

She stood up. "I'm bound for the attic again. Please see that I'm not disturbed. That includes you. You've seen quite enough of my legs for one day."

She enjoyed the beginnings of Tristan's blush. He rose and opened the study door for her, and she sailed out, nose high in the air.

That worked until she had to climb all the stairs to the attic and had to watch where she was going. A loose carpet on a stair tread was almost her undoing. She couldn't run away if she was bedridden with a broken leg.

Aha! If she couldn't escape tomorrow, she'd have to pretend to be ill. Maybe she could even enlist kind old Dr. Oakley's help. Surely he wouldn't want her to be forced into a marriage no one in their right mind would want.

And that was a problem. Tristan would suspect she was just playacting again. He'd probably send for a doctor from London. A hospital full of them: Specialists who would look straight into her eyes and down her throat and know that she was faking.

Lots of things to consider. Sadie had a headache already and she hadn't even dined with her father or the man he insisted she marry.

But maybe it was the damned brandy. She'd never had any before today, and still couldn't see what the fuss was about.

Chapter 14

"Fucking hell." Tristan usually tried not to swear, or to show any emotion, really. He'd had enough of unfettered emotion—ducking vases and crockery and flying books for the five miserable years of his marriage and even after when Linnet had come to weep and plead for him to cease the divorce proceedings. When the tears hadn't worked, she'd resorted to her old tricks, and Tristan bore a scar in a very private place to prove it.

But he was not going to have a bastard carry the Sykes name, and the way Linnet had been going, that was all too probable. He'd been as hard-hearted as he knew how to be.

He had no way then of knowing she had a cancer of the womb, and that conception would never have been possible. She'd died, alone and in disgrace.

Tristan carried the guilt still. If he'd somehow been able to please her—

No. It was pointless to try to change history. To change his nature, or hers, for that matter. Linnet had been a born coquette—flighty, irresponsible, impassioned. Perhaps she'd somehow known her life would be cut short and tried to experience all of the forbidden. She had been much too young when they married, barely seventeen, and had never really grown up.

But by God, he had to change the present, because, according to the furious telegram from the Duke of Islesford, his fiancée had done a bunk.

Tristan knew he shouldn't have trusted Lady Sarah to behave in his absence. A shopping trip to Stroud for bride clothes indeed. With three blasted chaperones he'd deputized—a maid, the Reverend Fitzmartin, and his wife. Five if Old Fred the coachman and his son, Young Fred, were counted. He would have been better off shackling her to Anstruther, although the sight of a woman's unmentionables in a dressmaker's shop might have caused the man an apoplexy.

A wasted day. All those papers he'd signed at his solicitor's and bank, so many his hand grew tired. The useless special license in his pocket. Tristan looked around his London flat to see if he'd overlooked anything. A hansom cab was waiting downstairs to take him to the railway station. He'd arrive on the very last train as planned, in preparation for tomorrow's wedding-that-would-not-be.

He raked a hand through his hair and clapped a hat on his head. Where in hell could she have gone? Lady Sarah had no money and no clothes. As far as Tristan knew, she had no friends in Gloucestershire to help her. Stroud was unfamiliar, although the station was easy enough to find. She could have boarded a train to anywhere.

Damn it. As head of the Puddling Rehabilitation Foundation's governors, Tristan was responsible for her well-being. The Duke of Islesford would make a stink that would impossible to cloak with all of the Sykes House's garden flowers.

But the duke *was* right there in Puddling. He should have been in charge of his own daughter, shouldn't he?

Fat chance. No one was in charge of Lady Sarah. Tristan wasn't going to skate away so easily.

The dark trip home seemed endless. He tried to distract himself by reading the architectural contracts he'd brought with him by the train carriage lights, but all the words and numbers fuzzed together.

The madwoman would be the death of him. If he couldn't concentrate on his work, what would become of his reputation? It had been difficult enough to redeem himself in the eyes of society after the divorce. A man who couldn't control his wife—well, how could he be trusted to oversee the building of a house? Workmen were known to be wayward too.

Tristan was met at the station by Old Fred and his son, who practically pulled their fetlocks and apologized profusely for letting Lady Sarah get away this morning. He checked his watch—a long twelve hours ago. Twelve hours was a lot of time to get up to mischief.

"It wasn't anyone's fault but mine. I should have locked her up," Tristan said, halfway meaning it. The princess in the tower—he imagined her shouting the walls down, or worse, donning trousers and descending efficiently to her escape.

Puddling was quiet as they passed the locked gates that closed the town off from the main road. If the other governors had been notified of Lady

Sarah's disappearance, there was no obvious sign of distress. No villagers with flambeaux were beating the bushes or marching off to Stroud.

Less than a mile beyond, Old Fred turned into the long avenue that led home. Tristan saw that Sykes House was ablaze again, every window lit. These damned Marchmains were costing his family too much money.

He'd steeled himself to deal with the duke, or so he thought. But he hadn't expected the man to burst from the house as if he'd been shot out of a cannon, if one wore a paisley dressing gown to fly across the air.

Tristan didn't wait for the carriage steps to be put down before he dropped to the driveway. "Any news, Your Grace?"

"Not a word! What are you going to do to bring my daughter back?"

"I'll go in to Stroud first thing tomorrow morning." The station master's office had been closed when Tristan got off the train, otherwise he would have asked questions.

"Your man already did that. Made up some story, but I didn't believe a word."

"Anstruther?"

"I have no idea what the man's name is. Looks like a ghoul."

"I'll go home and speak with him."

"What do you mean?"

Tristan attempted to be patient. "I already explained I do not live in my father's house. I have a cottage on the property. And if you don't mind, it's very late."

The duke's face flushed in the lamplight. "You dare to talk of sleep when my only child is missing? She could be lying in a ditch this very moment! Dead or, or decapitated!"

The duke's imagination was working overtime. Frankly, after the things Lady Sarah had said about the man, Tristan was surprised Islesford was as upset as he appeared to be. If Lady Sarah was indeed unhappily headless, her fortune would go to her father, wouldn't it?

"Lady Sarah is a very resourceful young woman. Let's not borrow trouble. I will do my utmost to find her—you have my word."

"Pah. As if your word means anything. You all promised to protect and fix my little girl, and where is she now? You don't know; no one knows. What kind of a place are you running anyway? I'll see to it no one of quality is ever snookered by any of you again! I've cabled my solicitors again, *and* a detective agency in London. Their man should be here tomorrow."

"Excellent," Tristan lied. *Damn*. If word got out that Puddling had lost a Guest, it would harm their entire operation.

And he didn't want Lady Sarah lost. He might not want to marry her, but he realized he didn't want one copper hair on her head harmed. "I'm sorry Lady Sarah went missing, but I understand that it's not the first time, Your Grace. Her previous, shall we say, *adventurous* history is familiar to every Puddling citizen." Lady Sarah had been running away from home for years.

"All the more reason for you to have taken better care of her," the duke grumbled.

"I couldn't be in two places at once, Your Grace. You insisted on the special license."

"You'll marry when she's found. Or else."

Not if she was headless. Tristan sighed. "I'll see you in the morning. I'm sure the staff will be delighted to provide you with whatever you need to make your night more comfortable and ease you to sleep." Brandy, or possibly a well-aimed cricket bat.

Tristan bid the duke goodnight, grabbed his satchel and walked briskly through the gardens to the Red House. The air was perfumed with the last of the roses, and he breathed deeply. But his peace would be cut up until he got his hands on Lady Sarah Marchmain.

And when he did, would he cuff her or kiss her?

His cottage was in darkness, which was odd. Usually Anstruther left a lamp burning on the rare occasions when Tristan came in late. He lit the candle in the entryway and found Anstruther's note, which appeared to be written in haste:

Have taken the liberty of pursuing a lead on Lady Sarah. A woman of her description was reported to have bought a ticket to Gloucester. Returning to Stroud and taking the train. Will inquire with utmost discretion. Staying at the new Station Hotel tonight. Will keep you informed.

The Freds had said nothing about Anstruther leaving either time. But bless the man for his initiative.

Tristan picked up the candle, shedding his clothes as he made his way down the hallway. He was too tired to tend to them tonight and would do so in the morning. He was not in general slovenly, although it was hard to fully eradicate the dirt from beneath his fingernails. But he hated to wear gloves in the garden—the touch of roots and leaves always calmed him.

He'd need to *live* in a hollow tree in the garden once he and Lady Sarah were married. Like one of those hermits people hired to make their properties more picturesque.

If they married. He'd have to retrieve her first. So imagine his shock when he got to his bedroom and found her curled up in his bed.

Chapter 15

It had been a perfectly dreadful day. Watched by Mrs. Anstruther and a fleet of maids and footmen once she came down to breakfast, Sadie had been unable to smuggle out any valuables beneath the voluminous folds of all her clothes. Not even a teaspoon—Mrs. Anstruther had held out her hand at Sadie's brazen attempted theft without saying a word. It had been awkward to even climb into the carriage, and both Fitzmartins had given her a rheumy-eyed look at her sudden bulk.

Her revised plan had been to escape once in town, find a secondhand clothes shop, divest herself of the layers she had dressed herself in, and accept whatever coin was offered. Her gown would be the first to go—it was as shapeless as a sack, and it would be far more convenient to ride the rails dressed as a man.

Sadie hadn't been able to cut her hair off. It was a moral failing on her part, but she was very fond of it and the effect her riot of red curls seemed to have upon some gentlemen. But she'd squashed a cap in her reticule— empty of any money—and planned to cover up her crowning glory as she fled her future.

Nothing had gone as planned. She *had* managed to duck out the back door of the dress shop Mrs. Fitzmartin took her to—a terribly inferior place—on the pretext of needing to use the loo in the narrow walled garden. The wall had proved remarkably tricky to scale. But once she was free on the unfamiliar streets of Stroud, Sadie had been unable to find a pawn shop of any kind. She had been wretchedly hot in all the clothes she'd donned, too. And the worst of it—she could hear a locomotive's whistle not far from where she stood. The train station was close, but might have been on Mars for all the good it did. She had no money at all for a ticket, and now bitterly resented buying that cinnamon raisin bun earlier this week at the Puddling bakery with the last of her allowance.

So she had wandered aimlessly for what seemed like hours, considering her options, ducking into alleyways when she feared discovery. Her best bet was to climb into a cart and take her chances as to the destination. The object was to get away, wasn't it? It didn't much matter where. Sadie would throw herself at the mercy of a stranger. She was not going to be forced into a marriage of convenience, especially since it only convenienced her father, and any kind, charitable person would agree.

It looked as if her luck had changed when an elderly but pleasant looking farmer parked his wagon if front of the apothecary where she had been studying the glass bottles in the window as if they contained the answer to the universe. She watched as the farmer conversed with the man behind the counter.

Time was of the essence. One of her minders was bound to discover her if she waffled any further. Sadie ducked under the tarpaulin in the back of the cart and held her breath—there had been an odiferous passenger there before her. A goat? Chickens? There were traces of feathers and other substances Sadie really didn't care to examine more closely.

One had to do what one had to do. She had curled herself up into a bulky ball and found the jolting on the country road almost soothing, as she had not slept very well the night before. She had been very close to nodding off when the wagon made an abrupt stop and she rolled into a corner like a billiard ball.

There was conversation, and the creak of a gate. Sadie could make out nothing of the words spoken, though it lasted quite a while. Eventually the wagon resumed its journey and she was thrown again into the corner as it descended what felt like a mountain peak.

This time the wagon rolled to a gradual stop, and Sadie felt the vehicle shift as the farmer climbed out. He whistled, and Sadie had heard a happy yap from a distance, which turned into a growl as the animal came nearer. The previously delighted dog hurled itself into the cart on top of the canvas, its paws scrabbling over her and its teeth nipping through the fabric.

So much for a stealthy arrival.

"Ho, Moll, what have we got here?" the farmer had asked.

He then exposed her cowering body as the border collie revised its method of attack, licking her face with exceptional vigor. The man clucked like a worried hen, and shook his head the whole time Sadie, fending off the dog's misplaced affection, tried to explain her predicament.

And predicament it was. She was right back in Puddling's village limits. Up the steep hill, she could see men working at the charred end of Stonecrop cottage, and even the elegant proportions of Sykes House and its gardens a little way beyond the town. Her old farmer, Ham Ross, was the very fellow she had stolen pumpkins from in what now seemed like a very juvenile prank.

Of course he was in no mood to assist her. Besides the pumpkin thievery, he shared in Puddling's economic fortune. An escaped Guest would do no good to the foundation's reputation, and so he told her. The entire village would suffer. And why wouldn't she want to marry Mr. Tristan? He was a fine young man. Handsome, too, even with the Sykes eyebrows.

She sat in her wretched stinking clothes with Moll on her lap while Mr. Ross lectured her on her perfidy. Nothing Sadie said in her own defense could save her. No one "in their right mind" would help her, according to the fellow.

So she would have to save herself. Sadie put the dog aside and inched her way off the bed of the wagon. Surely Mr. Ross was too elderly to chase her? She could hear the rush of Puddling Stream to her right. So what if she got a little wet?

Sadie had not counted on Moll. With one command from Mr. Ross, the black and white dog ran circles around her, causing her to trip. She was usually not clumsy, but perhaps wearing three or four different layers had something to do with her winding up facedown in the farmyard.

Moll wagged her tail and snuffled at her neck. Traitor.

"Now look, Lady Sarah." Mr. Ross's tone had been stern, although she could tell he found her situation amusing. "Come in for a cuppa, and then we'll see about getting you back to Sykes House in one piece. They must be up in arms."

"I don't want to see my father," Sadie muttered into the dirt.

"He'll be worried."

"Good. Let him stew."

Mr. Ross helped her up. "The Bible says you must obey your parents."

"If Moses knew my father, he might have made an exception on the tablet," Sadie said, brushing off her skirts.

One cup of tea had led to three, and a substantial platter of remarkably good scones with homemade strawberry jam. It had been so easy to talk to Ham Ross, who was not quite eighty and had seen and heard a great deal in his life. He proved to be sympathetic up to a point—he was not going to assist in any escape, however. But he did agree to bring her to Sykes House the back way, and to stop by the Fitzmartins to tell them she was all right—Sadie did feel a bit guilty there. Word would travel through the village, and everyone would sleep soundly tonight. He promised to say nothing to Tristan's staff, for then her father would be blistering her over his knee, or trying to. She thought she could outrun him, but was frankly exhausted.

This time Sadie was concealed in a swept-out wagon between two lavender-scented quilts. Ham Ross was stopped at regular intervals as they moved through the village, and he discovered that Anstruther had left the Red House with a satchel, off on the train for a fruitless search for that duke's daughter.

He brought her to the back gate of Sykes House, wished her joy of her impending marriage, and gave her a grandfatherly pat on the head.

He was such a nice man. Sadie had not been so comfortable with anyone in ages. Reluctantly, off she went, heading up the winding path through the gardens to the Red House. She would be safe there, at least until Tristan returned.

And she'd been so very tired. It had been simple to shed her layers of clothes, wash, curl up in his bed and nap off the tea and scones, all as the sun dipped behind the Cotswold Hills. She must have slept for hours, for it was fully dark, save for the candle flickering in Tristan Sykes's hand.

"What the bloody hell!"

The sharp planes of Tristan Sykes's dark face were illuminated. Was this the face she would have to wake up to every morning? He looked somewhat satanic, and as weary as she had been before her refreshing interlude in his bed. She supposed she should have hidden in Anstruther's monastic little room, but Tristan's massive carved bed had called to her.

Sadie raised herself up against the feather pillows. Maybe he wouldn't notice that she was wearing one of his linen nightshirts. *She* couldn't help but notice he was only attired in a pair of drawers. "Good evening, Mr. Sykes."

"Good evening? Good evening! This is what you have to say for yourself? My entire household has been upended because of you! Your father wants to ruin me!"

"Oh, he's always cross at the least little thing. You really shouldn't let him cow you."

He looked as if he would like to strangle her—she was familiar with that sort of look—but then thought the better of it. Slapping the candle holder on the bedside table, he growled, "Move over."

Chapter 16

"What?" she squeaked. Tristan was pleased to see her sleep-rosy cheeks pale.

She should be punished. Swiftly. Hard. His palm itched. Her curly coppery hair was braided like a schoolgirl's, and he longed to grab one of the plaits and shake her.

Ever since he got the damned telegram, he'd spent the day rushing to get home, dying a little of impatience for every mile of countryside the train clacked through. Worrying and feeling helpless, the duke's crumpled telegram in one pocket, the special license in another.

Tristan had imagined worse things than a beheading befalling her. A woman traveling alone with no resources? She'd been reckless in the extreme escaping like that. Absolutely anything could have happened to her, even in this quiet corner of Gloucestershire. Tristan had no great confidence in the saintliness of mankind.

With the exception of the estimable and ancient Fitzmartins, who could have dropped dead from failing to do what they perceived as their Christian duty to chaperone her. Clearly Lady Sarah had been allowed to run wild for far too long. She respected nothing, no one, not even the safety of her own person.

She needed to be tied up and isolated until she knew her proper place. Fed stale bread and water if necessary. If she thought Mrs. Grace's cooking was bad, she hadn't seen anything yet.

The future of Puddling was in his hands—and the thorn in its side in his bed. She was not going to run away again.

"You heard me." Tristan barely recognized his own voice.

She pulled the covers up. "You cannot talk to me like that."

"Really? You are in my bed. We are to be married tomorrow. I'm tired."

She darted away as he sank into the mattress. It was a good thing her side of the bed was flush against the wall. Lady Sarah Marchmain was going nowhere unless she tried to crawl over him.

Let her try.

"I—you—"

"Shut up, Lady Sarah. Haven't you caused enough trouble for one day? You will apologize to the Fitzmartins before the ceremony for you causing them so much distress. To poor Anstruther. To my driver and his son as well. Whichever maid you ditched, too. Was it Hannah or Audrey?" They were twins and he sometimes mixed them up.

"H-Hannah. And we are not getting married!"

Tristan raised an eyebrow. It was usually enough to strike terror in the observer's heart. "Oh?"

"There's no need to knuckle under to my father. I thought about his absurd demands all day. You do *not* have to marry me."

She was the one being absurd. She was in his bed, in, by God, his own nightshirt, which looked much sheerer on her than it did on him. They were entirely alone in the house, with not even old irascible Anstruther for company.

Indeed he had to marry her, if only to live with his own conscience. He could see the pink of her nipples.

Quite pretty they were, too.

"I do, or he will contrive to put an end to Puddling's success. I cannot let the village down." Tristan blew out the candle for his own protection. If he couldn't see her, he wouldn't want her so badly.

In theory.

Bloody hell. What was wrong with him? He wasn't some young Etonian looking at a naughty French photograph cadged from a wicked uncle. The madwoman should not appeal to him at all, even if she was within a foot of him, scrabbling at the covers. She was mad, after all.

And so very—singular. All that blazing red hair. Those very long legs. The odd gooseberry-colored eyes. Her impressive br—

Tristan punched his pillow down. He smelled lavender. Wasn't that supposed to be restful? However, not an inch of him felt at peace, particularly his manhood.

Which was expanding by the second.

Men were indeed pigs, just as Lady Sarah believed.

"Lie down and go to sleep. We have a busy day tomorrow."

"You can't tell me what to do! And I will not sleep in here! It's not proper."

Tristan's lips turned up. Imagine Lady Sarah lecturing him on propriety. She, who was infamous throughout the country for her hare-brained exploits.

"You've already been asleep in here," he reminded her.

"But you weren't home!"

He rolled onto his back. "You might as well get used to sleeping next to me."

She gasped. "Didn't you say just yesterday that you had no intention of consummating this marriage that is being forced upon us?"

"Did I? That was short-sighted on my part. I must not have been thinking clearly—you do seem to have that effect on me." Tristan sighed, enjoying himself far more than he thought possible. "I'll need an heir eventually. My duty, as it were. I may only inherit a baronetcy, but it's very ancient, you know. Wouldn't want to let the ancestors down."

"Duty!" Lady Sarah uttered the word as if it were a hairy spider to be spat out. "I'm not some broodmare."

"Didn't you and Roderick Charlton plan on having a family?"

"We never discussed it. One doesn't. It's not—"

"Proper?"

She hit him on the shoulder with a pillow. "Oh, you are an awful man."

Dear God, she wasn't going to turn violent like Linnet, was she? He'd had enough of that in his life, thank you very much.

Apparently God had a sense of humor that Tristan didn't share. He snatched the pillow and tossed it to the floor. "Behave yourself."

"I don't know how!"

And then the mattress shook. At first, Tristan thought Lady Sarah was bouncing to be annoying, but he realized she was crying. Without any sound. The bed was like a ship in a storm, heaving and rocking.

He was not going to take pity on her. She was in a coil of her own making. Everything she'd done since she came to Puddling had been meant to cause trouble, and now she was reaping what she'd sowed.

Oh, hell. He sat up and edged over to her. She was stiff and unyielding when he drew her close. Her tears were hot on his bare shoulder, and slid down his chest, little rivers of scorching despair.

"Don't. It won't be so bad."

No. It probably would be worse. Tristan was not suited to be anyone's husband, and Lady Sarah was no one's idea of a comfortable wife. Thrown pillows would be the least of it, he was sure.

"I want H-Ham," she stuttered.

Why was she speaking of meat at a time like this? "What?"

"H-Ham Ross. The farmer in the valley. He knows you and says you are n-n-nice," she wailed, attempting to push him away with not very much effort.

"You are not going to Ham's. My guess he's asleep by now." The old man was a wonder, running the farm with such vigor as if he were half his age. He rose before his rooster told him to. "How do you know him?" Apart from stealing the man's prize pumpkins.

"I climbed into his wagon in Stroud."

Tristan let out a bark of laughter. "From the frying pan into the fire. I expect you didn't think you'd wind up back here."

Lady Sarah shrugged in his arms. She'd stopped shaking and batting at his chest, resigned to his embrace. But he could still feel the tears flowing.

This was all kinds of wrong. She didn't want to marry him—she didn't want to marry, period. Her father was a buffoonish bully who had no right to manipulate their lives and threaten the livelihood of Puddling.

But Lady Sarah was in his bed, barely clothed. He'd seen more of her in the past few days than many men did of their own virtuous wives. Tristan had never seen Linnet completely nude in all their years of marriage, and now that seemed absurd. He'd been an idiot.

He was still an idiot.

He wanted to finish that kiss she had started the other evening. He'd almost returned it. True, it had been unexpected and at the time unwanted. He'd stopped following through with it when he'd come to his senses.

Oddly enough, he didn't want to be sensible right now. But someone must be.

Gently, he set her back into the pile of pillows. "I'll go sleep in Anstruther's room." He wondered what her expression was—he couldn't see in the dark. Was she relieved? She must be.

"But you must promise me not to run away again. We're getting married tomorrow."

He felt the mattress shift. She was silent. Somewhere in the distance, an owl hooted, reminding him he was not much of a nocturnal creature. He needed to sleep.

"Lady Sarah? I need your word."

"I cannot give it." Gone was the weepy woman. She sounded quite forthright. Determined.

Hell. So much for Morpheus turning up anytime soon.

"You would run away in the dark?" he asked, incredulous.

"If I have to. I'm only here because Mr. Ross made me come back. And I was so tired. I smelled, too."

She didn't smell of anything now but lavender and his own bergamot soap, a heady fragrance that was playing tricks with his senses.

"You took a bath in my tub?" Against his will, Tristan pictured her, snow-white skin, endless legs, and her breasts bobbing in the bubbles—he stifled a groan.

"I had to. There had been a goat, you see."

Of course he didn't see. The only thing he saw clearly was that he'd need to stay awake all night with this infuriating—and intriguing—young woman.

Chapter 17

She should never have come here.

But here she was.

Sadie should have lied, said of course she'd stay the night. Of course she'd marry him tomorrow. She was relatively good at lying, had honed her skills on her nannies and governesses and father. Her untruthfulness was one of the reasons there had been such a turnover in the staff as she was growing up. Until Miss Mackenzie, who was built like a stevedore and could swear like one too.

Nothing naughty Sadie did escaped Miss Mackenzie; the least little infraction was always punished. Sadie believed her father had stolen the governess from a women's prison. She might have even been an inmate for all Sadie knew. Miss Mac was a terror.

And long gone to her reward, wherever that might be.

God hates a liar. Miss Mac's favorite words as she blistered Sadie's ruffle-clad behind.

God probably was not all that pleased with Sadie now either. She had caused a commotion running away, frightened her elderly minders, and had not even managed to get anywhere.

What were her chances setting out at night on foot from Sykes House? Sadie peeked out the casement window. There wasn't even a moon, just a spatter of stars in the velvet-black sky. Her borrowed clothes were in a terrible goat-infused state, and she still had no money.

If she hadn't been so filthy and exhausted earlier, she would have secreted away a pair of Tristan Sykes's candlesticks to sell somewhere once she ran away again. He had some lovely things in this little house. Evidently he was a man of some taste and discernment, which was only fitting for an architect and garden designer.

Did he look upon her as a collector might? It was too dark to tell now that he'd blown out the candle. Was she one more pretty thing to put on a shelf? Some men thought that's all a wife was—a decorative object who was meant to keep her mouth shut and her legs open.

He didn't really want to marry her either. Why was he so insistent upon it? Just because he was afraid her father would make a stink about Puddling's propriety and efficacy? No one with any sense would pay attention to her father.

"Fine. I won't run away again. But you can help me leave." She could borrow some money instead of steal from him. Once she was on her feet somewhere far, far away from her father, she'd repay him, of course.

"I will do no such thing. I've made a promise, and I intend to keep it."

"Why?" Sadie cried. "Because of this stupid village?"

"'This stupid village,' as you call it, depends upon me. I am temporarily the head of its board of governors. It is due to my failing that the life's blood of Puddling could dry up in an instant."

"Pshaw," Sadie said. "My father is a bankrupt."

"But a well-connected one. He is a duke, Lady Sarah, and dukes have sway, no matter how disappointing and duplicitous they might be. We cannot survive any rumors, my dear. Our unimpeachable reputation has lasted almost eighty years. We've done an awful lot of good in that time. I'll not be the one to let Puddling down."

"But it's your life! Your future! We don't even know one another!" How could he willingly martyr himself to silence her father's bluster? It wasn't as if he were a soldier who had to fall on his sword to save his country.

"I'll manage," Tristan said shortly. "You will too."

No. Sadie didn't want to *manage*. She wasn't going to lie underneath a virtual stranger for the convenience of Puddling, no matter how attractive he was.

And she had to admit that Tristan Sykes was a very good-looking man.

But that didn't matter. She hardly knew him, and he didn't know her at all. Did he know her favorite color or fruit or what she liked to read?

"I don't understand you at all," she said.

Tristan sighed from across the bed. So far, with the exception of trying to console her when she briefly lost her composure, he was keeping a scrupulous distance. "No, I don't expect you do. We men have our sense of duty and honor beaten into us from the time we're in leading strings. You ladies may complain the male sex has all the advantages, but there are disadvantages as well."

She waved a hand between them. "This is all ridiculous." Although hardly a laughing matter.

"Is it? Marriages have been built on shakier foundations. At least we've met."

"Just a few days ago! We have nothing in common."

He chuckled. "We don't know that, do we? We both may be mad for...plum pudding."

Stir-up Sunday. Sadie used to help with Christmas preparations at the castle, such as they were. Her father had rarely been home for the holiday.

"One cannot live on plum pudding." She did have an excellent recipe, though.

"Right. It's much too rich to eat every day. We'd have to buy you a new wardrobe to accommodate your growing *avoirdupois* if that was all that was on the menu. Well, *a* wardrobe in any event. You do need one, although you missed your chance today."

Why was he making fun? Sadie had thought of him as a serious person. A bit boring and stodgy, actually.

She felt herself tearing up in frustration again. Perhaps she should try to go back to sleep. Maybe some sort of miracle would occur tomorrow morning and all this difficulty would disappear. Her father might choke on his toast....

Oh, she would be punished for breaking that pesky respect-your-parents commandment. And truly, she didn't wish her father ill. She just wanted him to go away and leave her alone.

"You're crying again!" Tristan accused. He must have particularly acute hearing, since one couldn't see one's finger in front of one's face, it was so dark in the cozy bedchamber.

"Am not." Sadie sniffled.

"Blast it. Come here." He patted the space between them as if she were an obedient dog.

"I'm perfectly fine."

Tristan snorted. "No one in this room is perfectly fine. We've both had a wretched day. Let's make the best of this, shall we?"

"And how do we do that?"

"I think I have to kiss you."

Sadie's heart stuttered to a stop. She remembered that last kiss. If one could call it that. She'd wound up on her bottom in the dirt. "I beg your pardon?"

"You know what a kiss is. Our lips will brush against each other oh-so-gently, then still and glory in the touching. You might open your mouth just a little out of curiosity. Our breaths will mingle, and the hair on the back of your neck will rise. You might actually shiver a bit, and I'll want to warm you. Stroke your shoulders and arms. Cup your cheek. My tongue will enter your mouth and seek yours. You'll be so surprised when they make the softest contact possible that you'll forget your troubles and relax in my embrace. Enjoy yourself. Get into the spirit of the thing. Kiss me back. Feel a flood of heat from your scalp to your toes."

She felt hot right now with his every reasoned word. "Dream on!"

"Well, all right. We won't kiss, though it seems a great pity. We'll just go to sleep together. Next to each other. But I don't trust you not to flee, so I'm afraid—" He stopped talking and got off the bed. Sadie could hear him rummage in the chest of drawers.

"What are you doing? I already said I wouldn't run away!"

"We all say things we don't mean, you more than most. Don't forget, I've read your dossier."

So had Sadie, even if it had been a bit butter-smudged at the baker's. Talk about a pack of lies. Well, exaggerations. Her father had not stinted in describing her behavior in the worst possible light. No wonder Puddlingites gave her the side-eye as she walked down the five streets on her daily constitutional.

Tristan fiddled with his tinderbox and the candle sprang back to life.

And then Sadie bit back that tongue which was supposed to tangle with his. Dangling from his hand was a set of shiny silver manacles.

Chapter 18

Tristan had never used the cuffs before. In fact, he'd forgotten all about them, bought on a lark for a fancy-dress party he couldn't attend after all. He'd intended to go as a Regency-era Bow Street Runner, red waistcoat and all.

But the prospect of staying awake all night watching Lady Sarah Marchmain had reminded him that help was, so to speak, at hand, in case he couldn't keep his eyes open after all.

Now where the devil had he put the keys? Anstruther might know, but the poor fellow was off on a wild goose chase.

"You cannot be serious!" The horrified look on her face was worth every moment of agony he'd experienced today.

Served her right. It was best to begin as you meant to go on. Tristan would have to assert the upper hand in this relationship or the saucy Lady Sarah would run him ragged.

Goodness, he was chock-full of hand references.

"I am. Would you prefer to be attached to the bed or my wrist?"

"Are you insane?" she spat. She was like a cat, hackles raised. Even the loose tendrils of her red hair looked like it was standing on end.

"I don't believe so, although dealing with you might predicate the eventual loss of one's mind. Hmm, I suppose the bedpost is a better option—it would be awkward to have company in the bathing chamber. Speaking of which, perhaps you should avail yourself of it before I limit your movement." Surely the keys could be found tomorrow morning. If not, Tristan could take a hacksaw to the metal before the wedding ceremony.

Or not.

"I am—you are—I don't need to go!" Lady Sarah spluttered.

Tristan shrugged. "Suit yourself. It's practically morning anyway."

Lady Sarah leaped out of bed, putting Tristan in mind of a gazelle he'd once seen in a zoo. "You are not to touch me! I will tell my father what you planned to do!" She backed herself into a corner, and her legs were very much in view.

"No doubt the old boy will applaud me and wonder why he never thought of it himself. Really, how else am I to get a wink of sleep?" He fought back a yawn. Perhaps just the threat of handcuffs would induce her to lie down and behave herself.

"You are barbaric! Criminal!"

"Let's not get carried away with the name-calling." He twirled the manacles, and they glinted in the candlelight. "Fine. What do you suggest then? Would you prefer rope? One of my neckties?"

"I would prefer my freedom! In all things. In four years I am to come into a substantial sum, and I want no husband to take my money away from me!"

"I have no interest in your money. Your father and I have already discussed that in our negotiations. You are to spend what you want, and leave the rest of it in trust for our children. If we have any, which at this point remains doubtful. The solicitors are writing up the formal contracts."

Lady Sarah gave him a goggle-eyed stare.

"By the way, your father thinks *I'm* crazy," Tristan continued. "It's a pity I can't take advantage of a twenty-eight-day sojourn in Puddling to cure myself of my magnanimity."

"Oh." There was quite a lot of emotion in that one syllable.

"Did you really think I was such a villain?"

She tucked a loose strand of hair behind an ear. She had braided her hair before bed, two long ropes that fell over her breasts and down to her waist. Tristan tried hard not to look at her ankles or her calves or any parts north. "Roderick wanted my money."

He shook his head. "I don't think that was all. Your father says the man loves you to distraction." Tristan wasn't sure why, exactly. Yes, Lady Sarah was rather glorious to look at, yes, but she wasn't precisely *lovable*.

But then, he wasn't either. He could be a right moody, dull sort of bastard, or at least Linnet had thought so.

Bah. He should not be thinking of poor Linnet hours before he was to get leg-shackled again. Maybe this time would be different.

Maybe it wouldn't.

"So." She paused, working her long white fingers together. "You and my father have sorted all this out?"

"I hope so. I saw my solicitor in London today. Your father has been telegraphing his." At Tristan's expense, no doubt. The completed paperwork was due to be delivered tomorrow—this—morning by special courier.

"And you won't keep my money."

"Not a farthing." He had more than enough for his, and a wife's, needs. She still didn't look happy. Maybe it wasn't just about the money. Maybe she didn't want to live as any man's wife. Was she afraid of intimacy?

Tristan though back to her spontaneous kiss the other night. A grandfatherly kiss, according to her, meant for his cheek until his lips got in the way. A short while ago, she had trembled under his touch like a startled fawn.

He faced her from across the room. "Has Charlton kissed you?"

Her russet eyebrows knit. "What?"

"Have you been kissed, Lady Sarah? Do you remember my description?"

"One could hardly forget it," she replied dryly.

"Shall we put it to the test? Seal your pledge to not run away tonight?"

Her eyes slid away from his. "My word should be good enough."

He raised an eyebrow and she flushed. As the pink stained her cheeks, Tristan felt an unaccountable urge to trace the color to her collarbone. She looked very, very fetching in his nightshirt.

"J-just one kiss. And then you will go to sleep in Anstruther's room like you said and leave me alone."

Tristan didn't want to leave her alone. The idea of securing her to the bedpost and having his wicked way with her was tempting beyond belief.

But how much better would it be if she came to him willingly? Sought her pleasure freely? He wondered if that would ever happen. If it didn't, they were both facing a future of emptiness. A marriage in name only. Unlike her, Tristan kept his word, although it would be hell not to ever touch her. He'd only mentioned heirs to rattle her since she'd given Puddling—and by extension him—such grief today.

If he wanted her in his bed at some point in time, he would have to woo her, and frankly, that seemed like a lot of trouble. Too much trouble. Tristan was tired of jumping through hoops.

He was just plain tired.

But he walked across the room, dropping the manacles to the carpet, palms open. "See? No coercion."

She was very still, almost rigid. He could almost hear the argument within her. She'd agreed to the kiss only to get rid of him, but there was something...

Did she find him as attractive as he found her? His physical response to her was treacherous. Surely she could see the bulge in his smalls.

Because men were pigs. Tristan was only confirming her opinion. He was at the mercy of his body because, God help him, she was a lovely disheveled vision of young womanhood. Innocence. She might have been wearing a plain man's nightshirt, and her glorious hair was confined to two meandering braids, but he'd never seen anything lovelier in his life than his doubtful, devious fiancée.

Tristan recognized the abyss when he saw it. And he was about to jump into it, for better or worse.

Chapter 19

It was only one kiss. Contrary to what Tristan Sykes thought, Sadie had been kissed, and sometimes it was even she who had initiated the kissing. But that was years and years ago, when she was a foolish, lonely young girl. Before her heart had hardened to the world and men's monetary machinations. The most recent of her many suitors had gotten nowhere near enough to touch their lips to hers. Roderick had only kissed her hand, and she had immediately rubbed it clean on her skirt every time he did.

Roderick. He would not be pleased at this course of events, but that was her father's problem to deal with. At least if she married Tristan Sykes, she would not have the urge to brush crumbs from Roderick's ginger mustache for the rest of her life. Happily, Tristan was clean-shaven, though his face was shadowed by dark bristles at the moment.

She wouldn't touch them.

Sadie took a step forward and wobbled a bit. She really didn't feel quite steady on her feet, but it was best to get this kissing business over with.

Tristan had been married, so he must know how it was done. Her previous kisses with Dermot were inexpert to say the least, and six years ago. Once her father had discovered their budding liaison—thanks, she knew now, to Dermot's treachery—Dermot had been sacked from Marchmain Castle. Sadie had long stopped wondering what had become of him.

One couldn't marry the groom when one was a duke's daughter. Even Sadie knew that.

Why was she thinking of Dermot, with his straw-thatch hair and the friendly little gap between his front teeth? By now, he probably was the father of a houseful of children with some accommodating country girl. He'd had such a way with horses and women it was inconceivable to think he wouldn't have fallen on his feet, found employment and female company. And the money her father had given to shut him up would have helped to get him settled somewhere.

Not that they'd really done anything irrevocable—Sadie was boringly intact as far as she was aware—but Dermot had claimed they had, armed with all the stupid letters she'd written to him. Had he even known how to read?

Her first betrayal. The bastard. Which was accurate in all ways.

Don't think, Sadie. Regret was too bitter a taste, and led to indigestion.

She wasn't going to let herself feel, either. She wasn't going to look into Tristan's careful blue eyes, or notice the tic at his jaw. Nor would she look at his broad bare chest and the springy dark hair that wended down below the waistband of his smalls.

She shut her eyes reluctantly. It seemed the only way to get through this.

Sadie heard him move across the floor, a telltale creak that he was too near. She felt the heat of his body, smelled bergamot and man and a greenness that was always present about his person.

A roughened fingertip lifted her chin. She wouldn't look.

At first she wasn't sure she'd understood him correctly. His mumbled words vibrated against her temple, causing a chilly lick down her spine.

God help me.

This was an odd time for him to pray, wasn't it? And surely the god of the Anglican Church had no interest in two betrothed—if unwillingly—people kissing the day before their wedding. It was all very regular. Unexceptional.

Until his mouth claimed hers and Sadie's knees buckled.

His lips were hot and hard. There was no preliminary tentativeness, no gentle exploration. This was a kiss meant to conquer, to destroy all doubt. His tongue swept her mouth open and found hers, smoothing its way across the soft tissue with complete confidence. Sadie parried back, surprising herself. She was grateful he held her shoulders with iron fingers so she wouldn't stumble, though she wondered if she'd be bruised by morning.

The kiss showed no sign of lessening or lightness. Tristan was making a credible, thorough, very respectable job of making Sadie swoon. Lose all sense of time, propriety and dignity. Make her limbs turn liquid and her blood sing a song she couldn't understand. There had never been a kiss like this before in the history of her world.

One corner of her disintegrating mind made her realize that Dermot was not the established Romeo she had once thought him to be.

Who could imagine one's mouth could be so sensitive? That something as blunt and ugly as a tongue could work such magic? That this man, who was a stranger who didn't even *like* her, could make her feel—

No. She wasn't going to feel. This was simply a physical reaction, like putting your hand down on a hot stove and scorching yourself. Nerves or synapses or something—she hadn't really paid attention when Miss Mac lectured her on the natural sciences. Of course her body was responding, but it did not mean her head and heart had to.

But, oh, she would let him do this for a little while longer before she shoved him to *his* arse.

He showed no sign of wanting to stop either. One of his hands had left her shoulder and was snaking through her bound hair. The nape of her neck lit with fiery joy. Just more action and reaction, Sadie reminded herself. It didn't mean anything, though his touch at her scalp had an adverse influence on her nipples, which were suddenly erect. But he wouldn't know that; there were still some inches between their bodies, though their faces remained attached to each other.

Tristan was a very deliberate man, attentive to details. Well, he'd have to be, wouldn't he, since he was an architect. One needed strong foundations to support pillars and posts and what-not. He licked her teeth and the inside of her cheek. Both of them. Her palate, too. His tongue had been completely given over to her pleasure, dancing across it with adeptness.

Mr. Sykes was nothing but adept. In fact, he was dangerous.

Sadie felt an alarming heat skip through her body, a desire to eliminate those inches between them and press herself against his bare chest like the hoyden everyone thought she was. But there would be grave consequences, for once Sadie embarked on one of her harebrained ideas, she usually couldn't stop herself.

And it was definitely harebrained to fall into Tristan Sykes's clutches like some moony schoolgirl. Yes, he was handsome as blazes. And skillful with women, if this kiss was anything to go by. She could easily imagine his rough hands running over her naked skin and having no objection whatsoever.

"Unh." The groan just slipped out. She'd always had an overactive imagination.

Tristan took it for permission, wrapping a braid around his fist and drawing her closer.

Oh dear.

And there it was. They were front to front, and every marble plane of his masculinity was imprinted upon her. She certainly couldn't miss his manhood jutting into her belly, and he probably was not missing her diamond-hard nipples, either.

Inconceivably, the kiss became even better as their bodies touched, when Sadie could have sworn it had been perfect as it was. Tristan's remaining hand relinquished her shoulder and cupped her misbehaving breast. He thumbed the naughty nipple, soliciting another groan from Sadie.

This was all too much yet not enough. Why were they still standing up when a perfectly good bed was a few feet behind them?

No no no.

Sadie pushed him away with remarkable feebleness. She, who was known for her strong right hook, even if she was left-handed. She stood gasping, hot and cold, elated and miserable.

Tristan's bronzed face was flushed, his blue eyes hooded. His hands hung at his side, hands that were apparently as magical as his tongue.

"Stop," she whispered.

"As you must notice, I already have." His voice was grave.

"Well, now I've promised. You can go," Sadie said with false brightness.

"Can I?" He made no move to leave the room.

His room. Maybe Sadie should sleep in Anstruther's.

"W-we had a deal."

"Did we?"

Why was he being so obtuse?

"Yes, we would kiss, and I wouldn't run away." Tonight, anyway. She could barely stand up, her heart was racing, and her mind was total mush. How far could she get? She doubted she could find the front door of the Red House at the moment.

"You know we did! I only kissed you to make you go to bed."

His lips quirked. They were still swollen. "I'd love to go to bed." He raked her with a look that sent shivers to her toes.

"Well, go on then. Anstruther's gone off to look for me, as you know, and his room is available."

"Is it?"

"Stop asking these damnable questions!" she cried. "Go away!"

He shook his head. "I think not. It wouldn't be wise under the circumstances. Now that you've experienced true passion, you might be frightened and renege upon your promise. I'll stay to comfort and reassure you."

Ridiculous, wretched man! "I'm not afraid of you or anyone. And passion? Pooh!" Sadie tried to snap her fingers but failed.

"Nevertheless." He blew the candle out and the room was in full darkness. What the devil would he do next?

And would she let him?

Chapter 20

By the saints and all that was holy, Tristan was in trouble. Why didn't he walk out the door and bed down in his valet's monastic little cell?

Three words: Lady Sarah Marchmain. A few more: a cockstand that wouldn't quit. He doubted he'd be able to walk anywhere for a bit. Let her get settled back onto the bed, then Tristan would thrust—unfortunate choice of words—a pillow between them and try to get some sleep before the wedding day arrived. He still didn't trust her not to escape. No kiss could constrain her innate wildness and poor judgment.

The kiss had frightened her. Hell, it had frightened *him*. He was not unfamiliar on how to arouse a woman, despite his youthful failure with Linnet. Lady Sarah had been aroused and then some. He had never in his thirty years felt such a violent, desperate desire for a woman, and he was fairly sure that desire was reciprocal.

And now he thought to sleep chastely beside her, separated only by a pillow and his gentleman's sense of honor? He was a hopeless optimist.

Or a first-class fool.

The sky outside was turning gray. His white nightshirt on her luscious body was visible in the gloom, though Lady Sarah's face was in shadow. She wasn't gliding toward the bed like an obedient future wife, but standing stock-still.

Tristan sighed. "Please, Lady Sarah. The cock will crow any minute now." Hopefully his own cock would quiet down.

"I don't want you here!"

"Can't be helped." He was so exhausted he didn't trust himself not to sleep through any attempt on her part to flee. Would he hear the quiet snick of the front door or a creaking floorboard? But if she had to crawl over him, now that would surely wake him up. Her strong, long legs, her soft bum brushing by—

"I won't kiss you again!"

A pity.

"That's quite all right." Tristan couldn't withstand another burning encounter and keep his wits about him anyway. They were more or less wandering as it was. He gave in to a yawn without covering his mouth. She couldn't see him or his tonsils.

"I don't like you at all." He imagined he could see her scornful pout. The little liar.

"Again, that can't be helped. Maybe one day you won't find me to be such an ogre. Now, do be a good girl and get into the bed."

He knew that was a mistake as soon as the words came out of his mouth. Lady Sarah Marchmain hadn't been a good girl since she was a little one, and probably not even then. By her own admission, she didn't know how to behave. He ducked her fist with an agility he didn't know he possessed at this late hour.

She was shouting at him now as he darted about the room trying not to trip on anything. Where was the soft, sensual woman of their kiss? He had no interest in subduing this virago by placating words or gestures.

He'd have to grab the bull by the horns. Or grab the cow, since Lady Sarah was most definitely female. Not a flattering appellation, and he had the good sense not to state it out loud. He tackled her as she came at him and tossed her onto the bed.

There was a great deal of squirming and invectives. The latter did not bother him, but the former did nothing to squelch his lust. It was like wrestling with a slippery if seductive eel. Because of her height and slenderness, she was very difficult to get hold of, but Tristan and Wallace had wrestled as part of their youthful fitness regime. Lady Sarah was no one's little brother, however, and it took far too long for Tristan to remember the basics.

"If you do not cease this at once," he growled, "I will not only manacle you to the bed, but gag you. Enough!"

She stilled too quickly under him. What trick was she contemplating now? Did she know how to unman a man? It seemed very likely, and Tristan adjusted his position accordingly.

"Let me go."

"Not a chance."

"You are a brute!"

"Name-calling never solved anything." He could think of a few negative names for her himself. Shrew. Provocateur. Imp.

Goddess. Oops. Where did that come from?

"You cannot make me stay!" Her voice was wobbly, and Tristan knew what that meant.

Don't cry, don't cry, don't cry.

He was only a man, and she had unmanned him without benefit of a knee. So he kissed her again, tenderly this time. At first she sniffed and didn't open to him, but he was patient and she relented. The kiss was very sweet, almost innocent. Except they were lying down, and nature was definitely taking its course. She was trembling beneath him, and Tristan sought to soothe her. His hand slipped under the nightshirt to her satiny skin and she gave that delightful groan again.

She was warm. Soft. Precious. And his for the rest of his life, however long that would be. She might decide to kill him in his sleep or over the breakfast table. Her temper was unpredictable.

He'd gone through this once before. What had he done to deserve such abuse?

He needed to stop touching her. Kissing her. Tristan needed to get control before Lady Sarah Marchmain took advantage of his state of insanity. Would the Puddling Rehabilitation Foundation give him a discount?

The handcuffs were on the floor somewhere. It was almost light enough to find them without a candle. Withdrawing gently, he gave the corner of her mouth a final lick, tasting the salt of her tears, and laid his forehead against hers. It was unfortunate he couldn't tell what was really behind her alabaster brow, but maybe he didn't want to know.

He felt her eyelashes bat his cheek as he centered himself for the task ahead. And then he sprang with sudden alacrity off her supple body, snatched the cuffs from where he dropped them, and bound her wrists together in a feat of considerable skill and stealth.

Her shriek was inevitable.

"Hush. We are going to sleep now. In about four hours, we'll become man and wife, and then you can yell at me all you want. I'll need my rest to cope with it."

"Cope? How can you do this? It's evil! Depraved!" She rattled the chain between her hands. He hoped she wouldn't try to garrote him with it while he slept.

"Not so very. It's just a precaution. I'll remove the manacles for the ceremony." If he could find the key.

The bed roiled as if they were at sea in a Shakespearean tempest. Tristan placed a hand on her shoulder and she bucked away. "Good night. Good morning, really." He turned his back to her, taking up more than half the space on the bed. Deliberately he didn't try to roll against any part of her body, but he could sense her heat and fury.

Perhaps he'd bitten off more than he could chew. It was difficult to imagine sharing a bed with such a spitfire in the future, no matter how delicious her kisses were. He could buy Lady Sarah her own domicile, or better yet, build one to her specifications. He owned some land on the other side of Puddling, just waiting for improvement. She might look upon him more favorably, and one day could possibly come to some sort of affectionate accommodation toward their forced marriage.

And...there was always divorce. He'd survived one failure. Why not another? He was older now, and his heart wasn't engaged this time. The duke wouldn't be pleased, but damn the duke anyway. Tristan would have lived up to his responsibilities to Puddling, and Lady Sarah would no doubt be relieved to be left alone. She'd thrived on scandal ever since her debut, hadn't she?

A divorce would show her true scandal.

What a grim view of his impending nuptials, planning for dissolution before the wedding day dawned. The last time, Tristan had been almost too eager, and impossibly naïve. Twenty years old. He'd been a baby. He knew better now.

Willing his breathing to slow, he closed his eyes against the weak gray light coming from the casement window. He hoped his staff had the preparations in train. He'd left a specific set of instructions before he'd left for London. Flowers in the family chapel, a hearty wedding breakfast, a proper bouquet for his bride, which he would do up himself. It was a shame she'd found nothing to wear, but there wouldn't be many wedding party guests to notice.

Lady Sarah was remarkably silent behind him. The bed had ceased to pitch, too. Excellent. Tristan gave in to another yawn and tucked the blanket under his chin. Just a catnap would do the trick.

The clock on the mantel ticked away, bringing them both closer to their fate. Tristan relaxed, and slipped away into an uncertain dream.

Chapter 21

Sadie had tried to sustain her anger. She'd been kissed into quasi-submission and then ignominiously shackled by the beastly baronet's son, two good reasons to call for blood or some good old-fashioned bludgeoning. But somehow listening to the regular, lulling breaths of her captor—she wouldn't call them snores, exactly—Sadie fell asleep.

She woke to the gunshot of rain on the roof, a heavy downpour that was entirely suitable for her unwanted wedding day. Her wrists itched from the metal bracelets, and her temper re-flared.

Tristan's side of the bed was empty.

Perfect. A little rain wouldn't hurt her. She might not have clothes, but if she could find her shoes she would take this opportunity to flee.

Sadie bounced out of bed. No noise came from the adjacent bathing chamber. She peeked in, pleased that she could relieve herself in private. Taking care of necessities, she splashed water on her face with her joined hands. The mirror revealed unraveled braids and a mouth that was chafed from those wretched, remarkable kisses.

She couldn't do anything about her hair with her hands in their current state, but out of spite she used Tristan's damp toothbrush and splashed a little of his bergamot cologne on her neck to freshen up.

The house was silent apart from the beating rain. Sadie didn't trust her luck, so time was of the essence. She managed to fish out her half-boots from the pile of goat-scented clothes and stole a frockcoat from Tristan's wardrobe to toss over her shoulders. If she could manage to do up some buttons, it would keep the worst of the weather off her unbound breasts. There was no question of tying corset strings.

Sadie felt no guilt whatsoever stealing from Tristan Sykes. She found a silver-backed brush and comb set, scissors and a pair of onyx cufflinks lying carelessly on the dresser, and stuffed them into a coat pocket. Even if she looked like a tramp, she would have something to barter with. Somehow, she'd get the handcuffs removed, too, even if she had to bite them off herself.

She turned the bedroom door handle, but nothing happened. She was locked in!

Ooh! Once she got her hands on him, he would be sorry for the rest of his miserable, manacle-loving life.

Sadie sat back on the bed, her mind whirring. If she stood on a chair, she could climb out the window. It would be tricky to fit through it, but she was thin enough.

Her stomach rumbled. *Too* thin at the moment. She was starving. Ham Ross's scones and jam were ancient history as far as her stomach remembered.

She needed to get of here first before she worried about breakfast. Sadie shoved a worn leather chair beneath the window, hopped up and opened the latch. A blast of rain hit her in the eye, and she blinked.

It certainly was coming down. Anyone mad enough to be out in this would be soaked to the skin in an instant. Sadie hoped Tristan was off drowning somewhere.

No. Not really drowning. Maybe floating in a torrent of wild water, being swept out to sea where he couldn't kiss or confine anyone else for a long, long time. If he wound up on a deserted island with rotten coconuts, it would serve him right.

Someone knocked on the door, and she heard the rattle of keys. Jumping from the chair, she prepared to give her jailer a very large piece of her mind.

It wasn't Tristan, but the twin maids Audrey and Hannah, who were very wet indeed. Sadie had given Hannah the slip yesterday, and had the grace to blush at both of them, since she wasn't sure which was which.

"We've come to help you get ready, my lady," one of them said with some firmness, putting a case and a basket on the bed. Sadie could smell coffee. She would have preferred tea.

"Ready for what?" Sadie cracked.

"Your wedding," said the other. "Mr. Tristan's in the chapel waiting, since it's bad luck for the groom to see the bride before the ceremony. The carriage is outside to bring you to the chapel. Young Fred and Old Fred are in the parlor, and you're, um, not to get any funny ideas about running away, because Mr. Tristan has authorized them to take any measures necessary for your safe delivery."

"Like tie me up and spank me?" Sadie asked, incredulous.

"Whatever it takes. Oh, and he apologizes, but he did not find the key to the handcuffs."

Sadie was appalled. "I am to be escorted to my wedding like a convict?"

"Yes, my lady. I'm sorry." This must be Hannah. She didn't sound sorry at all. "You are to eat a bite of breakfast. There are fresh rolls."

Sadie raised her arms. "And how am I supposed to eat and get dressed? I can't marry in a nightshirt!"

"No, indeed, my lady. We're going to feed you, and then cut off Mr. Tristan's, um, nightshirt." She pulled a pair of evil-looking scissors out of her apron pocket. They could easily double as a weapon, and were far superior to the scissors she had stolen.

Sadie realized her proposed flight and entire arsenal of over-reaction was useless in the face of the determination of the twin maids. Tristan had obviously warned them to beware. Audrey held a roll to her lips and Sadie took a vicious bite, just missing the maid's fingers. A sip of hot coffee from a jar came next.

Everything tasted like lead. She shook her head when offered more, and the twins shrugged.

"Get on with it."

Sadie was silent while the garment was sliced off her. She should not feel embarrassment to be naked before staff; she'd spent most her life relying on others to help her get dressed and undressed, even when her father couldn't afford to hire proper maids. But she knew her face was red, mostly from anger.

"What's in the case then?" she asked. Hopefully not any of the tiny outdated garments from the attic.

"Some lace curtains, my lady. Audrey is clever with a needle and will fashion something suitable."

Curtains? *Yellowing* lace curtains. Unbelievable! Dusty, too. Sadie coughed as the maids shook the fabric with vigor.

The twins sliced up a plain shift and sewed her into it. Then came a pretty corset, a corset cover, stockings, and too-tight satin slippers. A cage bustle petticoat was tied around her waist. My word! They though to make her a fashionable bride in used curtains? It was too absurd.

She held her cuffed hands out straight in front of her and they cut and pinned fabric on her as if she was a dressmaker's dummy. Sadie was afraid to say a word they stitched, half-expecting Hannah to poke her with a needle to get back at her for ditching her yesterday.

Audrey stepped back after a half hour of hard labor. Her forehead was damp, and she spat the pins out of her mouth into her hand. "Not bad, considering."

"It's brilliant, Audrey, and you know it! Now for the hair."

Hannah was none too gentle as she pressed Sadie down into a chair and dragged a brush through her tangles. In the meantime, Audrey attached a swath of lace to tarnished diamante combs. They had thought of everything.

Hannah brought a large velvet box from the case. "The deWinter diamonds. Mr. Tristan insists that you wear them. They belonged to his grandmother, and are his wedding gift to you."

And were ancient and ugly, Sadie decided. The necklace felt heavy and cold on her throat, the ear drops threatened to pull her earlobes to her shoulders, and the tiara gave her an instant headache. She supposed all the glittering diamonds were well enough, but the jewels would benefit from a new setting.

"This is ridiculous," Sadie complained.

"Do you think so?" Hannah pushed her toward the mirror on the back of Tristan's bedroom door.

Well. Perhaps not so very ridiculous. It was not immediately obvious that she was wearing curtains, and not even her father could sniff at the large diamonds she was decked out in. She looked good. Beautiful even, with the irritated flush of color bright on her cheeks.

She rattled the chains between her wrists. "What about these, then?"

"The bouquet will cover your hands. Mr. Tristan made it himself."

He did, did he? He'd been a busy boy this morning.

The maids escorted her from the bedroom to the parlor, where the Freds were keeping watch over an enormous spray of fragrant white flowers lying on the sofa. Sadie recognized them at once. They were from the garden Tristan had created for his dead brother, and she felt something turn in her heart. He must have picked every one.

"Lively now," the older man said, opening an umbrella in the entryway.

"Bad luck, Pa. You shouldn't open an umbrella indoors," his son said.

"Old wives' tale. We don't want Lady Sarah to get wet now, do we? Anyhow, rain on the wedding day means fertility." Old Fred gave her a wink.

"Talk about an old wives' tale!" Young Fred said.

"You'd better stop arguing, or there will be no young wife," Sadie said acerbically.

They hustled her into the carriage, the twins holding her train aloft from the sodden grass. The vehicle squeezed through the garden paths, which had been designed for foot traffic only. The rain pummeled on the carriage roof, branches tapped against the windows, and a bright bolt of lightning landed quite near. Sadie felt as if she was in the middle of a Gothic novel and expected Frankenstein to jump out of the bushes at any moment.

Instead, it was Mrs. Anstruther who greeted her on the steps of Sykes House, with two footmen racing down with more umbrellas.

"You look lovely, Lady Sarah," the housekeeper shouted over the wind. Hannah—or Audrey—caught the veil before it could get stuck on the potted boxwood topiary at the door.

Sadie noticed the fresh flowers in the front hall, the gleaming black and white tiles. Her every sense was alert, smelling beeswax and furniture polish and rain. Her pulse was erratic, and her breathing tight.

She realized she was afraid.

According to Tristan, her money would remain her own, so it wasn't that. He'd promised her independence. Within reason. Whatever that meant.

Sadie didn't want to marry a stranger, even if he kissed like an angel. Or, more accurately, a devil. So she would not say "I will" when the time came, no matter how much her father raved in the Sykes family chapel. No one could make her change her mind or open her mouth.

Chapter 22

Considering the last-minute nature of his nuptials, the servants had made a concerted effort toward perfection. The house was always well-run, but everything seemed to have an added sheen today. The chapel itself, even with all the gloom of the heavy rain outside, was alight with candles and lamps, and the altar was covered in flowers.

Mr. Fitzmartin stood before the altar in his cassock, looking a touch anxious. But Lady Sarah wouldn't be running away from him today. Mrs. Fitzmartin was there too to serve as organist and witness. Tristan's childhood friend David Warren, whose hobby was photography, would arrive later to immortalize the occasion.

Tristan wondered if, when he was old and gray, he and his wife might sit of an evening and admire photographs of themselves and their wedding day finery. If the old drawing room curtains could be considered adequate dress material. He'd thought them inspired when he'd hit upon the idea, but perhaps Lady Sarah was not in agreement. He himself was in a proper morning suit, complete with top hat.

The rest of the Puddling Rehabilitation Foundation governors had not been invited. The Duke of Islesford sat in the front pew, checking his timepiece for the eightieth time. He had been relieved to discover this morning that his daughter had been found, but not even curious where. "What's keeping her?"

Tristan had watched the carriage make its laborious journey through the gardens. Did she notice the horses' bridles were tied with soaked white ribbons? He'd tried to make this day tolerable, despite his own reservations.

"They should be arriving any minute, Your Grace. Perhaps you'd like to wait in the vestibule to walk her in."

The duke grumbled something but got up.

The air in the chapel seemed lighter without him. Tristan stuck a hand in his waistcoat pocket, feeling for his grandmother's wedding band. Gold, with a square emerald surrounded by diamonds. Lady Sarah might think it was a reference to her eyes. If she didn't like it, he was prepared to buy her something she would. He was perfectly ready to compromise on some things—within reason.

Tristan considered himself to be a modern man. He had no interest in tying a wife down to cater to his every whim, which was fortunate. Lady Sarah seemed unlikely to cater to anyone.

But tying her down might be fun. Tristan was beginning to worry at the direction his mind was taking regarding Lady Sarah, and tried to think of something else instead.

He heard the scuffle outside, then the duke's yelp.

The man should have ducked.

Lady Sarah marched in without him, cheeks crimson and eyes sparking. Mrs. Fitzmartin had no hope of accelerating the music to match her stride. After a few discordant notes, the woman gave up.

His bride was magnificent. Hannah and Audrey had achieved the unachievable. No one would ever guess the bride was wearing the old drawing-room drapes. The dress conformed to every inch of her body, with puffy sleeves and a low but not immodest neckline. Tristan looked forward to removing it as soon as it was possible.

The duke dashed after her, rubbing the scratches on his cheek, putting a halt to Tristan's daydream.

"Sadie, you hellion!"

Tristan's future wife ignored her father and stopped in front of Tristan. *Sadie.* The name suited her far better than the staid "Lady Sarah." The bouquet he'd made her with such care trembled, although one side was somewhat squashed where she'd clubbed her father with it.

She was nervous. And angry. Well, so was he.

"We'll have none of that nonsense, now, shall we? We must begin as we mean to go on." He spoke quietly. Firmly. And gave her that Sykes look that usually quelled rebellion.

"What the devil does that mean?" Lady Sarah—Sadie—asked, not bothering to lower her voice.

He took her elbow, wishing he were not wearing gloves. "It means we will approach this thing calmly. Like adults, not recalcitrant children. No tantrums. Definitely no fisticuffs."

"Calmly? Have you forgotten I am shackled like I'm a murderess?"

she hissed.

She looked completely capable of doing him in with whatever was handy. The altar cross? The silver chalice of Communion wine? Best she was unable to get to them, and held fast to her elbow. Preventive measures.

"Hush. I'm sorry about the key. When Anstruther gets back, I'm sure it will be located. Or—we'll find a hacksaw," Tristan said, somewhat desperate. She looked as if she'd hit *him* with the bouquet next. It had once looked lovely, one of his best efforts. Flower arranging was women's work, but Tristan enjoyed it anyhow. "Your father doesn't know of that unfortunate state of affairs. He promises to leave before the wedding breakfast."

"In this weather? Dream on. You won't be rid of him for days. He'll want to stay and celebrate that he's gotten his way. Drink every bottle of expensive wine in your cellar. Eat every scrap of food that's in the larder."

"Then you won't want to give him any additional reasons for celebrating and drinking and eating. Wouldn't he think it was a lark knowing your movements were hindered? He would have saved himself many a clout over the years when you lost your temper if only your hands had been tied."

"If I lose my temper, I am always justified." There was a martial glint in her eye.

"Well, I wish you wouldn't lose it today. Let's think happy thoughts."

Sadie snorted, and the vicar cleared his throat. "Ahem. Are you two ready to begin? This conversation is very irregular."

"Sorry, Mr. Fitzmartin. I'm afraid all of this is very irregular." And a far cry from his first wedding ceremony, with St. George's in London full of well-wishers, and his young bride in a Worth gown.

But Sadie was much more breathtaking than any bride Tristan had ever seen.

Begin as you mean to go on. Concentrate on the future, not the past. Make the best of this "irregular" situation. Find common ground.

A kiss would be a good first start. Tristan knew that was how some wedding ceremonies ended, although not usually with people in his class. One didn't display one's affection in public.

If one had any.

He thought he...might, confusing as it was. A sliver of affection, only. One had to admire Sadie to some degree. He was a mere mortal, and she was beautiful.

Why wait to kiss her until the very end?

He caught her by surprise, steering her toward him. Bending, he covered her lips with his, stealing her breath, tasting her sweetness. She kissed him back with no hesitation, surprising *him*.

This attraction between them was more than pleasant. It promised something rather spectacular if they didn't ruin it. Tristan resolved to do his best to be patient. Understanding. Sadie was still under the care of the Puddling Rehabilitation Foundation, and deserved every consideration.

Like kissing. Even if she was a hellion.

Tristan heard the duke sputter behind him, and a mild clucking from Reverend Fitzmartin.

"Yes, we definitely should begin before—well, before." The vicar rapidly rattled off a few of the requirements of the prayer book. The duke agreed to give his daughter away with unseemly alacrity. Tristan and Sadie murmured their assent to everything, although she did not meet Tristan's eyes. The ceremony was seconds from being over—and another kiss—when the doors of the chapel burst open.

Tristan turned to the red-bearded stranger. "What is the meaning of this?"

"I might ask you the same question, you bounder! I object!"

"Too late for that," Fitzmartin said, thumbing through his book. "We're a few pages past that point. Oh, dear. I've lost my place now."

"I don't care! Lady Sarah is my fiancée, and I do not release her from her obligations!"

"Honestly, Roddy, you're making a fuss over nothing," Sadie said, looking pale, her every facial freckle visible. "You're better off without me."

Roddy? Ah, Lord Roderick Charlton, the spurned suitor. Was Sadie Tristan's wife yet, or did they have to go through this rigmarole all over again? He hadn't gotten much sleep, and was tired of standing up when he'd much rather lie down in a soft bed with his new wife.

If she *was* his new wife. Come to think of it, he still had the ring in his pocket, even after promising to cherish, etcetera.

Hah. Old Fitzmartin might be past a lot of points.

"Duke, I thought you notified him of the change of circumstances," Tristan said, drawing Sadie closer to him.

"And so he did, by a bloody telegram, but he neglected to pay me back all the money he owes me!"

The slippery devil. Tristan thought of all the funds he'd just poured into the duke's bank. "This is about money?"

The man colored. "Not only that. I'm very fond of Lady Sarah. You don't have to marry this country bumpkin, Sarah. I will give you everything you need."

"I doubt it."

Well, that was a good sign. Tristan could not imagine his lace-clad bride in the arms of this red-faced fellow. Apparently, she couldn't either.

Tristan remembered to be insulted. He lifted a severe Sykes eyebrow. "Country bumpkin?"

"This is the back of beyond, isn't it? I don't care who your father is. *I* am a viscount."

The other eyebrow raised. Tristan had practiced alternating them in front of a mirror in his aimless youth. "So?"

"So, Lady Sarah deserves a title."

"And she will have it. Mrs. Sykes. Eventually, Lady Sykes, when God forfend, my father passes on."

"Pah! You're only the heir to a baronetcy. She is a duke's daughter."

Reverend Fitzmartin tapped Tristan on the shoulder. "Do you want me to go on with the ceremony? As far as I can tell, this gentleman has no standing, viscount or not."

"By all means."

"I do not recognize that our betrothal contract has been broken. My solicitor awaits your pleasure in the drawing room," Charlton said.

"I don't care how much paper you throw at me. Sadie is mine," Tristan growled.

"I am not! I am nobody's! I'll not be pulled apart between you beastly men like some ragdoll. I—I—I want Ham!" Sadie cried, tugging herself away from Tristan's embrace.

Charlton's confused face was a sight to behold, though Tristan didn't waste much time looking at him. "This is hardly the time to want to eat, my love," the viscount said.

"She is not your love." Tristan lifted Sadie's chin. "If that is what you want, I will take you there myself. Only let the vicar say the last words."

"N-no. This is all a big mistake. I—I didn't mean to agree to anything. But then you—oh!—and I forgot."

Tristan was not sure what she was talking about, but he knew one thing. "I don't think it's a mistake. Remember last night."

"When you bound me and forced me to spend the night in your bed?"

"What's this?" The duke rose from his seat. "What's going on?"

"Only this." Sadie dropped her bouquet and raised her shackled wrists.

Chapter 23

Sadie hadn't meant for poor Mrs. Fitzmartin to slip from the organist's bench and swoon to the floor. She hoped the woman didn't break anything—old bones were difficult to mend, and the floor was made of stone.

Between her father's roar and Tristan and the vicar springing to her assistance, Sadie saw her chance and dashed down the chapel aisle, only to be thwarted by her previous intended who was blocking the door.

"I will rescue you," Roderick said, grasping her shoulders.

"Don't be ridiculous. I will rescue myself." Sadie had been all too lulled by Tristan's kisses and had completely forgotten she was going to refuse to be married. She had stood like an automaton, mindless and parroted every word the vicar said. What had been wrong with her? "Let me go."

He shook his head, and his fingers dug into the lace. "I know my duty. I must take you away from here. This town is a veritable madhouse. Do you know they lock themselves in like some medieval walled city? I had a devil of a time getting someone to open the gate. Cost me a fortune."

"You can afford it," Sadie replied, unmoved. "Let me go, I said!"

"Not after your father has weaseled away all my money!"

"You shouldn't have trusted him. It's your own fault." She bucked sideways, but the viscount hung on like a barnacle.

"But I wanted to marry you!"

"I can't understand why. I'm not very—nice." She had gone out of her way for years to not be nice.

"Unhand her!" Tristan's words echoed off the stone chapel walls. Miraculously, Roddy's hands relaxed and fell to his sides.

"How is Mrs. Fitzmartin?" Sadie asked, turning to face him. She could tell how *he* was, and she shivered.

"As well as can be expected. She's lying down on a pew. What were you thinking to expose yourself like that? We had an arrangement."

"If you didn't want people to know, you shouldn't have done it. That's what Miss Mac always told me," Sadie said primly

"Your governess, if I recall your silly tale to the Stanchfields. Right before she spanked you, I imagine. And how I'd like to follow in her footsteps."

Sadie shivered again. She could picture Tristan putting her over his knee with very little effort at all.

"She doesn't want to marry you." Roddy didn't sound quite as brave now.

"We are already married. Aren't we, Mr. Fitzmartin?"

The vicar was invisible behind the high-backed pew, hunched over his incapacitated wife.

"Fitzmartin!" the duke shouted. "Are they wed or not?"

The vicar's head popped up. His skin looked bleached with worry. "I think we should send for Dr. Oakley. Helena is not as young as she used to be."

"None of us are," Tristan mumbled. "I'll go find a footman and send him to the village. You must promise me if I leave this chapel that you will not run away."

Sadie's eyes slid to Roddy and she sent him a silent message. Was he smart enough to understand it? "I promise."

"You little witch. Come on." Sadie found herself propelled by the chain on the cuffs as Tristan dragged her through the chapel door and into the hallway.

"I am not some dog to be exercised!" she cried. "Slow down!"

"When Mrs. Fitzmartin's life is at stake? I thought you better than that." He broke into a run and she had no choice but to follow.

"Robert! William! Anyone!" he barked.

Footmen poured out of the halls. Tristan shouted instructions, and soon Mrs. Anstruther bustled into the chapel with a vinaigrette, a jug of water and a cloth. Tristan still hung on to Sadie in that vile, proprietary way, and she was unable to shake loose from him.

"Sit."

"As I said, I'm not your dog."

"If you were my dog, you'd be better behaved."

Sadie was breathless with rage. "How dare you!"

"I dare because it's true. And you are my wife."

"I am not."

"She isn't," Roddy said from a neighboring pew.

"She'd better be!" The duke scowled. "Spent the night in his bed, did you?"

"Nothing happened," Sadie lied.

"All of you shut up!" Hearing such harsh words from the elderly vicar surprised the lot of them, and silence reigned until Dr. Oakley arrived.

Sadie was relieved to see Mrs. Fitzmartin sit up. Mrs. Anstruther was mothering her as Dr. Oakley gave her a gentle examination.

"I think she'll be fine, Virgil. A day or two of rest. No excitement. No outside irritations." Dr. Oakley seemed to be glaring at Sadie rather specifically.

"I'll have my driver take you both home," Tristan said. "Anything we can provide for you—calves' foot jelly and whatnot—I'll leave to Mrs. Anstruther's good judgment." He whispered a few words in the housekeeper's ear, and she rushed out.

"Not so fast! The ceremony isn't over," the Duke of Islesford reminded them.

"And it doesn't have to be, Sarah. My solicitor—"

"Damn your solicitor, Charlton! You're too late, in all ways. Are you questioning my honor? Lady Sarah spent the night in my bed, as she has admitted herself. In my nightshirt, I might add, and a most fetching sight. Which *you* will never see. It is my obligation—"

"Obligation? You owe me nothing but the key to these horrible things!" Sadie was sick and tired of hearing about legalities, duty, and obligation. She felt like a bone tossed between two dogs—three, counting her father—and she was picked clean. "I don't want to marry anyone."

Mr. Fitzmartin cleared his throat. "I'm afraid it's a bit late for that, Lady Sarah. You did follow the service, didn't you?"

Not really. Sadie had been in an utter haze, her heart beating, her lips swollen, her head filled with cotton wool.

"There's not much left to say but I-now-pronounce-you-man-and-wife," the vicar said hurriedly. "And what God has joined, let no man put asunder. We can sign the register tomorrow when my wife is recovered. I must get her to bed. Let's go, Helena, my dear. We can journey back in the good doctor's carriage. So sorry to miss the wedding breakfast."

Lying hypocrite! And he was supposed to be a man of God!

Sadie did what she did best. She sank to her knees and howled. But somehow Tristan Sykes got tangled up with her and joined her on the chapel floor.

He raised one of his damned eyebrows. "Really? Again? Have you no new tricks to torture me with?"

"You are horrid! Get off me!"

"You didn't mind so much last night. Or should I say this morning?"

"Ooh!" It wasn't much of a comeback, but it was all Sadie could think of.

"Hold still."

She felt him jam something on her finger and blinked. An emerald set in chased gold winked back at her. Very large. Very bright. A halo of diamonds around a huge stone.

Very lovely.

Although the ring itself was a touch too tight. She tried to pull it off but failed.

"I'm afraid old Fitzmartin is getting a little forgetful in his dotage. I think he skipped a few paragraphs."

"Then we're not really married."

"Oh, I think we are. There were witnesses. Under the circumstances, I think everyone would agree the deed has been done. We wouldn't want to hurt Mr. Fitzmartin's feelings, would we?"

"I don't give a rip. What about Roddy's solicitor? He'll object and find some way out of this."

"I sent him off back to London or wherever he came from. Mrs. Anstruther and the boys are taking care of it even as I speak."

"Ooh!" Sadie was becoming repetitive.

"Come along now. If you continue to writhe under me, we'll have to consummate this marriage on the chapel floor."

Sadie stopped herself from saying one more "Ooh." She'd never been so angry in her life. Outmaneuvered. Outnumbered. Outdone. Tristan Sykes was no one to be trifled with.

"We are not consummating anything."

"We'll see about that. But first, some bacon and eggs. I'm starving. Aren't you?"

Chapter 24

Tristan was almost enjoying himself. A skeleton key had been found for the handcuffs and his bride was picking at her shirred eggs with her own fork. It had been amusing to feed her at first, but the duke had been so furious it had spoiled Tristan's appetite.

In Tristan's opinion, the man's concern for his daughter came far too late. The fact that he'd even considered Charlton as her life mate showed his poor judgment.

Ah, yes. The fly in the ointment, the pebble in the shoe, the unwelcome guest at the wedding banquet, such as it was. Charlton was refusing to leave without money, Sadie, or both. Damned if Tristan was going to throw more money away, although it seemed very likely he would have to. One thing he would *not* give up was his wife.

Charlton had been given a room in a distant wing, where he could rave to his heart's content. Apparently the solicitor had left with his carriage, intimidated by Tristan's burly footmen. So the viscount was temporarily stranded. Hopefully, he'd leave with the duke when the weather calmed down.

Which it showed no sign of doing. Sykes House's walls rattled with the rumble of thunder above; bright flashes of lightning illuminated the dining room windows at regular intervals. Rain came down in sheets. Tristan hoped the gardens wouldn't be flattened.

"Quite the storm, isn't it?"

"You are going to talk to me about the *weather*?" She stabbed a sausage onto her fork. She was probably imagining it was his thigh.

Or worse.

"Why not? It's hours before bedtime, and we must pass the time of day in some way."

"Well, I'm not going to talk about the weather. Or go to bed with you."

Tristan leaned back in his chair. "Surely you don't want Charlton to have a case against us."

"What do you mean?"

"If the marriage is not consummated, what's to stop him from saying we're not married at all? Claim grounds for an annulment? His solicitor could drive a carriage through some loophole or other. Would you rather go off with the viscount? I would think you'd be more discerning." In truth, Tristan was not entirely complacent about the irregularities in the service and its legality. Or the grounds for an annulment. He certainly wasn't going to subject himself to an examination for impotence. He might not have indulged in any recent fornication, but he remembered how to.

And was looking forward to getting back in the saddle again, as it were.

But they hadn't signed the register yet. He wouldn't relax until—

Well, likely he was never going to relax. Keeping up with Sadie and her antics were apt to turn his hair gray. Or make it fall out.

"Oh."

"Yes, *oh*. I cannot be certain, but if he keeps asserting the betrothal contract has precedence, we might be in for a wrangle."

Sadie picked up her champagne glass and took a long swallow. "I hate you all."

Tristan chose not to believe her. Anyone who kissed him as she did had to have some positive feelings for him.

"Have I told you how exquisite you look? My friend should be arriving any time now to take some photographs."

"Of me in the curtains?"

"No one would ever know. Charles Worth himself could not have done better."

"I don't know how you're going to get me out of them. I'm sewed in."

Ah. So she was thinking ahead, was she? That was a hopeful sign.

"I'm very good with my hands. As you might remember." He had plucked at her nipple until it was as hard as a cherrystone last night.

"Pah," she dismissed.

"I am! Look at the gardens. And I build things. I'm quite a nimble creature."

She turned to him. "Do you dance?"

"Dance?" The word felt foreign on his tongue.

"You know, the waltz. The mazurka. The gallop. I love to dance."

Did she? He knew very little about her.

"Um. I haven't danced in some time."

"Why not? Don't you go to parties? Even *I'm* invited to parties, though there's no telling what I might get up to once I'm in someone's drawing room. Filch the silver. Set the rug on fire. Kiss a footman."

Kiss a footman? She'd better not try anything like that now they were married. Or sort of married. Really, he would need to check with the vicar first thing tomorrow morning.

"There are very few amusements in Puddling, as you know." Puddling was designed to be as boring as it possibly could be. Most of its young people left the first chance they got, money or no money.

"But what about when you're in London?"

She seemed genuinely curious. Did she imagine she'd spend time kicking up her heels in the city? Shopping and gossiping?

"I hardly ever go to London. I have responsibilities here." She was one of them.

Her russet eyebrows met. "Do you mean to lock me up in this house as I was locked up in Stonecrop Cottage?"

"You weren't locked up. You had total freedom of movement. Enough to steal trousers and pumpkins and tarts." And raise general havoc amongst the villagers. How would they feel once they knew mad Lady Sarah Marchmain was now Mrs. Tristan Sykes? Sadie was likely to upset the calm quiet of the town, that soothing atmosphere which was so essential for their Guests' mental health and physical well-being.

Perhaps he *should* take her to London and leave her there.

How had his grandfather dealt with his grandmother, another duke's daughter who chafed against the restrictions of society? The short answer was that he hadn't. Lady Maribel did pretty much as she pleased, and poor Grandpapa followed behind to clean up her messes and admire her backside.

Tristan had no intention of following in his grandfather's footsteps.

"I prefer the country," he said in a clipped voice. He'd spent enough time in London chasing after Linnet.

"How do you handle your architectural commissions?"

He was surprised that she cared. "Easily. You have heard of the post, have you not? The occasional telegram. I have trusted deputies who carry out my instructions. A very dedicated crew of workers and artisans. Every now and again I go to town for business meetings. More often, my clients come to me."

Tristan wasn't about to brag, but he had a sterling reputation and too little time to take on every project that came his way.

She scrunched up her nose. "So we'll be buried here."

"Not buried. Happily ensconced, I should say."

"Where will we live?"

Tristan had given this matter some thought as he lay awake in the too few hours before dawn in his Red House bedroom. He gestured toward the yellow wallpaper. "I suggest you remain here at Sykes House, where there is greater space, more amenities and a full staff at your disposal. I shall, um, visit you."

"Visit me."

"Yes. For conjugal relations." He cleared his throat of an enormous frog.

Her eyes were wide and rather lovely. "You don't intend for us to live together."

"Not at first. We are, as you have pointed out on more than one occasion, strangers. I will—ah—court you so we can get to know each other better."

Sadie threw back her head and laughed, almost losing the tiara that glittered from her red hair. Tristan stopped it from flying backward, tangling his fingers in her hair and veil. She batted him away, still laughing until tears were coursing down her cheeks.

"What is so amusing?" he asked. He was making a good faith effort here, and bristled under her ridicule. The servants were beginning to stare, and the duke gave him a fearsome grimace from across the room.

"I think you have the cart before the horse. One is usually courted before one is bedded."

"We are in unusual circumstances."

"I'll say." She wiped her cheeks with a monogrammed linen napkin. "Who is that gorgeous man who's just come in?"

For a moment he wondered if it was Islesford's detective, who would come much too late to discover Lady Sarah's whereabouts. He turned, but it was his friend. David was looking well-put-together, in a morning suit even though he'd missed the ceremony. "David Warren. I haven't seen him in an age, but sent for him to take photographs. I mentioned him to you."

David knew him as well as he knew himself. Knew where all the bodies were buried. David had stuck with him through everything.

"To c-commemorate this sterling oc-occasion." Sadie hiccupped. Had she drunk too much champagne? She was verging on hysterics. He prayed she wouldn't say or do anything embarrassing, although David would probably just shake it off if she did.

"David! Thank you for coming on such short notice."

"Is this your bride? Another beauty, you lucky bastard. No wonder you've been hiding her away, not letting any chaps you know of your good fortune. The stories I could tell on him, Mrs. Sykes. You never would have married the blighter!"

"It's Lady Sarah, actually," Tristan said, putting a possessive hand on Sadie's lace-clad shoulder. David had an overabundance of charm, and women were always susceptible. Even Linnet. Especially Linnet. But David, to his credit, had resisted. "That's my father-in-law, the Duke of Islesford, down the other end of the table." Still not far enough away, but out of hearing range at least. Tristan wished the man was in the next room. Or Jupiter.

His friend whistled. "I'll repeat myself, Tris. You are a lucky bastard. I'm so pleased to make you acquaintance, Lady Sarah. I say, wait a moment. Islesford! You're Lady Sarah Marchmain? *The* Lady Sarah?"

Sadie gave him a thin smile. "The very same."

Tristan gave his friend a sharp look, but David was not to be distracted. "Good Lord! Old Tris will have his hands full if only half the stories are true. However did you two meet? I was under the impression you were engaged to—what's-his-name? Reggie Something?"

"Roderick. Lord Charlton. As you can see, I changed my mind. Tristan simply swept me off my feet."

Tristan had never heard her sound so much like a duke's daughter, all frozen hauteur. David was too stupid to realize he had icicles forming on his earlobes.

"Well, my felicitations, Lady Sarah. You are obviously a woman of sound judgment." David looked down on their empty plates. "Shall we begin the photographic process? I set my equipment up in the drawing room."

"There is wedding cake to come." Sadie pointed to the three-tiered confection that Mrs. Anstruther and her kitchen staff had so painstakingly assembled under the shortest of notice.

"Oh, by all means then. I'll have a piece too, what? But I don't mean to horn in. I see this wedding breakfast is very private."

The irate duke and the bridal couple. It was a pathetic turnout, really. Even Anstruther would be welcome to lend some support. Where was he?

"More people were expected, but the vicar's wife took ill," Tristan said.

"Bad luck. May I sit next to your wife, or are you too jealous?"

"I trust you. I trust you both."

"You shouldn't," Sadie murmured.

Chapter 25

The cake had been delicious. Sadie ate four pieces, mostly to delay the photographs, which she knew would be awkward and time-consuming. She had taken an unjustified dislike to Mr. Warren, who was altogether too smooth and charming for anyone's good. And she didn't care for the speculative gleam in his eye now that he knew who she was. Perhaps she was justified after all.

Like Tristan, he was untitled, but heir to the Earl of Summerton. Unlike Tristan, he had no employment. Photography was his hobby, and he seemed to be efficient at it. She had sat still as a statue, unsmiling, as he positioned his tripod. He handled the glass plates with dexterity, was clear in his instructions, didn't hurt her eyes with his lights or offend her nose with his chemicals.

But after half an hour, Sadie had had enough. She was tired, and the tiara weighed upon her head like a boulder. Warren's and Tristan's cheerful banter was more than annoying. She rose abruptly, brushing Tristan's hand off her shoulder.

"I think we are done."

"Whatever you say, my lady," said the unctuous David Warren.

"Right then." Sadie hesitated. She'd expected an argument.

"You probably want to take a rest this afternoon. I'll have Mrs. Anstruther bring a tray to you."

Sadie felt like resting at least until tomorrow, possibly the day after. Alone.

"Thank you. Would you please send either Hannah or Audrey to me?" She'd have to be cut out of the curtains before she could nap.

"Of course." She could tell by Tristan's face he preferred to be the one wielding the scissors. Well, it was best to begin as she meant to go on. She'd have to lock herself in.

Hours later, after a hot bath, a refreshing sleep and another substantial meal, Sadie heard the rattle at her door.

She didn't care who it was. "Go away!" She was right in the middle of a very interesting chapter of one of Baroness X's books. The villain, a tall, dark, and handsome gentleman who reminded Sadie of her alleged husband, had just been buried in a mudslide. No one was apt to shovel him out.

"Not bloody likely. Open the door, Sadie."

Sadie almost smiled. She liked to hear her nickname on Tristan's lips. It was so much friendlier than Lady Sarah, not that she wanted to be friends with him.

She put the book face down on a pillow and went to the door, making sure the key was firmly in its lock. "I have a headache."

It was *almost* true. The ugly tiara had been a trial to her for hours. The diamond-encrusted set was now back in its velvet case on her dresser, perfect for Sadie to pack and abscond with. It was a pity the jewelry was so old-fashioned, but she was sure she could find a jeweler who wasn't too particular.

"Do you remember what we talked about?" Tristan wasn't shouting, but his words were very clear and measured through the wood.

How would old Roddy ever know what transpired on their wedding night? Were they expected to display the bloody sheets out of a Sykes House window?

"We don't have to do anything," Tristan said, his voice softer. "But for appearances sake, we need to spend the night together."

"I suppose that's what you say to all your wives."

There was utter silence from the hall. Sadie had forgotten the man had been married before.

Oops.

"We may not even be married." Sadie added. She really wasn't quite sure, or so she told herself.

"I'm not going to fight with you. Or beg."

"Good. I'll see you tomorrow at breakfast." Hopefully the rain would stop by then and she could make her escape. She had diamonds to bargain with now.

But then the key in the lock clattered to her feet and the doorknob turned. It was too late to push a chair in front of the door, or scream her head off.

Who would come anyway? The staff was loyal to Tristan.

He waggled a ring of keys at her. "I came prepared."

He was wearing a striped silk robe in masculine shades of brown and navy. His feet were bare, and Sadie suspected he wasn't wearing anything on any other part of him either beneath the robe.

"You can't just sally in here!" she hissed.

"Oh, I think I can." He bent to pick up the key and turned it back in the lock. "Now we won't be disturbed."

Sadie was disturbed already. "I don't want you in here!"

"Why not? The bed is big enough for two. Possibly three, although that sort of thing has never been of interest to me. I guess I'm too old-fashioned." He gave her a lopsided grin that should not have the effect it had on her, and proceeded to sit down in a wing chair in front of the fireplace.

Her chest felt tight. "You promise not to touch me?"

He shrugged. "If I must. I admit the prospect of ravishing you has its appeal. We *are* married. I'd be within my rights to insist."

Let him see how far he'd get *insisting*.

"Has your friend gone?"

"Yes. Hours ago. We're down to your father and your ex-fiancé. Oh, and some inquiry agent who practically swam here this afternoon. He was supposed to find you, but here you are. You should have joined us for dinner. Jolly good fun." His expression told her otherwise.

"Ugh. Poor you." Not that she really had much sympathy.

"The only thing that could have made it worse would have been my father returning home from Paris. Not that he'd object to you as a daughter-in-law—"

"I should hope not!" Duke's daughters didn't fall out of the sky and into baronets' sons' laps every day.

"But he wouldn't care for the commotion. My father is a stickler for propriety. He's got quite a stick up his, um, anyway, he likes things to be calm. Settled. The ceremony would have made him break out in hives. And the dinner company—let's just say Paris or perhaps Patagonia would have been preferable."

"Was Roddy still an ass?"

"The man refuses to see the writing on the wall."

Or the writing in the parish register. If Sadie legged it tomorrow, her marriage would certainly be invalid without her signature.

Would the de Winter diamonds still belong to her? They were his "wedding gift." Tristan might have her prosecuted for theft.

Maybe she shouldn't run away.

The idea was such a revelation she had to sit down on the bed.

Tristan brightened at her new position. "Tired? It has been a long day."

"I am wide awake." She picked up her book but couldn't understand a word. Out of the corner of her eye, she could see Tristan rise from the chair and stretch, his robe gaping open.

His thighs looked very strong.

Oh, merciful God. She shut her eyes and now she really couldn't read.

"Scoot over. You may want to burn the midnight oil, but I confess I'm exhausted."

She heard the robe slither to the floor. What a conundrum. Should she open her eyes now, or wait until he was under the covers?

By the time she rolled to the side and decided to look, he was safe under the matelassé coverlet, punching a pillow into submission. All she saw was a brown shoulder and the curl of the shaggy dark hair on the back of his head.

So, clearly no pajamas or nightshirt. She was wearing her usual maid's hand-me-down, billowing rough cotton and very un-wedding nightlike. Sadie realized she *still* did not have clothes of her own.

Something must be done.

She put the book aside. "Could you turn down the lamp, please?"

"Certainly." He reached over, and the room was cloaked in darkness. Much better. She didn't want to see brown shoulders or curly hair.

Oh, who was she kidding? She wanted to see it all.

Chapter 26

Tristan had taken a risk coming to her in nothing but his robe and smalls. She might decide to bash him with her book. He was almost too tired to fight back.

Last night he'd been wearing his smalls too, and it had been a near thing not to strip and have her right then and there. For too brief a time, she had been soft. Approachable. But he hadn't lied—he *was* old-fashioned. He hadn't wanted to take advantage of her distress, or the kiss that had been so cataclysmic.

Most men of his acquaintance would encourage him to storm Sadie's castle. He was her husband, was he not? Entitled to exercise his rights and appetites.

And God knows, Tristan wanted her despite knowing that his lust was likely to be his downfall.

There was a great deal riding on their marriage—Puddling's security, for one. He didn't trust the Duke of Islesford farther than he could throw him, and throwing the old geezer was very tempting at this moment. The man had almost ruined Sadie, made her obstinate. Oppositional. Obdurate. If he weren't so sleep deprived, he could probably think of more words.

He and Sadie had to make this marriage look real to her blasted father and that idiot Charlton. It was a compromise to come here tonight with no intention of taking her innocence.

No. Wrong word. Sadie was not innocent, but a sly, conniving imp. He could feel her breathing at his back, stirring his loins like they hadn't been stirred in ages.

Tristan was just a man, after all. He punched the pillow again.

"Do you plan to spend the whole night here?" his nemesis asked.

"I think it best. I know people like us do not traditionally share a bedroom with a spouse, but my parents did. One of the few ways my father ever broke a rule. If we are to silence gossiping tongues, you'll have to put up with me."

"I don't care about gossip."

"No, you actually enjoy it, don't you? I've had quite enough of it in my life, thank you very much." How he had hated to read all the blind—and not so blind—items about Linnet in the gutter press. Their divorce had splashed his misery all over the front pages. His architectural practice had suffered until poor Linnet had conveniently died. He was no longer a divorcé; he was a widower to those who believed that man and law courts could not dissolve a marriage.

"You? I've never met such a proper man. A proper stick-in-the-mud," she added loud enough for him to hear.

He rolled onto his back. "Yes. I expect my placid, boring nature is no virtue to someone like you. Would you like it better if I throttled you when you misbehaved?"

"You wouldn't dare!"

"It would be out of character, but you might drive me to it." Tristan did not believe in physical brutality toward women, or even men. He saw himself as a reasonable, cerebral man. But Sadie made him lose his reason. He could easily see spanking Sadie's lovely bare bottom.

At least he assumed it was lovely. All signs pointed in that direction, and he'd like to see if for himself.

"One can never blame another person when one loses one's temper," she said tartly.

"Really? So then your entire life has been predicated on your own lack of control. Your weakness."

Sadie bolted up. "I am not weak! And I've always been in control! I did things—planned things—so I would not—" she trailed off.

"Would not what? Be considered normal?"

Sadie smacked his arm. "What is normal for a woman? How would you know?"

"I had a mother." And a wife, but he didn't say it. Linnet was hardly normal anyway.

"Was your mother forced to marry your father?"

"Good gracious, no. It was a love match, although I've never been precisely sure what she saw in him. My father can be difficult. Not as difficult as yours, obviously. But he's stiff, I suppose you would say. Full of his own and the family's consequence."

"The apple doesn't fall far from the tree," Sadie said too sweetly.

Tristan bristled. Just because he had standards of acceptable behavior didn't mean that he was like his father.

"I admit I observe the conventions. I find life to be easier that way."

"Well, you would, wouldn't you? Nobody's making you get mar—" She stuttered to a stop, realizing how very wrong she was. Tristan had been maneuvered into this mésalliance as much as she had.

He found her fist on the coverlet and gave it a squeeze. "Look, I've said it before. We must make the best of this for our own sanity. I choose happiness, Sadie, or at least some pleasant accommodation. We don't have to live in each other's pockets. I won't ask to hear your every thought." In fact, her thoughts were apt to be pretty hair-raising, if her past was anything to go by. "And you know I won't touch your money," he added for good measure.

"It all sounds too good to be true," she said, the doubt thick in her voice.

Tristan chuckled. "That's me. The paragon of manly virtue and understanding."

Suddenly, he wasn't so tired anymore. He continued to hold Sadie's hand in his, and could feel it tremble. Tristan had an overwhelming urge to soothe away her fears.

A kiss was called for. It was their wedding night, wasn't it?

He drew her fingertips to his lips.

"What are you doing?" she squealed.

"Tasting you." He licked the next digit, and inserted her forefinger in his mouth, sucking on it at first with gentleness, then more determination.

"Stop it. That's disgusting." She made a halfhearted effort to pull her hand away.

"Every inch of you was made to be kissed."

"D-don't be silly."

"Do you doubt me?" He nuzzled her palm. "Your throat. Your earlobes—perhaps even inside the shells of your ears. Your eyelids. Your shoulders. Your beautiful breasts."

"Aha! You felt no need for any adjectives before when naming my other body parts. You men are all alike."

"Guilty. Probably. No man could withstand your glorious bosom, madam. It was one of the first things I noticed about you, apart from your noisy histrionics on the Stanchfields' floor. I would very much like to see those breasts when they're not corseted or covered in white cotton."

"Well, I have no intention of showing them to you."

"Pity. I'll have to use my imagination then." He thought back to the afternoon in the attic as she stood in a shaft of sunlight wearing little more than a scarf, her white skin glowing with tiny golden spangles. Last night at the Red House when he had touched her, the exquisite fullness of her breast filling his hand. Tristan sighed, and licked a finger again.

She sighed back.

What would she do if he kissed her breasts? Through the fabric, of course—he didn't want to rush her.

Much.

Nothing ventured, nothing gained. She was still sitting up, so he slid up and leaned against his smashed pillows. There was scarcely a foot between them. He could feel the heat of her body, smell her rose-infused perfume, hear her shallow breathing.

There was no point to overthinking what would come next, but he'd need both hands. He set hers carefully down on the bed, then erased the space between them. Tristan silenced her gasp, his mouth covering her lips. After a few long seconds, she responded.

Ah, this was more like it. Warm woman, mild September night, the future unfolding kiss by kiss. She allowed him to embrace her and loosen the tail of hair that was tied by a plain ribbon. His fingers were nimble even in the dark, and he lost himself for a moment in its scarlet silk.

Focus, Tris. Her chest was touching his, and he edged her away so his hand could perform his heart's desire. Her softness was everything his touch had told him before. Her nipple peaked under his care, and he broke the kiss to attend it.

Sadie's stifled groan was most gratifying. She might pretend to be aloof, to have no interest in the physical side of their marriage, but Tristan knew better. She was as responsive as any husband could wish for, relaxing in his arms. Her fingers curled in his hair, keeping him in place.

As if he wanted to be anywhere else.

The nightgown was thin, presenting no serious barrier to his indulgence. The fabric tasted sweet, but not as sweet as her bare skin would, he wagered. He laved until the wetness revealed the pink underneath the white, and he suckled harder. She bucked against him.

"Easy, my love," Tristan whispered. "There is much more to come."

Chapter 27

Sadie couldn't take much more. Honestly, she couldn't. It should have been repulsive having a grown man at her breast but somehow it wasn't. Each tug and touch shot fire straight to her center, traveling a secret, sensual path she'd heretofore never known existed.

She was not a total innocent. There had been Dermot, clumsy and earnest. But she *was* a virgin, and had planned to stay that way until a time of her choosing. She'd always defied convention—why shouldn't she take a lover once she came into her independence, if someone worthy was to be found?

Four years from now.

Tristan definitely had other ideas. And if she didn't stop him, she would lose her virginity in approximately four minutes.

But no. He'd made no effort to divest himself of his smalls, nor had he eased her nightgown over her head. He seemed perfectly content doing that extraordinary thing with his tongue over her fabric-shrouded nipple, and she had half a mind to ask him to do the same thing to the other one.

Half a mind. Face it, Sadie, you have no mind left at all.

And he had promised not to...not to ravish her, although the prospect of ravishing did not seem entirely unappealing.

Sadie had always believed sexual congress to be somewhat violent. She'd seen enough of nature amongst the animals at Marchmain Castle, and had been vehemently warned by Miss Mac all through her adolescence, not that she'd paid attention. Dermot was proof of that.

But whatever Tristan was doing was not violent. His hands smoothed over her body, which was still completely covered by the rough cotton. The friction was almost like a tickle, but she wasn't laughing. In fact, Sadie was making sounds she'd never made in her life.

She felt the panic rising. "You mustn't—"

He placed a finger on her lips and raised his head. "I know. I won't. It's too soon. But trust me." She thought she could see his smile in the dark.

Each short sentence confused her further. She needed to be left alone, or something awful was going to happen.

And then it did. His hand slipped under the hem of her nightgown, which was somehow now at her knees. Up her thigh it crept, until it touched the dark red curls of her mons. She twitched as one finger dipped into the seam.

"You're wet."

"I-I'm sorry," Sadie said, mortified.

"Don't be. It means I've been doing my job." His finger stroked carefully between her nether lips, smoothly navigating her inner skin. The rubbing felt peculiar. Wonderful.

"Oh! Stop!"

He didn't. "Do you really want me to?"

Sadie was silent, and Tristan took it for the permission it was. He continued the delicious torture until she bit her lip to stop herself from crying out, and then shifted his body down on the mattress.

She shivered as he lifted the nightgown, grateful it was dark. This was so embarrassing. So wrong.

So right.

He was going to kiss her *there*. She had never in her life expected to find herself in this position.

Legs splayed.

Wanton.

Willing.

Her stomach did a flip, and she held her breath in anticipation.

"Down *there*? Really?" she yelped.

"Really."

Trust me, he had said. For some reason, she did. She just didn't trust herself.

Both hands were parting her now, and she could feel his warm breath on her body. Tristan's tongue licked a hidden spot and she thought she would simply die of lust.

For that's what this was. He'd made no claim to love her, not that she would believe him if he had. They'd agreed that romantic love was not for the likes of them.

But *once* he'd loved. Could he again? Would anyone love Sadie for who she was, faults and all?

So far, no one had.

She would take these next few minutes as a substitute. Pretend he truly cared. Any man who was as talented as he was with this kind of kissing—and the conventional one, too—was worth a bit of fantasy.

Sadie kept her eyes shut and allowed herself to feel everything. She cupped her own breast, shocked at the hardness of the point she strummed to even greater heights. Her body was a jangled combination of rigidity and languor, alternating as Tristan worked his magic.

Tristan's mouth was around something inside her she had no name for, swirling and suckling until she thought she would go mad.

Then that madness strained, rose, and slipped free.

Sadie was tossed into unknown territory. Wave upon wave of incredible sensation crackled through her, right to her toes. It was fire, it was ice, it was a sort of heaven that owed nothing to angels.

She might have screamed. Hopefully no one would come rushing in to save her from her devilish husband.

Sadie didn't want to be saved.

He seemed to know when she could endure no more. Returning to the pillows, he folded her trembling body into his arms and kissed her forehead.

Sadie was speechless. Witless. So this was what the fuss was all about. All the giggling and blushes amongst her married female acquaintances. If such could be achieved with a mere tongue, what would happen to her when Tristan's member was put to use? She could feel it now against her hip, iron and unyielding. If she could move her hand, she'd be tempted to touch it, to bring him the kind of joy he'd given her.

How very frightening to think along those lines. Years of virtue—or semi-virtue—thrown away in the aftermath of carnal pleasure. She would need to guard herself against such brazen behavior. It would only result in her humiliation. Tristan would think she was weak, putty in his hands or beneath his tongue. She would lose herself, her very Sadie-ness, become just one more simpering woman suffering from infatuation.

She'd been there. Done that. She'd found a way to repel men and keep her independence, even if it had resulted in society thinking her a madwoman. That's why she was here in Puddling, wasn't it? But could she keep Tristan Sykes out of her bed?

Did she want to? Was there a way *she* could seduce *him* and protect herself?

It was a conundrum that would require further thought, and right now Sadie was in no position to make sense of her conflicting emotions.

"All right?" he asked, a certain roughness in his words. He released her and rolled a few inches away.

She willed herself to sound normal. "Quite." She nearly managed to pronounce the one syllable without a hiccup.

She could feel his examining gaze in the dark. Thank heavens the light had been extinguished; she must look a wreck. Guilty, too. What they had just done—what *he* had done—couldn't be considered proper. Her response to it was also disturbing.

She had lost all self-control.

My God. Did all married couples throughout England engage in such play? Sadie wouldn't be able to meet Mr. and Mrs. Stanchfield's eyes for weeks. Even worse, ancient Mr. and Mrs. Fitzmartin? The mind boggled.

Of course, if see was seeing them around the village, that presumed she truly was not running away with her diamonds. That perhaps she would go to the store on an errand for Mrs. Anstruther. Sit in the humble Norman church and repent for her sins. Live in Puddling-on-the-Wold because she wanted to.

Because she was Mrs. Sykes.

Sort of.

Sadie was absolutely sure that, unlike his employer, Mr. Anstruther would never partake in such activity with his wife. Perhaps that was why they were separated. She clapped a hand over her mouth to stifle a laugh.

"What is so amusing?"

How did he know? She hadn't made a sound. Maybe he could see in the dark, like some large feral cat.

"Nothing."

"As I've already said, I think we should begin as we mean to go on. Speak the truth when at all possible. We owe each other that much."

How could she tell him the direction in which her mind was running without total mortification?

"I know you have a history of falsifying things," he continued, reminding Sadie of a schoolmaster. "I warn you, I will not tolerate that sort of betray—um, behavior."

"I only lie when I need to," Sadie said, irritated. How had he gone from lover to prig so quickly? She remembered the disapproving man she'd met that first day in the Stanchfields' store. The one who had looked down on her.

Literally. From his great height, those expressive eyebrows indicating his disgust. He had been so very disdainful. So cool. Icy, really.

Bollocks. She didn't want to be married to *that* man.

"You will not need to anymore. Your father is out of the picture, at least after tomorrow. Your previous fiancé as well. You'll have two less men to bedevil. I expect you to deal honestly with me."

"I'm not sure I remember how." She wanted to stick out her tongue, but he probably would see that somehow.

"I'll help you along. Did you enjoy that?"

Was he fishing for compliments?

"What?" she stalled.

He chuckled, the smug bastard. "The cunnilingus."

"I have no idea what you're talking about. My governess never mentioned that word in my studies."

"I imagine not, or your father would have sacked her. When I kissed you. *Down there*, as you put it."

He was making fun of her. Sadie couldn't help it if she was ignorant of sexual terminology. Women were supposed to be ignorant. It was a wonder she knew as much as she did.

"The truth? Yes."

"You won't elaborate?"

"What else am I to say? It was very shocking. But pleasant."

He snorted. "All right. I guess I deserve that. But I want to make you happy in bed, Sadie. You must tell me what you like, what you want, and I shall endeavor to do it."

She sounded like a chore to him. "I am hardly one to direct you. You have far more experience than I. *You* have been married before, after all. I am just a virgin ninny, dependent upon your manly expertise."

It was so *unfair*. Sadie had never felt less sure of herself.

He went quiet for what seemed like forever. "We won't consummate the marriage until you are ready. But for all intents and purposes, to the outside world, we have."

"Lying, Mr. Sykes?"

"Reluctantly. A necessary evil. But no more lies from you to me."

Truth was what he liked. What he wanted. But Sadie wasn't sure her heart knew the truth.

Chapter 28

His bride snored. Tristan had noticed that last night as well as he'd alternated fitful sleep with wakeful rumination. He hadn't done much of the first and too much of the latter.

Well. His first encounter as a new husband had had its ups and downs. Tristan knew he had to be conscious of Sadie's mixed feelings—she had resisted marriage ever since her debut. It had been less than twenty-four hours before she'd run off at the thought of it after Islesford's ultimatum, and Tristan liked to think it wasn't because he was such an awful prospect.

He wouldn't take it personally. She had a long history of being rebellious. That was why she was here in Puddling, for heaven's sake. It would take more than one month in the Cotswolds and one masterful kiss *down there* to change her mind.

He didn't quite trust her not to leave again, although this time the handcuffs would stay in their drawer. They'd caused enough trouble. Unless, no, he really could see Lady Sarah Marchmain as anyone's willing submissive. More than likely she'd prefer to tie *him* to the bed, and that thought gave Tristan an unexpected frisson. He could easily picture her over him, having her wicked way, all white limbs and sinewy grace, her red hair tumbling down.

Only in his fantasies.

In reality, he needed to persuade her to stay by other methods, to accept her fate, and had gone some way in that effort tonight.

That persuasion had done nothing for his own needs, however, and he was still hard as stone.

Tristan was adept at taking care of himself. Since Linnet's death, he had deliberately not sought out a mistress or a compliant widow. His celibacy was his way to assuage the guilt that he felt for the utter failure of his marriage.

The punishment was not so severe after all—he was still very much alive, unlike poor Linnet. He had a hand, and a good imagination. And since his father had left him in charge, Tristan had had no opportunity in Puddling to alter his singular state, not that there was anyone suitable in the locality who held his interest. The village's former schoolteacher Rachel Everett had been sweet, but not for him.

She had been his brother's first and only love. Tristan hadn't wanted to court his father's disapproval twice over. And anyway, she was a viscountess now.

Good for her.

His abstinence was a thing of the past. Or might be, when Sadie resigned herself to their situation.

How grim. Surely he wanted her to be more than resigned. An enthusiastic partner. Tristan felt she had the capacity. She'd shown fire both tonight and last night, which boded well for their future. At least they would find some comfort in their mutual physical attraction.

He heard her gentle snuffles, could feel the warmth radiating from her body. And he could smell her too—roses and arousal.

Dear God.

He turned away from her and gripped his cock. It wasn't difficult to bring himself off. He remembered how she lay open before him. How she tasted. How soft her skin was beneath his hands and mouth. The fullness of her incredible breasts. The helpless cries as she came. He had to bite his cheek to prevent his own as he came hard onto the sheet.

His heart turned over. How long could he keep away from his own wife? He wanted to respect her reservations. Knew he had to, if they were ever to forge ahead. They had to get to know each other, if not in the Biblical sense.

He knew already that she was not the spoiled, self-centered girl he once thought her to be. Her upbringing had been difficult, and caused her to cope with her misery by doing foolish, self-destructive things.

"What are you doing?"

Bloody hell. He thought he'd been quiet enough.

"Saving you from my carnal appetites. I made a promise, but one part of me did not quite agree," he said lightly, hoping she'd go right back to sleep and assume this conversation was a dream.

"Your—your cock, you mean. You were touching it."

Just hearing her say the words made him stiffen again, which should have been biologically impossible. "Just so."

"May I see it?"

Good God again. He was not in his prime at the moment.

"I'd have to get up and light a candle. Perhaps we should wait until morning." He usually awoke to a magnificent cockstand.

"I may have changed my mind by then."

"And that will be fine. I'm not going to rush you into intimacy." Damn it all and his honor.

"Looking is not precisely doing. I confess I'm curious."

Young ladies were not supposed to be curious. What had Tristan expected? His new wife had been unusual all her life. And, to be fair, many women her age were married and mothers.

"Surely you've seen books. Visited museums."

"Well, of course. But I've never had the opportunity to explore a living man before. Examine all the nooks and crannies. Without those pesky marble fig leaves."

"I should hope not."

The covers rustled, and his bride sat up. "What if I had? Would you divorce me?"

A cloud of dread swirled around him in the dark. Lady Sarah Marchmain had gone out of her way to test boundaries. Had she truly overstepped? He couldn't—no, God would not be so cruel to curse him twice.

"What are you saying?"

"Why is it all right for men to have experiences, but a woman is expected to remain pure until she marries?"

She sounded absurdly naïve. "You do understand about conception? There's a very practical reason men seek virgins, or at least someone who has been sufficiently chaste. Another man's son should not inherit."

"Oh."

"I agree ignorance is not always bliss for the woman. But a good husband will cherish her and teach her—"

"Teach? How very odd that sounds. 'Put your hand there, my dear... Move this way or that.' Like some puppet master."

Tristan raked a hand through his disordered hair. "Perhaps teach is not the right word. One would hope the couple would discover their pleasure together. As I told you earlier, I want you to be happy. Satisfied. I would not want you to do something you didn't like."

"Like what?"

He could think of quite a few things she might object to, and his cock twitched hopefully. "Really, Sadie. Now is not the time to discuss all this. Aren't you tired?"

"Not after you woke me up doing whatever you were doing."

Tristan's ears were hot, therefore they must be turning red as they always did when he was embarrassed. Good thing they were having this hideous discussion in the dark. "Have you never touched yourself?"

"As you did to me *down there*? No. If I'd known it was possible, I believe I would have. But no one ever said—"

"Maybe Miss Mac should have added that to the curriculum," he joked. He conjured up Sadie on her bed, long legs parted, russet hair tangled on the pillow, and the topic became very serious indeed.

"I can't imagine her even knowing such a thing. This is what I'm talking about. I just feel so *stupid*."

He drew her closer. "You are very young still. And perfect just as you are."

Sadie laughed. "Liar. I thought you always wanted to tell the truth."

"Perhaps not perfect, then. But mine."

She grew still. "Yours? I belong to no one but myself."

He remembered her words in the chapel. "Of course you belong to yourself. Just as I belong to myself. I shall never seek to have dominion over you." Fat chance of accomplishing that anyhow.

"So I don't have to obey."

He saw where this was heading. "Look, Sadie. I'll phrase this the way your new friend Ham might. We are yoked together now. If you lunge too far to the side, you will drag me right along with you. Likewise, if I pull away, you'll have nothing to do but follow me, kicking up your heels, no doubt. We have to find a path that will be mutually beneficial so that neither of us will strangle to death."

"So we're a team of horses. Or oxen."

"Let's just say a team."

She was quiet. Tristan had grown to understand that her histrionics were planned out to shock—there was a great deal of mischief tumbling about in her pretty red head. What was she thinking of now?

Chapter 29

Sadie had never slept next to another person. If she'd ever been tucked against a nurse or her mother when she was an infant, she had no recollection of it. And lying beside Tristan Sykes for the second night in a row was unnerving.

She couldn't believe she had fallen asleep after he had...kissed her so. But her body had been limp, and she was utterly worn out from fighting against her fate all day. She wasn't sure what had woken her, but she'd lain still as a mouse as he—

Well, what precisely had he done? Stroked his member? The room had a scent she was totally unfamiliar with, not unpleasant, but very specific.

She had a right to see her husband, didn't she? The words Reverend Fitzmartin mangled must have included some vaguely couched terms to that effect. She was Tristan's wife.

More or less. Sadie supposed until the register was signed, the issue was not entirely settled.

She really should take advantage of this situation tonight, if only to expand her education. Who knew if he'd ever spend the night in her bedchamber again once her father and Roddy were gone? Perhaps she could bend Tristan to her will after all. Thus far, she was the one who had been twisted into a willow branch chair.

"If we are to be yoked for eternity, as you so crudely put it, I think you should light that candle."

Tristan sighed. "Very well. I warn you, I'm not at my best."

"I wouldn't know the difference now, would I? That's what this is all about."

He rose and fumbled with the tinderbox, finally lighting one smallish candle. The light it threw would not go very far to aid in her observation.

His dark form was limned with its pale glow, and then he turned, holding the candle near his chest.

His smalls were low on his hips, and he tugged the drawstring with his free hand to prevent them from slipping further. He seemed amusingly modest all of a sudden.

"I've seen most of you before," she reminded him. "When you were in the bath." It seemed like years ago. How discomfited he'd been, and how much had changed in that short space of time.

He almost smiled. "I remember. You are the first woman to ever invade my bathing chamber apart from my nanny."

Had his first wife not ever peeked? How odd.

She didn't want to pry, and Tristan had seemed reluctant to discuss her. But at some point, she would need to know something about her predecessor—she didn't even know her name!

"Come closer so I can see you properly." Her voice had taken on an unexpected husky quality, and she cleared her throat.

He took a few steps forward. Tristan really was rather lovely, tall with broad brown shoulders, hair lightly dusting down his torso to the waistband of his smalls. His nipples, she noticed, were not flat. Was he aroused by her gaze? Her own breasts were responding to his, peaking with an odd ache. He was staring right back at her, his shadowed face serious.

"Aren't you going to disrobe for me?" she reminded him.

"I will. If you will."

That was not part of her bargain. But why shouldn't she? It was only fair. Her skin flared with heat, making her nightgown feel irrelevant.

"You first."

He shook his head. "Uh-uh. I don't trust you to follow suit."

"Fine. We'll do it together. On the count of three."

"Let me put the candle down." He set it on the bedside table, where it sputtered gloomily. "One."

Sadie fingered the hem of her white nightgown, inching it up over her thighs. Tristan released the loose knot on his drawers. "Two," she whispered.

Tristan shut his eyes, his fierce eyebrows meeting as if he was in pain. "Three."

His smalls dropped, and Sadie forgot to pull the nightgown over her head. Oh my.

She must have spoken out loud. "See? I knew you would cheat." He stepped out of the puddle of linen at his feet.

"I—" she croaked. She felt light-headed all of a sudden. His member was not as beautiful as the rest of him, but was compelling nonetheless, growing larger the longer she looked at it. How very fascinating.

"Your turn, Mrs. Sykes."

"Oh. All right." Her hands shook, but she managed to take off the nightgown after getting it tangled in her hair and toss it to the floor.

She had never felt so naked in her life. Exposed. Vulnerable. Cold, but strangely hot, too. Neither of them spoke for a few minutes. He never came any closer to where she sat on the bed, but his eyes swept over her, raising gooseflesh on her skin. He seemed unperturbed by her shy visual exploration, holding his arms behind his back so she could look her fill. Sadie wished he'd get back into the bed so she could touch him.

Touch *it*. There was no marble fig leaf to constrain her.

Sadie wanted, well, she wasn't sure she knew quite what. Maybe some touching. A kiss or two or three. But they weren't ready to become man and wife in truth. They had an agreement about that, didn't they? She hardly knew this man, and some of what she did know she didn't much care for.

His familiarity with handcuffs, for example.

"Thank you. You may dress now," she said, hoping she sounded steady enough.

"Are you sure?"

"I rarely say things I do not mean."

He stepped back into his smalls and tidied himself. "Is that so? I was under the impression you said a great deal of nonsense to trick people."

She was famous for it. Up until a few days ago, it had worked like a charm. But Sadie discovered she didn't want to trick Tristan Sykes. She really didn't know precisely what she wanted to do with him.

For once in her life she was stumped. She had an unwanted husband who nonetheless was a very fine figure of a man. Intriguing. She could have stared at him all night long, and only wished for more candlelight to do so. But he was blowing out the candle stub at this very moment, and she still had to find her night rail.

She scrambled off the bed, dragging her fingers across the floor until she came to the rough cotton. She couldn't make heads or tails of the garment in the dark.

"Here. Allow me." He took it away from her and shook it.

"How can you see?"

"I've always been blessed to be able to see pretty well in the dark. It comes in handy on occasion."

Sadie pictured Tristan tiptoeing out of women's boudoirs like some large cat, avoiding slippers and husbands. He slid the nightgown over her head as she stood still, gently pulling her hair out over the fabric. It must be a mare's nest by now, her braids history.

"You can do the rest, right?"

She batted about, found the sleeves and stuck her arms through. There. She was proper again.

Unfortunately.

"Now what?" she asked.

"I believe we should try to go to sleep."

"Is it still raining?"

He moved across the room and opened one window. "No. Excellent. That means our wedding guests may go home, barring any other unforeseen disaster."

"It was an odd sort of wedding," Sadie said as she sat back down on the bed. He probably thought that *it* had been a disaster.

"I'm sorry if it didn't measure up to your girlhood dreams."

"I didn't have any! I knew I was not meant to marry."

"Indeed? How wise a child you must have been, and how disappointed you must be as an adult. Move over."

"Can't you go to your house now? We've been together for hours." Sadie didn't really want him to leave, but he had that tone back in his voice that set her teeth on edge.

"I don't want to take the chance. We shall emerge from our honeymoon suite arm in arm tomorrow, just in time to say goodbye to your father and Charlton before they depart."

Sadie didn't want to see either of them. "Do you think we will really fool them about our marriage?"

"You have a large freckle over your left breast, rather like a bird in flight. If I have to describe it, I'm prepared to."

She wanted to throttle him. "You are a beast!"

"Calm down. I won't do anything to embarrass you. Many married couples never even disrobe during the act of coupling."

That seemed strange. Sadie had longed to feel Tristan's skin against hers. Was she somehow unnatural?

She rolled to her side of the bed and tried to lie still. Tried not to ask the questions banging away in her brain.

It was hopeless.

"Your wife—did she keep her nightgown on?"

"What?"

"Your w-wife. I don't know what she was called. I don't know anything about her."

"And there's no reason to," he growled. "The past is the past. She has nothing to do with us."

"But you loved her."

"Damn it, Sadie! I am not going to talk about Li—her with you. Ever. Now go to sleep."

Li. Linda or Lisbeth. Lysistrata. Sadie didn't dare say one more thing. But she would find out somehow.

Chapter 30

Tristan had been married less than twenty-four hours and he was ready to strangle his wife. Or himself. But that wouldn't work now, would it? Once he began to lose consciousness, his hands would fall away and the deed would never get done.

He had jumped through various hoops all day trying to please the uncommon cast of characters that were currently occupying Sykes House. He was tired. Frustrated. And had the bluest of blue balls, despite masturbating less than three-quarters of an hour ago.

What in hell was he going to do with his wife?

This one. He had no interest in discussing Linnet with her. His first marriage had been a disaster, and most of the time he pretended to himself that it had never happened. His friends and family were usually too polite to bring the subject up.

Did he owe Sadie the truth? She would think less of him, knowing he'd been a cuckold. A man who hadn't satisfied his wife—

Ha. He'd pledged to satisfy Sadie. Had touted his ability. Just words, when it had yet to be proved that he could.

Perhaps it was for the best that they would live apart.

But at the moment she was scarcely a foot away. Now that he'd seen her body—and its charming freckles—he was in a state of lustful agony.

He waited to hear her light snores, but the wait was in vain. He could practically *feel* how awake she was, vibrating with energy. If he told her just enough, they might put his past to rest, and then *get* some rest.

Tristan cleared his throat of gruffness. Best to make this simple. Unemotional. "Her name was Linnet. Her father was a viscount. We married much too young. She was hardly seventeen and not at all ready to settle down."

"What happened to not talking about it *ever*?" Sadie asked, moving closer.

"You're like a terrier with a rat. I might as well tell you some of it before you wear me down with your chewing. It's not something I particularly relish doing." An understatement if there ever was one.

"Thank you. If I had a husband, I'd tell you about him."

And I wouldn't want to know. "Men and women are different dealing with such things. You ladies like to chatter until our ears fall off."

"And you men keep everything to yourselves until you explode."

"Maybe you are right. At any rate, Linnet and I were unhappy almost from the beginning. She preferred the gaiety of London. I like a quieter life."

"But you said you wanted to marry her. Why could you not make the sacrifice to stay in the city?"

"I did. For a time. Then things became too painful for both of us, and we divorced."

"And then she died."

"Yes."

"And that's all?"

"Yes."

She paused, and he hoped she was done. No such luck. "It's very sad, isn't it?"

"Yes."

"Is that the only word you can say about it?"

"Yes. Now, if you please, can we try to go to sleep? I shall try to answer any other questions you might have at a reasonable hour, but there's not much left to tell." Nothing more he wished to divulge at any rate.

"Was she beautiful?"

Tristan knew whatever he said would be wrong. "That's enough, Sadie."

"But—"

She needed distracting, and a kiss was a good way to do it. But this time, he was going to mark her, so there would be little doubt of the consequences of their wedding night. He grasped her shoulders, drawing her to him. "Enough, I said."

He covered her mouth with his and felt a tremor. His or hers, he wasn't sure which. He thrust his tongue deep, deliberately giving her no chance to stop him.

She didn't seem to want to, which was gratifying. Sadie was pliant in his arms, making those soft noises that drove him mad with desire. She returned his kiss with equal fervor, and Tristan knew he would be lost in seconds. Abruptly he turned his head and nipped her long white throat, causing her to shriek and torture his eardrum.

Hearing was overrated anyway, wasn't it? He continued to bite and suckle and stroke her breasts until she was frantic, clawing through his hair, scratching his bare back. They were marking each other, and let Roderick Charlton try to prove they had not consummated their hasty marriage.

She was writhing and sobbing, straining against him. She wanted to finish this, or at least he thought she did. He knew what he wanted, had never wanted anything so much.

But he'd made a promise.

"Enough," he whispered.

"Damn you."

He *felt* damned. Doomed. His cock was definitely cursed.

"Have you been reading Polidori's *The Vampyre*? What on earth was that?" Her voice shook as she buttoned her nightgown up to her chin.

"Love bites. I don't believe I drew any blood, though." He'd been careful, but her throat would be covered with rosy welts for all the world to see.

"It was b-barbaric."

"Forgive me." Better to ask forgiveness than permission. He tucked her head on his shoulder and smoothed her hair. "Go to sleep. It's very late. Or very early, depending upon your perspective."

No more questions about Linnet. No more talking about anything. A cool rain-scented breeze wafted in the open window, and Tristan began to plan the day ahead as he lay cradling his wife. His number one priority— to say goodbye and good riddance to Charlton and Islesford.

He would have to meet with the Puddling Rehabilitation Foundation governors and explain their Guest's newly altered state. Altared state. He smiled in the dark at his pun. Check on the progress of the renovations of Stonecrop Cottage. Propose new construction somewhere in the village to expand the program.

And sign the parish register. One mustn't overlook that. Really, that was the first order of business. He'd go to the parsonage and bring back old Fitzmartin. The rest could wait.

He felt Sadie's lips buzz against his skin. "May I finally go shopping for clothes?"

He'd really prefer she never wear anything again. How delightful it would be if he confined her to the Red House bedroom where he could feast his eyes on her all the day long.

Except he didn't have time for that indulgence. "Can I trust you not to run off?"

"I don't know. Maybe you should come with me to make sure I behave."

"Not if you're wearing my old suit. Tell you what. I have several things to take care of tomorrow—no, *this* morning. I'll take you into Stroud in the afternoon. All right?"

"I suppose." She snuggled against him, her long limbs tempting him unmercifully.

It was peaceful to lie thus. One could almost imagine they were a happily married couple on their honeymoon, apart from Tristan's iron erection. If he was truly on his honeymoon, he'd be doing something about that.

Perhaps one night, but not this one. She might be more than amenable to his kisses, but the rest could wait. Tristan didn't want Sadie to feel forced any more than she already did and turn resentful. Her life had changed far beyond what she had ever planned.

As had his. He supposed he had thought he might marry once again— many years in the future, when an heir was needed. He might have found someone obliging. Docile. Two words one would never ascribe to Lady Sarah Marchmain.

Chapter 31

"You owe it to him, my girl."

How dare her father try to make her feel guilty, when this impossible situation was all due to him and his high-handed finagling! If anyone owed anything to Roddy, it was the Duke of Islesford, who had neglected to reimburse his ex-future son-in-law for the loans he had made. Tristan had assured her the viscount would be adequately compensated, and that his solicitor was working out the details. A breach of promise suit would be one more embarrassment that he wanted to avoid.

Sadie wished she could avoid everyone and everything. But she had found herself at the breakfast table with her new husband, her dreadful father and her former suitor, the most awkward meal imaginable. She had barely been able to swallow her tea while the gentlemen treated each other with arctic politeness over the poached eggs.

Tristan had excused himself to go into the village on business, promising to return shortly. He gave her a very thorough kiss in front of his departing guests which would leave no doubt in anyone's mind—other than hers—that he and Sadie were a committed couple. She had added a kerchief over another servant's dress—gray, this time—to cover the livid marks on her neck.

She should not have enjoyed being nibbled like a pastry, but she had. Sadie found her reaction to her married state inexplicable. Tristan Sykes was—

Confusing. She might have thought of more words if she possessed more than half a brain.

"I don't see why Roddy wants to speak to me. He should hold me in aversion." You too, she added silently to her father. She wouldn't want to share their carriage ride.

"He cares for you, Sadie. I believe he wants to assure himself that you've made the right choice."

"I didn't make a choice at all, Father," she said coldly. "You insisted on this marriage."

"What was I to think, finding my little girl half-naked in a man's arms?" the duke blustered.

"I haven't been a little girl in a decade." Sadie had shot up alarmingly as a child, and was a good four inches taller than her father now. She stared down at him, hoping to make him feel like the lowly worm he was.

"I am not talking about your size, you ungrateful chit. You are my daughter, and I worry about you."

"You have an odd way of showing it, selling me off to every creditor that comes along."

"It was never like that! You needed a husband's strong hand to control you. I admit I was a failure at that."

"I don't want to be controlled!" It was all Sadie could do to refrain from punching her father's veiny nose this instant. It was obvious he'd indulged in what the Sykes's wine cellar had to offer last night.

"You'd better get used to it. That Sykes fellow is no milksop. You may think to run him ragged now, but he'll soon set you to rights. I've had him investigated. That man who was here yesterday—well, you didn't see him and he left at first light, but he knows what's what."

"The inquiry agent? I'm surprised you spent the money."

"I've been throwing money away on you ever since I paid off that groom when you were fifteen."

Her father had never believed her about Dermot. The hurt of his doubt was still as sharp, but there was no point in Sadie letting her father know he'd scored another hit.

"So sorry to be a bother."

"None of that. It's what you live for. I hired the fellow to find you when you ran away. But I killed two birds with one stone. The information he provided was invaluable. If you think to be up to your old ways, think again. Sykes won't put up with any funny business from a wife. The first one learned that soon enough."

Linnet. Sadie wouldn't give her father the satisfaction of knowing she was still curious about her predecessor.

"Tristan's told me all about it," she said airily.

"Then watch your step if you know what's good for you." He sighed dramatically. "I had hoped you would make a brilliant marriage, but here you are in this wilderness. You've made your bed, now you must lie in it."

Ooh, her father was insufferable. With any luck, she wouldn't see him again until—

Goodness, she was about to think of his grandchild's christening. A baby, hers and Tristan's. If and how that was to be managed was a task for another day.

"I'll just do that, Father. Tell Roddy I will meet him in the conservatory in ten minutes. Have a safe trip." She didn't angle her cheek for a kiss.

Her father left, grumbling. With every step he took, Sadie's shoulders relaxed until she felt almost calm.

How had her mother endured him? Had she been so dazzled by his title she threw away any good sense she had? Sadie had a feeling her mother had been manipulated by *her* father, who had wanted to advance his woolen mill by his relationship with a duke. At least her grandfather had been wise enough to protect his daughter's money from her rapacious husband.

Sadie supposed she had access to those funds now. They were to be released upon her marriage or when she turned twenty-five. What would she do with the money? It had been a dream for years. But any fantasy she'd had butted up against the reality that she was Tristan Sykes's wife. She couldn't buy herself a castle or a cottage and acquire some cats.

Or could she? If marriage to Tristan proved to be impossible, she might have recourse.

She checked her herself in a mirror and was dismayed. Her scarf had come loose, and purple bruises climbed to her jaw. No wonder her father had been so disdainful. She couldn't remember the last time he'd looked at her with anything like joy.

She'd seen to that.

Sadie entered the conservatory, her favorite room in the house. It was truly an amazing place, Tristan's green fingers evident everywhere. The air was thick and hot despite the gray skies outside, and she sat on a wicker chair to wait.

Her husband had skills unusual for a gentleman. He did, after all, construct wedding bouquets. She'd seen some framed architectural renderings in the Red House during her incarceration. Tristan's house designs were clean-lined, yet warm and inviting. She wondered if he ever thought to create a real house for himself, something larger that his converted garden folly.

Why should he? He'd inherit Sykes House one day, and it was a rather lovely property. No doubt he'd add his own touches to it when the time came. Would she still be here to see them?

She was so lost in thought that she didn't hear Roddy enter until he cleared his throat.

Sadie didn't rise. "You wanted to see me?"

He took the chair opposite. "I did. You know you can depend on me, Sarah, if you change your mind about Sykes." He gave her an earnest look that she couldn't meet.

"Thank you. I shall be fine. Have a pleasant journey home." There. He could go.

He twirled his signet ring in the heavy silence, and cleared his throat again. "You've had poor judgment about men in the past."

Sadie felt a flash of irritation. "What do you mean?"

"I know about your youthful indiscretions. I decided to forgive you when I asked you to marry me—it was all so long ago, after all."

"Forgive me? I don't need your forgiveness! Nothing happened with anyone!" There had been Dermot. Two other rejected fiancés. None of them were worth tuppence, and they hadn't got much further than misbegotten kisses. Kisses that she knew now were the work of amateurs.

"You have a reputation, Sarah. I was willing to overlook it. I assume Sykes is aware of what he's gotten into."

"If this conversation is supposed to make me sorry for not marrying you, it's failing in spectacular fashion. How dare you criticize me!"

"I am not criticizing! You are a spirited woman. I had hoped to tame you."

"Tame me?" Sadie's palms itched, always a bad sign. "As if I were a filly to be broken to bridle?"

"I am a patient man. I waited for you for a year, Sarah," he said with reproach.

"More fool you." Had it really been that long? Sadie had tried to ignore her father's machinations, and Roddy had never really registered with her, apart from noticing his rust-colored moustache and beard. She wasn't even sure what color his eyes were, and he was sitting right in front of her.

"I didn't agree with the duke that you should be sent here, and I was right. Look at you."

"What's wrong with me?"

His lip curled. "That dress. You look like a housemaid. Does your husband plan to keep you in rags like a bumpkin Cinderella? He cannot have wanted this marriage. Your father explained how you trapped him." He shook his head in mock sympathy. "You would have been a viscountess. I would have spared no expense in providing for you."

She was the one trapped! "A diamond bridle, perhaps? A tooled Spanish leather saddle? I will be happier here." *Maybe*. Or maybe she'd run off again. Why not?

"Just remember I warned you. And should your husband or you come to your senses, you have only to summon me. I will take you back, of course not as a wife but a mistress. You'll have everything you would have had, save for my name. You've made that impossible, I'm afraid." He stood. "I'll see myself out, but how about a kiss for old time's sake? I had always held off any show of my affections, respecting you too much. I see I underestimated your warm nature."

Sadie didn't trust herself to speak. She'd held rein over her temper for a remarkable amount of time, and was trembling with rage. When Roddy bent to kiss her goodbye, she socked him in the jaw with her left fist and he fell backwards at her feet. There was a loud crack as his head hit the brick floor.

"Oh, dear. Tut, tut."

Sadie looked up, rubbing her hand. Both Tristan and Reverend Fitzmartin were in the doorway, and neither looked happy.

Chapter 32

"You could have let him kiss you," Tristan said, not really meaning it.

It would have been so much easier. Charlton would be gone, Islesford would be gone, he and Sadie might be in Stroud clothes-shopping right about now. He could be sitting in a chintz chair in the modest dressing room of Madame Elyse's dress shop while his wife displayed her very considerable charms to him, and him alone.

Instead they were waiting for Dr. Oakley to come downstairs and give his opinion on Charlton's injury. There had been a fair amount of blood on the conservatory floor, which some unfortunate soul was mopping up under Mrs. Anstruther's direction. Fitzmartin hadn't been pressed into giving Charlton the Last Rites yet, but he was lingering about in the library just in case. Tristan had no idea where the duke was, which could bode ill for them all.

At least Tristan had signed the parish register, as had his wife. It was the last thing she was going to do with that bruised hand for a while. Mrs. Anstruther had wrapped it with an ice pack, and Sadie sat nursing it glumly.

And Anstruther was home, quite shocked to discover the missing duke's daughter was back and had become Mrs. Sykes right on schedule. The woman he chased to Gloucester had proved to be a red-headed grandmother of five.

"He said I could be his mistress!" she hissed. "You would have hit him too."

Tristan poked at the fire in the drawing room. The day had turned unseasonably chilly and damp, and the room was cold. Whiskey would be welcome, but it was still early in the day and he needed a clear head in case of more calamities. "He was only saving face, Sadie. You've obviously hurt him. Besides the punch."

"*I* didn't hurt him! It was my bloody father's idea to break the engagement and for me to marry you!"

Tristan had wondered if she was getting used to the idea. It appeared not.

"Nevertheless. You can't go around hitting people. I won't have it."

She looked up to him sharply. "Am I just to nod and simper and be agreeable to everything?"

He returned the poker to its stand. "It couldn't hurt." As unlikely as it would be. "Look, I understand he angered you. The man is an idiot. But now we're stuck with him—and your father—for the foreseeable future. There are consequences for your ill-advised actions."

Tristan knew he was lecturing, but he couldn't stop himself. Did she realize the seriousness of the situation? They had been on the cusp of putting her past behind them, settling with Charlton so they wouldn't get sued, getting rid of the dreadful duke so he could carry on his louche life. If Charlton was mortally injured, Sadie's life would be ruined.

And Tristan's too.

"I didn't expect him to fall down," Sadie said, mulish.

"And he didn't expect to be hit. I daresay if you gave him some warning, he might have managed himself better. Found his footing."

"Are you saying if I tried to hit you I wouldn't succeed?"

She looked like she wanted to hit someone or something very badly. "Don't try it. I boxed at university." A stupid thing to do for a young man who hoped to earn his living with his hands.

From the time he could remember, he built things. First with blocks, then with boards to house dogs, rabbits, and other creatures. A playhouse for his younger brother. He shadowed the estate carpenter on school holidays until the man had probably wanted to hit him on the head with a hammer. Tristan sat back down on the sofa, several feet away from his bride. Some honeymoon this was.

"What's taking Dr. Oakley so long?" Sadie asked after an interval.

"Stitching up Charlton's head, I should imagine." Let's hope that's all he was doing. No pennies on Charlton's eyelids yet, pray God.

"I'm going up there."

Tristan shook his head. "You've done enough damage for one day. You are to stay here."

"Is this how it's going to be? You telling me what I may or may not do?" Her eyes were very bright.

"Don't be childish. I merely meant you'd get in the way. Anstruther is up there helping. He knows his way around a sickroom."

"Ugh. I wouldn't want *him* to take care of me if I was ill."

"He's very competent. He may not be a handsome fellow, but his heart is in the right place."

Sadie picked at the fichu around her neck. "He hates me."

"He hardly knows you. And if he hated you, why would he go to Gloucester to look for you?"

"Probably to push me under a train so you could be saved from me and my wicked ways."

"What a bloodthirsty imagination you have. Come here." He patted the space between them, but she stayed stubbornly put. Tristan sighed. "Do you want a cup of tea while we wait? I'm told it works wonders."

"Tea, the cure-all to everything," Sadie muttered. "No, thank you."

Tristan needed a cure—for his temperamental wife. That was why she had been shipped to Puddling in the first place, to give her tools to deal with life's frustrations in a more satisfactory manner. She couldn't continue to solve problems with her fists, and Tristan didn't particularly relish the thought of her turning those fists on him.

Women had few ways to assert themselves, despite the fact that a queen had sat on the throne for forty-five years. Men ruled their households, and Tristan knew if he wanted to live in any sort of peace, he'd have to make some accommodation with his independent bride.

After meeting the Duke of Islesford, he was beginning to understand his wife. Sadie needed someone to listen to her. Value her. No wonder she was so violent and willful, when those around her had simply tried to order her around. Including him, Tristan thought ruefully. "Tell me what he said again."

"Oh! If I repeat it, I'll want to go upstairs and pummel him all over again."

Tristan gave her a grave look and she flushed. "All right, all right. First he told me if I ever needed him, he would come. Innocuous enough. I thanked him and tried to send him on his way."

"But he didn't leave after his chivalrous offer."

"No. He wanted to have a few more last words. Let's see—he said I looked like a drudge in this horrible dress. There was something insulting about my high spirits and how he'd thought to tame me once we got married. As if *he* could." She unwrapped the bandage and put the ice pack on a decorative plate on the end table.

"The man is an ass. Go on."

She tapped her chin as if she was lost in thought. "Hm. Basically he called me a whore, offered to keep me as his mistress when you got tired of me and my whorish ways. There. Satisfied?"

Good God. No wonder she had decked him. "He should be shot. But not today. I'll wait until he's recovered and challenge him to a duel."

Her mouth dropped open, just the effect he was seeking. "What? You cannot do that! It's—it's not legal! And Roddy is a fair shot. I've been to house parties with him where he bagged more grouse than anyone."

"I am not a game bird, Sadie. Your honor needs to be avenged, and Charlton needs to learn to shut his mouth." If the man besmirched Sadie's character publicly, they might not recover from the disgrace. Sadie would be unable to take her rightful place in society, not that she'd shown much interest in doing that so far. However, that had been her rebellious choice. Someday she might see the advantages of conventional behavior, and it would be too late. The choice would be lost to sour grapes and scurrilous gossip. The Beau Monde had a long memory.

As for Tristan, he'd gone through all this before with Linnet. He really couldn't live through it twice. He'd be a laughingstock. But more important, he would fail Sadie.

Failure was not an option.

She clasped her hands together in entreaty, wincing. "The scandal— oh, Tristan, you mustn't. I'm not worth it."

He reached for her and cupped her cheek. "That's where you are wrong. You are very much worth it." Charlton and people like him didn't know Sadie at all. Tristan might not actually fight a duel, but Sadie needed to think he *would*.

That supposed Charlton made it through his concussion or whatever it was. Tristan was tempted to go upstairs and put a pillow over the man's face to hasten his deserved demise, but Sadie would be deemed guilty.

She turned her lips to his palm and kissed it. Tristan felt a powerful jolt of emotion—possession? Empathy? He did not want to see Sadie hurt anymore.

Chapter 33

Tristan was being kind, and she couldn't bear it. Sadie wanted to cry her eyes out. It was most unlike her. But really, almost everything she had done these past few days was unlike her.

Not the running away, though. She was champion at running away, even if she never got very far.

If Roddy didn't get better, she'd have to run somewhere far, far away. The thought of jail—or hanging—was simply too awful. Being a duke's daughter wouldn't help her escape the noose.

If he lived—Tristan couldn't possibly be serious about fighting a duel. If she disappeared, that would put an end to that, wouldn't it?

She would miss Tristan and his expressive dark eyebrows. Miss his capable hands. Miss becoming his wife in truth.

Oh, Lord. What was happening to her?

She stopped kissing Tristan's palm. It was a silly thing to do, but then she specialized in silly.

"It will be all right, Sadie."

"You must promise me not to fight a duel. Swear it. I will never forgive you if you do." If he died because of her, she'd never forgive herself. She would have to try to kill Charlton all over again.

"My, you look fierce. All right."

"You're not just saying that to fob me off?"

"I'm a man of my word. Are you?"

"What do you mean? I'm not a man, you know."

"All too well. Yesterday we spoke vows in the chapel. I intend to honor mine as best I can. As far as you will let me. I expect the same from you."

Ah. The *obey* part. Sadie swallowed, and found herself crossing her fingers behind her back. For some reason, lying outright to Tristan was unexpectedly troubling. "I'll try."

"That's all I can ask." He got up from the sofa and opened a cabinet, coming back with a deck of playing cards.

"Cards? Seriously?"

"It will pass the time."

"I have no head for cards."

"You know how to count, don't you?"

"In several languages." Miss Mac had insisted to qualify as a lady, one must have mastery of French and Italian. If that's what it took, Sadie was all set.

"Good. We only need to count to twenty-one in English."

"*Vingt-et-un?*"

"Yes. Have you played it before?"

Sadie had not. Unlike many females of her class, she was not to be found in card rooms at parties frittering away her pin money. She liked to dance instead, although most of her partners were half a head shorter and a good deal less graceful.

She and Tristan sat at the fruitwood card table. He shuffled and dealt the cards deftly. Sadie lost every hand, asking for new cards when she should have been satisfied with what she had. Rather like her approach to life in general, she realized. The grass wasn't always greener, and the necessary card might be buried at the bottom of the deck.

"It doesn't hurt to be conservative," Tristan advised her, when she'd gone down to defeat yet again. "And you need to pay attention to the cards that have gone by. There are only four aces in a deck, you know."

He might as well be speaking Greek, a language she did *not* know. "I told you I was no good at this. Where in blazes is Dr. Oakley?"

Tristan checked his pocket watch. "It has been a while. I'll go check."

Sadie bit her lip. "You'll tell me the truth, won't you?"

"I will." He placed a brief kiss on the top of her head and was gone.

Sadie picked up the deck for a game of patience, something in which she was sorely lacking, but her hands shook too much to proceed. She tried to steady them, examining the uncomfortably heavy emerald ring. The square stone was substantial. Worth a lot of money. Again she tried to remove it with no success. If she had to leave, it would have to go with her.

She—didn't want to leave.

Puddling wasn't such an awful place. The surrounding countryside was beautiful. Sykes House and its gardens were perfectly delightful. Now that she was beginning to get to know Tristan, he was more or less delightful too.

Sadie got up and paced the length of the drawing room. She'd missed her prescribed daily walks, part of her rehabilitation plan. Her entire routine—her entire life—had been upended because of the fire. She could blame or thank Mrs. Grace, depending upon her mood.

Left, right, left, right. She spent a full five minutes going from one end of the room to another, and came no closer to finding out what was happening upstairs.

She couldn't wait for news any longer. Sadie wasn't sure where the footmen had carried Roddy. The house was a warren of wings and rooms which she had yet to explore. She was its mistress now, wasn't she, with a right to climb the stairs instead of feeling useless and guilty.

Or so she thought. A tall young man in the Sykes livery was guarding the staircase, looking just a tad nervous when she sailed out of the room.

"Sorry, Lady Sarah. Mr. Tristan left strict orders for you to stay down here."

"I beg your pardon." She tried to look down her nose at the footman, which was difficult as he was as tall as she.

He did not wither under her gaze or freeze at the chill in her voice. Tristan had picked well.

"If you will be so kind to return to the drawing room, my lady."

She wasn't feeling kind. Taking another tack, she flicked her eyelashes ever so slightly. She wouldn't want the poor boy to be overwhelmed. "What if I want to go to *my* room? To, um, freshen up? It has been an ever so trying day."

"Mr. Tristan told me not to be bamboozled by your charm or beauty, Lady Sarah. But if I was to succumb to your wiles, John and Henry are stationed outside Lord Charlton's door. You won't get in."

Damn Tristan for being so high-handed. But charm? Beauty? Those words were tiny sops to her irritation.

"What if you were to escort me upstairs to my room, just to prove I have no intention of trying to visit Lord Charlton? Why, I don't even know which room he's in."

"And I'm not telling you. No, my lady. You are to remain downstairs until Mr. Tristan says otherwise."

Sadie contemplated stamping her foot but knew when she had been bested. She returned to the drawing room and rang for tea. If she was stuck here, she might as well try to enjoy it. Breakfast was long ago, and she hadn't been able to eat very much with those three men glaring at each other.

Looking harried, Mrs. Anstruther herself answered the summons. "Yes, Lady Sarah?"

"Any news? What's happening, Mrs. Anstruther? And may I have a pot of tea?"

"Tea you shall have, but I have no idea. Dr. Oakley is taking his own sweet time."

Dr. Oakley didn't have much sweet time to take—he was nearly as elderly as Reverend Fitzmartin. He must have years and years dealing with Puddling's reprobate Guests.

"What are the servants saying?"

"Nothing, if they know what's good for them. Mr. Tristan hates gossip with a passion, especially after—" She stopped herself and colored. "We'll protect your reputation, Lady Sarah."

Protect her reputation? Sadie had been so worried about Tristan doing something irrational that she had quite forgotten her part in the situation. She couldn't even reassure Mrs. Anstruther that she didn't usually go about hitting people, because she did.

"Th-thank you."

"Would you like some sandwiches, my lady? Biscuits?"

The thought of food now soured her stomach. "No. Just tea, please."

According to Tristan, it worked wonders.

Chapter 34

"I'll wait for you outside. Don't be too long—we don't want the patient taxed. He is somewhat agitated and most anxious to speak with you. Anstruther, let me go over a few things with you while your master and the viscount have their *tête-à-tête*."

Tristan nodded to the doctor. Even a minute would be too long spent with Charlton, but it had to be done. He was not relishing this conversation, but the fellow apparently was determined it would take place, and in private.

The viscount lay in bed propped up on a mountain of pillows, his head swathed in bandages. Charlton would live, but shouldn't be moved for a day or two. Anstruther was to move in to the adjacent dressing room and monitor him for any signs of concussion.

"Are you sure you're not too tired? I can come back later this afternoon."

"No. This needs to be said now. I've finally had some sense knocked into me."

A joke? Tristan settled into a chair near the bed and waited.

"You are aware I've considered myself engaged to Lady Sarah this past year. The settlements were drawn up, and, fool that I was, I passed a great deal of money into the duke's hands on the expectation that the man was to be part of my family."

"You've made a lucky escape then. As I said, I will make good your losses, Charlton." They'd both grow old before slippery Islesford pitched in.

"I—I cared enough about Lady Sarah to overlook some peculiarities in her background."

Tristan smiled despite himself. "She does have a temper."

"I'm not talking about her temper. You have a right to know, and I have an obligation to tell you, as one gentleman to another. God knows,

Islesford won't be straight with you—I had to worm the information out of him bit by bit."

Was there more madness in the family than was already obvious? Some two-headed ogre locked in a turret at Marchmain Castle? A grandmother who'd signed a temperance pledge? "What the devil are you talking about?"

"You must have noticed on your wedding night. Sarah was no virgin bride."

Tristan felt the color drain from his face. And his fists clench. It wasn't cricket to beat a man who was already down, but tempting nonetheless. How dare Charlton speak of Sadie thus, and how could Tristan sit and listen?

How could he not?

"Are you saying *you* slept with her?" Impossible. If the man claimed it, Tristan would know him for a liar. Sadie would never—

Well, how was he to know what Sadie might or might not have done? She was not precisely consistent, and had run loose for years.

Charlton's lips twisted in distaste. "I? I'm a gentleman, Sykes. I would never anticipate my wedding vows. I gave her plenty of chances to come to terms with her earlier indiscretions and admit her faults. A year of chances, hoping she would be honest with me. I treated her with every respect for all the good it did."

Charlton was actually giving him a look of pity. Tristan was incapable of speech.

"What, you didn't know? She fancied herself in love with her groom. Her groom! She should know the requirements of a gentlewoman by now, but the earthy aspects of her mother must have come to the fore.

"An Irish groom, can you imagine? Islesford paid him off, but I tracked him down in Newmarket just to make sure he'd stay out of my way. Ghastly common fellow. Horse trainer now. Told me he's still in contact with Lady Sarah, had the letters to prove it, and if I knew what was what, I'd pay him off too. The man bragged he's left a litter of bastards up and down the British Isles, and it is only a matter of luck that—"

Charlton got no further as Tristan's bunched fist somehow encountered the viscount's yellowing teeth.

The man spat of mouthful of blood onto the counterpane. "What was that for? I'm trying to do you a favor! Ask the duke. Ask your bride. You'll need to watch her like a hawk. I'm well rid of her."

"I don't care what Oakley says. I want you out of my house," Tristan said, rubbing his knuckles. He and Sadie were now a matched pair. "If I hear that you have insulted my wife in any way, even to as much as utter her name with your filthy mouth, you will wish you were dead, and any money you hoped to recoup will be forever unavailable to you in hell. Is that clear? Anstruther!"

He was shaking so hard he could barely convey his orders. In much less than twenty minutes, Charlton was bounced down the stairs on a litter by four footman to a spare carriage. Tristan didn't care how far Young Fred had to travel to get the viscount away from Puddling, nor did it matter if the jostling trip would kill the bastard.

Tristan locked himself in his father's study and, despite the early hour, poured three fingers of brandy. Had Charlton told the truth?

What if he had? Tristan had certainly not been a virgin when he'd married the first time. He doubted Linnet was one either, God help him. In fact, the likelihood of that was remote—she had run wild, as he'd come to find out, and her parents had been anxious to wash their hands of her.

But Sadie, he'd been so reluctant to breach her defenses until she was ready. Had given her every opportunity to get used to the physical side of marriage. Had been so careful. So sensitive.

Was he a fool? Again?

If she loved another man, an Irish groom no less, there was little hope for them. No wonder her father had tried to restrain her impulses.

It wasn't that his rival's birth bothered Tristan; he was more democratic than most men of his class. But if her heart was engaged, there was no point in Tristan making an effort to woo his unwanted wife.

And the irony—Sadie didn't want him either.

He swallowed too much brandy. Could he be so wrong about her? Tristan remembered last night, and shook his head of the angelic vision she'd gifted him with. He'd been sure—

Well, he'd been sure before, and look where that had led him. He would get no closer to the truth swilling brandy in daylight. It was time to find the damned Duke of Islesford.

And then he'd deal with Sadie.

* * *

Islesford was easy to run to ground. He was in the billiards room, smoking a cigar, drinking Sir Bertram's best Scotch whisky, and hitting the balls in a desultory fashion. He seemed unsurprised to see Tristan.

"Care for a game?"

Tristan bit back a bitter reply and shook his head.

The duke returned the cue stick to its wall case, and settled into a plush armchair. "I understand you've saved me from traveling with Charlton. He'll live then, will he?"

"Unfortunately, yes. I see you're still here."

"I couldn't very well go until I knew things were settled and my girl was safe, and now it's a little late in the day to head for London."

"You could take the train," Tristan said, churlish.

"And leave my coach here?" The duke looked nonplussed.

"We'd send it on. As a matter of fact, we can get you to the station within the hour. I believe you have plenty of time to make the four o'clock train. You're still packed, are you not?"

"You *are* anxious to begin your honeymoon."

The duke winked at him, and Tristan wanted to punch him, too. Sadie's temper must be rubbing off on him.

Tristan took a breath. "Charlton had a few things to say to me before he was removed."

"Oh?"

"I think you know what they might be."

Islesford squirmed in the chair. "I? How should I know? I don't go around eavesdropping, and I'm not a mind reader."

"The. Irish. Groom."

"Who?"

"Don't play games with me, Your Grace. He told me Lady Sarah formed an unsuitable attachment to the man."

"Why, that's old news!" The duke reddened, and took a sip of his drink. "She cried her eyes out at the time. Swore he loved her. Loved her money, more like. He came to me, not to make an honorable offer—not that he could have—but to blackmail me for his silence. I burned all her letters. Romantic rubbish. She moped around the castle for months, not eating, behaving in the most shrewish manner, and I must say it was a relief when—well, you know. Nothing transpired. No half-breed brat arrived to sully the Marchmain name."

So it was true. Tristan shut his eyes briefly. He couldn't afford to show the weakness he felt.

Again.

But then, Sadie hadn't really betrayed him. Hell, she hadn't known he existed when she gave herself to the rogue . She'd never claimed to love Tristan; they had been forced into this impossible situation. He wasn't coming to her an innocent lad. Why should she be untouched?

"You needn't worry, Sykes," the duke assured him. "I gave the fellow a small fortune, and he'll keep his mouth shut if he knows what's good for him. I'm not so sure about Charlton, though. You may have trouble there. The man's a corkbrain. My Sadie would have run rings around him."

Sadie could run rings around most everyone. Even Tristan. He'd begun to—well, he could stop beginning. Go back to his old ways. He'd had experience shoving his finer feelings into dark corners for more than a decade.

"Who was this groom?"

The duke waved a hand. "Dermot Something. Ryan? Reilly? I forget."

"I'd like you to find out."

"Why?"

That was indeed the question. "I have my reasons." If only he understood what they were.

"Best to let sleeping dogs lie."

"Nevertheless."

The duke rose. "All right. I believe it's Reid. Dermot Reid. R-E-I-D. I suppose you still want to get rid of me."

"You are very astute, Your Grace."

"Tell Sadie good-bye for me again, won't you? We've already said it once today."

Tristan made the arrangements to get the duke to the railway station in nearby Stroud. In a few hours, the man would be in his London residence, ready to gamble away his son-in-law's largesse. With any luck, he wouldn't see Islesford until Christmas, if then. Tristan was under the impression that the duke and Sadie weren't much for playing Happy Families at the holidays.

Tristan's own father was annoying, but he meant well. The same could not be said of Islesford. Tristan stubbed out the smoldering cigar the man had left behind, careless to the end. All he needed was this house to burn down around him. Then where would he and Sadie go? The Red House was not big enough for the two of them.

Especially if they were not to share a bed.

Chapter 35

Waiting for Tristan, Sadie had drunk four and a half cups of tea. It was eventually necessary to make discreet use of the downstairs washroom under the watchful escort of the tall young footman. It had been mortifying to have him stationed outside the door, where he could hear her every movement. Sadie's temper had risen with every sip of tepid tea.

Where was her husband? *Husband.* The word had an odd cadence inside her head. She had watched Charlton get bundled out of the house almost two hours ago, so he must be well enough to travel. She hadn't killed him, which was more or less good news. Her father had also left in a Sykes coach not much longer after.

They were now alone in the house. Well, as alone as one could be with a fleet of conscientious servants. This was the first full day of their marriage, and she felt like a prisoner, worse than when she'd been sequestered in Stonecrop Cottage. At least Mrs. Anstruther was an improvement over Mrs. Grace.

Sadie paced the room. At this point she had examined every book and bibelot on the recessed shelves and tables. Anything worth reading must be in Sir Bertram's library. She picked up an empty candy dish, and considered aiming it at the door.

That was childish. But she felt childish. She did not feel like a married woman.

Perhaps because she wasn't really.

Sadie threw herself down on the brocade sofa instead. She examined each fingernail, traced each gore of her borrowed skirt. Looked in vain for a loose thread on the cushions, a speck of dust on the tea table. Everything was as it should be, a testament to a well-run household. But she was not the mistress of Sykes House yet, and might never be. Her father-in-law might bring home an opera dancer from Paris for all she knew.

Sadie didn't wish Sir Bertram ill. She did not even know the man. But his portrait hung in the library, and he looked a touch choleric. Unfriendly. Tristan had inherited his eyebrows.

Where was Tristan?

The drawing room door opened just as she was beginning to let her irritation get the better of her.

"Where have you been?"

"Attending to some family affairs. Yours, in particular." He did not smile. Probably he hadn't missed her as acutely as she had missed him this afternoon.

"I saw that you tossed my father out," Sadie said. "Thank you."

"It was my pleasure. I can move back to the Red House now."

Sadie's heart stilled. "What do you mean?"

"There's no more need for the marital pantomime. We do not have to share the same roof. As I've said."

Sadie cast her mind back to that conversation. It seemed like a lifetime ago. "You mean so you can woo me." He'd already made a spectacular start.

"I think we're past that point, don't you? You may remain in Puddling until the gossip dies down, and the novelty of our marriage no longer attracts attention. Then, I suggest, I will purchase a property for you, somewhere in another part of the country. Your choice. You've wanted your independence all your life, and you shall have it."

The rug was being pulled out from under her. She snagged it with a booted foot. "You don't wish to be married to me?" She sounded so pitiful she wanted to slap herself.

"No more than you do to me. We've fulfilled your father's demands, but I'll be damned if he ruins our life permanently. If you are discreet, you may pursue other interests. I will not stand in the way of your happiness."

Was he actually giving her permission to have affairs? Sadie, who always had the last word on everything, couldn't not find her voice.

"You'll understand that I'll draw the line at raising a bastard, however. There are precautions that can be taken."

Were there? The subject had never come up with Miss Mac.

"There is no reason we cannot be civilized about this," Tristan continued through her silence. "You are a duke's daughter, and will have more latitude than most women. You've already established a reputation for eccentricity. In any event, the conduct of our marriage is no one's business but our own."

"I see." Did she? No, she did not. She thought she was warming up to the idea of spending her life with this man, and thought he was getting used to the idea too.

He was only repeating what he had said before. Separate living arrangements. But he had completely omitted the courtship. Why did she feel he had thrust a knife in her heart?

He didn't want her.

Well, she didn't want him, either. What he was proposing was very much along the same lines as her own pre-Puddling goals. Autonomy. Access to her money. A quiet place of her own where she could do as she pleased. And apparently sleep with as many men as she liked. Except for the one that had briefly captured her interest.

"It's too late in the day to go shopping in Stroud," Tristan said, all businesslike. "I'll send a message to Madame Elyse. Perhaps she or her assistant can deliver some ready-made dresses tomorrow. Assess what you need."

"I need everything."

"Yes. Well." His eyes wandered away from hers and fixed upon the sluggish fire in the fireplace. "Are you warm enough?"

No. She felt a chill which had nothing to do with the temperature in the room. He had reverted to the cool, dismissive gentleman she'd first met in the Stanchfields' grocery. The one who brooked no nonsense.

Sadie was too dispirited to even attempt any.

"I'll see myself out then. Have a good evening." He hesitated at the door, as if he wished to say more, but thought the better of it.

And then he was gone.

This time, she heaved the candy dish with all her might against the door he'd just closed. Sadie hoped it was a priceless antique.

She heard a knock. Had he changed his mind?

Mrs. Anstruther entered the drawing room. "Are you all right, Lady Sarah? William heard—something." The housekeeper looked down at the shattered glass on the floor.

"Yes. I'm afraid I had an accident. I'm sorry." She hadn't stopped to think.

"Would you like an early supper? You've missed luncheon."

"That would be nice." Sadie had no appetite whatsoever.

"Would you like to dine downstairs, or do you want a tray in your room, my lady?"

Sadie did not relish sitting in the cavernous yellow-papered dining room alone. "A tray in my room would be just the thing, Mrs. Anstruther."

"Very good, my lady. I'll send a maid in here to take care of the... accident, and have your supper brought up to you in an hour."

"I've caused a lot of trouble today, haven't I? Blood and broken things. I shall try to do better."

"You've been under a strain, Lady Sarah," the woman said with kindness. "Everything will be better in the morning."

Would it? Somehow, Sadie had her doubts.

She crunched over the glass and went upstairs. Her bedroom was immaculate, with no sign of her wicked wedding night. A fire flickered cheerfully, and she stood before it, trying to get warm without success.

She removed her gray bodice and skirt and wrinkled kerchief, getting into her nightgown well before the sun thought to set. She should have rung for Audrey or Hannah, but didn't want to have to pretend that everything was normal. Although she was a famous liar, Sadie felt the current circumstances were more challenging than she was used to.

She moved to the window overlooking the vast gardens. Tristan was in the distance, speaking to a pair of gardeners. He used his hands as he spoke, windmilling about. Those forceful, magical hands that had unraveled her maidenly resistance. She watched as he trudged off up the slope to the Red House and disappeared behind the hedges. Would he enjoy dining alone? No doubt he'd feel relief he was well rid of her and the pretense of their union.

Sadie supposed she could go anywhere in the house she liked—the attics or the library. Find books to read or fripperies to place about her room to make it to her own taste. It was beautifully appointed, to be sure, but too perfect. Sterile. She nearly preferred the shabbiness of Marchmain Castle.

My goodness. She was homesick for a place she'd run away from at least a dozen times. It wasn't because she missed any of the dwindling staff—turnover was extreme due to her father's frequent inability to meet his financial obligations. All the friendly faces of her childhood had disappeared, one by one, off to work for employers that actually paid them. Only Cook was left, too elderly for a new life adventure.

Cook's receipts, which Sadie had copied so carefully over the years, had been lost in the fire at Stonecrop Cottage. Not that Mrs. Grace would ever use them. When Sadie had presented them in her naiveté, the woman had shoved them in the kitchen dresser drawer and forgotten all about them. Against the Puddling dietary rules, no doubt. Sadie had been beyond bored swallowing the tasteless pap she'd been served since.

She wiped a tear that seemed to be leaking from her right eye. Tears got one nowhere. She'd learned that lesson a long time ago. But neither, really, did anger.

What emotion was left in her limited arsenal?

Not fear. Sadie wasn't afraid of anything. Well, not counting spiders. She knew rationally they were good for the garden, but she couldn't like them. Marchmain Castle had far too many of them indoors, creeping up the curtains and bedcovers.

Was curiosity an emotion? For she was curious, and wanted to finish what Tristan had started in the bedroom. Find out what happened next. Bring things to their logical conclusion. They didn't have to live together as husband and wife, but for Tristan to leave her in this half-awakened state was not gentlemanly at all. She would simply have to seduce Mr. Sykes, whether he liked it or not.

And then she could go on her un-merry, unmarried way.

Chapter 36

Tristan had kept busy all day. He'd been hunched over on his knees for hours in what he called the Spring Garden, high up on a rise where it was visible from the main house, planting hundreds of bulbs. From overhearing the grunts and grumbles, he knew he was in the head gardener's black books for putting them in before the first frost. There were warnings galore—it was too soon in the season, animals would devour the bulbs in a gourmet buffet, they'd rot in the wet earth. But the work kept Tristan from going to go to Sykes House to see Sadie.

He was prepared to be generous with her, despite the repercussions to his own reputation. He'd written that letter first thing this morning, hadn't he? One of them should be happy.

It was more than he'd been able to do with Linnet, but he was older and wiser now. He couldn't countenance another divorce, however—he'd be ruined both socially and in business. Society would wonder how he'd gone so very wrong.

Where to start? Tristan had fallen under the spell of a woman who was not only completely unsuitable and unstable, but whose affection was fixed elsewhere. No wonder she'd rebelled, separated from the man she loved. Stuck in a crumbling castle, shunned by her feckless father who only remembered her when he needed money. *He* was the one who should have been sent to Puddling for rehabilitation.

Tristan was so immersed in digging a hole he failed to hear the rustle of skirts and the delicate tramp of a booted foot. The late afternoon sun disappeared all of a sudden, and he looked up into the face of his wife.

Holy God. She was not wearing trousers or servants' clothes any more. Madame Elyse had performed a miracle. Sadie was suitably dressed for the weather in a column of deep forest-green light-weight wool, her waist nipped in, a swath of gathers falling gracefully almost to the ground. She looked even taller than she was, especially with her red hair artfully swept up with green glass-tipped pins that shimmered in the sunlight.

"Good afternoon, Tristan."

He should have leaped up off his muddy knees, but all he could do was stare. She was magnificent.

"Your dress—" he croaked.

She smoothed a gloved hand down her skirt. "Yes, lovely, isn't it? Plainer than I'd like, but well made. Fortunately the dressmaker had enough extra material to add six inches to the hem. One would never know the ruffle wasn't meant to be there. Quite a needlewoman is Madame Elyse."

Tristan nodded in agreement. Who with eyes could dispute it? The dress was severely simple, yet Sadie had never looked better.

"She left me with several dresses to choose from until she and her assistant can run up the made-to-measure ones. No more Eton suits for me." Sadie smiled, and Tristan was nearly blinded. "There is even an evening gown. I have come to invite you to dinner."

"Dinner?"

"You sound as if you've never heard of the custom. Hot food on the table. Knives, forks, and spoons." She paused. "Wine."

"Anstruther—" Tristan began.

"Oh, I consulted with him first. I stopped at the Red House, and he told me where you could be found. He is not pleased to have to cede his cooking duties to his wife, but I persuaded him. Do they never speak?"

"Not to my knowledge." Anstruther hardly spoke to anyone if he could help it.

"How ridiculous. You and I may be estranged, but I do hope we can be civilized with each other. We haven't even been married long enough to have an actual fight."

"I don't think dinner is a good idea." For one thing, he might never be able to get up from the ground, slayed as he was by Sadie's regal presence. He'd never seen her full effect as a duke's daughter in proper clothing before, not even on their misbegotten wedding day.

"Whyever not? We both need to eat to keep body and soul together. And on the outside chance that someone is here spying for my father, it cannot hurt to share a meal, if not a bed."

Tristan's cheeks grew warm. "I doubt your father could suborn any of the Sykes servants."

"One never knows. Sometimes the man can become deceptively ducal. A person of lesser fortitude might succumb."

He supposed she might be right. And now that Islesford had a hefty purse filled with Sykes money, he could afford to bribe the entire village. Damn.

"Shall we say half past seven? Dinner will be served at eight."

What were they to do for those thirty minutes? Drinking was not recommended—Tristan wished to keep his wits about him.

And his hands to himself.

"I really don't—"

"Oh, come on, Tristan. Take pity on me. There I am, in that great big house, all alone on my honeymoon. I know you don't like me, but you don't have to. I imagine you know how to talk to people you have no interest in. You were raised a gentleman."

Not like? Have no interest? If only that was true.

"Very well." He struggled to his feet and brushed the dirt off his trousers. Now that he was closer, he could see the faint traces of lavender under her extraordinary green eyes. Had she slept as badly as he had last night?

She flicked her russet lashes at him. "Don't be late."

"I wouldn't dream of disappointing you."

He watched as she sauntered down the ridge, back straight, her bustle trembling provocatively with each step. Tristan wanted her to turn and give him a wave, but she didn't.

From his vantage point, he watched as she meandered through the gardens below, pausing to bend now and then over a flower or clump of ornamental grasses. He stood motionless for the time it took her to cross the acreage and climb the path up to Sykes House.

He was in so much trouble. He glanced at the half-empty basket of daffodil and tulip bulbs. Tristan's back ached like the devil had trod upon it. How many had he already put in the ground for his father's pleasure today? Would the man even be home by next spring to see them? Paris had its allure. And with the stock market crash and subsequent recession earlier this year, Tristan's frugal father found his English pounds went a long way to keeping him comfortable.

He picked up the basket and tools and returned them to one of the garden sheds that discreetly dotted the landscape. If he was to dine with his wife, a lengthy bath was in order. It's a wonder she hadn't covered her nose with a handkerchief while she spoke to him. He was dirty from his uncovered head to his boots.

Anstruther met him in the hall as he came in.

"I hope I did the right thing, Mr. Tristan. I told that woman where you were."

"*That woman* is my wife, Anstruther. You will treat her with every courtesy."

Anstruther looked paler, if that was even possible. "Of course, Mr. Tristan. I know my place."

"Oh, stubble it. You've been like a father to me. But your harsh judgement of Lady Sarah is unwarranted.

She's much more than the dossier you read about her."

Anstruther sniffed down his beaky nose. "If you say so, Mr. Tristan."

"I do. Most emphatically. She's had complications in her life. You met the duke. You should understand."

"But he's a duke!"

"An accident of birth. The man's a menace. I would think you to be more of a democrat."

The butler shrugged. "It's true, the world is changing faster than I can keep up with, but I know my place."

Doubtful. Tristan had been genially bullied by his butler for years. "I will be dining at Sykes House. Why don't you come with me?"

"I?"

"You might have a word with Mrs. Anstruther."

Anstruther straightened to his already imposing height. "I have nothing to say to her."

Tristan sat down on the hall chair and removed his mucky boots. "Surely whatever quarrel you had is in the past."

"Not far enough in the past for me," Anstruther replied.

"I don't mean to pry"—well, yes he did—"but what was the nature of your difficulty?"

"I have reason to believe Mrs. Anstruther's affections are engaged elsewhere," Anstruther said, picking up the boots and dropping them in a newspaper-lined box. Tristan's gloves followed, and he knew before tomorrow all traces of his day's labor would be removed.

He thought of his father's housekeeper, a rather rotund, wrinkled, gray-haired lady who must be every day of sixty. She was no *femme fatale*.

Nothing like Sadie. But he supposed love didn't discriminate.

"Was this affair of recent vintage?"

"A few years back. I was grateful of your offer to serve you here. Things were awkward."

Anstruther and his wife had served as butler and housekeeper-cook for his father as long as Tristan could remember. It was a traditional sort of arrangement, and Tristan wondered who the fly in their ointment had been. A fellow servant? A tradesman? It was all rather incomprehensible.

"Did you hash it out with her?"

"I wouldn't lower myself. She knows what she did. I shall run your bath now."

"You could be mistaken. Perhaps you should talk to her."

Anstruther sniffed and stalked off.

It was more conversation than the two of them had ever had in the months they'd lived in the Red House together. It was a pity that a marriage of such long standing had failed. But as Tristan knew well, marriage was not for everyone.

Especially him.

Chapter 37

Both Hannah and Audrey had been called in to assist Sadie with her toilette. There was no room for error. Nothing was left to chance.

Except for the evening gown. That couldn't be helped. Madame Elyse—whose name was really Eliza Smith—had made it for a young woman who had passed away, but Sadie was determined not to feel it was cursed. Or so pink.

It was *very* pink, a froth of moiré silk and lace in four different shades ranging from baby's bottom to its radish-colored trim. It fit her as if it had been cut specifically for her; nothing had been necessary but to add a lace flounce at the bottom to lengthen it. Deep pink satin roses and green leaves hovered over Sadie's bosom and at her waist and bared shoulders, which seemed a bit much after the austere green dress she'd worn earlier.

"Let's take these off," she said, pointing to the clump at her tightly-laced waist.

"We can put them in your hair," Audrey suggested.

Fine. She'd look like a rose bush. No, a rose tree, since she was so damned tall. "And take the flowers off the sleeves, too. Let's not gild the lily. Or the rose."

The girls giggled. Sadie was getting along with them better now that she was no longer running away or getting married against her will in handcuffs. Was that only two days ago? How time flew.

Once Sadie had seen the rose-studded confection of a dress, she knew what she had to do. Between fittings with the dressmaker, she had consulted Mrs. Anstruther about the menu. Perhaps it was too obvious. The oysters and truffles had been difficult to obtain, but even with Sadie's limited knowledge, she knew they were considered to be aphrodisiacs. There were figs and apricots in honey for pudding. Rich *pot de chocolates,* too.

Mr. Grimsby, the butler who had replaced Mr. Anstruther some months back, had been dispatched to Sir Bertram's wine cellar to bring up the very best vintages.

The prime difficulty was getting Tristan to agree to come, but she'd managed it somehow. Now all she had to do was feed and flatter him into bed.

She'd said the words at the wedding ceremony. Well, some of them. Signed the register. If she truly was married, it was time she ceased being a virgin.

"You look a treat, Lady Sarah. Just lovely," Hannah said, stepping back to admire her handiwork.

"I feel lovely. Thank you both."

Sadie remembered to stand tall as she descended the stairs at seven twenty-five that evening. She need not hunch over and try to hide herself—that was impossible anyway. She allowed Grimsby to pour her a glass of champagne, and drank it rather too quickly in her nervousness. Then she sat on the blue drawing room sofa, folded her hands, and waited. Her wedding ring sparkled under the lights.

The hall clock chimed the half hour, and a rap at the front door echoed it shortly thereafter. Tristan was on time to the minute. Surely that boded well, didn't it?

He bent to kiss her hand as she greeted him, except his lips didn't quite connect. He was resplendent in his black and white evening clothes. His hair, which had been so disheveled this afternoon, had been partially tamed with a fragrant oil. All of him, frankly, smelled delicious. Clean and woodsy and grassy. He could be a Green Man come to life, minus the ferocious beard.

"Good evening, Lady Sarah."

"So formal, Tristan? You know I prefer Sadie. It was my mother's nickname for me."

"Sadie, then." His blue eyes raked over her briefly. Too briefly, after all the trouble she had taken. "You are looking well. That dress is very becoming. But I thought you had an aversion to pink."

"It's this or nothing. Any port in a storm." But not the tight pink-and-white striped dress from the attic that she had torn. Although she supposed she owed her marriage to it. It was what she had been wearing when her father discovered them in their not-terribly compromising position. "Grimsby, you may leave us."

The butler nodded and left the drawing room, shutting the doors behind him. Sadie waved toward the champagne resting in a standing ice bucket.

"Will you do the honors, Tristan?"

"I see you've started without me."

"One glass only. I am as sober as a judge." Even if her heartbeat was erratic.

He refilled her glass and joined her on the sofa, sitting on its edge as if he would jump up any second and flee.

"None for you?"

"I've had an exhausting day. One drink, and I might fall asleep at the dining table. I'm sure you don't want that."

No. But she wanted him a bit looser. Playful. Right now, he was Tristan the Stiff. Her lips quirked, wondering if he was stiff in more interesting places than his spine.

Likely not. He'd made it plain he had no interest in her. Why had he changed so markedly from the other night?

"You worked in the garden?"

"Yes."

Sadie was pulling up one weed at a time. "What were you doing?"

"Planting bulbs."

Two weeds. "Isn't it too warm for that? It's only September." And he was supposed to be a great garden expert! Even Sadie knew better than to put bulbs in at this time of the year. The temperate weather might confuse them into blooming too early, only to get their new shoots frostbitten. True, it had been a little cooler today, and the scent of autumn had been in the air.

"Do you garden, Lady Sa—um, Sadie?"

"Not really. Marchmain Castle's gardens went to rack and ruin years ago. It's a shame."

"Perhaps your father will improve the property now."

Sadie snorted. "The only green my father is interested in is the baize on a card table. I expect you to discover that whatever amount of money you gave him, it will never be enough."

"We'll see." No doubt Tristan would stand up to her father better than Roddy had.

"I—I want to thank you for yesterday. For supporting me when I, uh, had the altercation with Lord Charlton."

"You are my wife."

Sadie leaned over the sofa cushion ever so slightly, pleased to see Tristan's eyes drop to her décolletage and then find their way back to her face. Normally, she didn't care for such inspection, but tonight was different. This man was different. "Am I?"

"You *were* in the chapel the other day, weren't you?" Tristan asked dryly.

"Under duress."

"There will be no more of that. No coercion. As I said, you are free to—do as you please." He was definitely not looking at her bosom now, but examining his hands. Sadie noticed they were reddened from scrubbing.

What if doing as she pleased involved kissing a man who wouldn't meet her eyes? It was too soon in the evening to pounce. The oysters needed to be given their chance to work, too.

"What exactly do you mean by that?"

"Don't make me spell it out."

"I'm afraid you'll have to. I find I'm all at sea regarding the rules of this marriage."

"There are no rules."

"No honoring or obeying?" She tried to flick her lashes, but he wasn't looking anymore.

"As if you would. I'm a practical man. I know when to give up."

Give up? Already? They'd barely had time to learn each other's middle names.

Tristan popped up off the sofa and went to the fireplace. A substantial fire was roaring to prevent Sadie from taking a chill—her bodice covered very little of her torso. Her shoulders and chest were exposed, the whole thing held up by boning and strips of fabric over her upper arms which really had no right to call themselves sleeves. However, it was so well-constructed it probably wouldn't slip down, which was a pity.

To think she'd spent most of her life trying to appear dowdy so she wouldn't attract the enemy. Well, here was one adversary she wished to entice, and he was back-to, his broad shoulders limned by the firelight.

Turn around. Turn around. Look at me.

Her directions did not manage to penetrate his cranium. He picked up the poker and stabbed at the logs, causing sparks to fly up the chimney. Glum, Sadie swallowed the rest of her champagne. The bubbles failed to ignite any sparks within her.

"I didn't mean to trap you," she said, her voice soft.

Tristan returned the poker to its stand but came no closer. "I know you didn't. This is your father's doing. But I promise I will not try to restrain you. It's time you have what you've longed for all these years."

Freedom. But somehow the word didn't resonate as it once did.

"Must I leave Puddling? I've come to like it." The mellow gold-gray stones, the hills dotted with sheep, the steep winding streets—they were all home now. Sykes House was beautiful and comfortable, and its gardens spectacular. She could see herself growing old here, like Lady Maribel de Winter.

"I can't have that," Tristan said flatly. "I'm not a saint."

Was she so offensive to his sensibilities? He'd liked her well enough when she was chained in his bed.

But he had disliked her at the beginning. Tristan had been cold. Dismissive. Too damned acute and on to her tricks. The futility of her intimate dinner was suddenly ridiculously clear. She'd been so naïve. Tristan wasn't going to be lured. He couldn't even be bothered to face her.

She wasn't going to beg to stay where she was not wanted.

"Where shall I go?"

"I rather thought Suffolk."

Sadie looked at him blankly. She didn't know a soul in Suffolk, but that was more or less the point, wasn't it?

"Close enough to London. Some sixty-odd miles, I think. I presume I'd be allowed to visit."

Tristan sighed with impatience. "Why don't you understand? I will not place any restrictions on your movements. You'll have all the money you'll ever need. Just don't—" He paused, disturbing his curls as he raked a hand through them.

"Don't what?"

"Make a spectacle of yourself."

She tamped down the flush of anger. "But that's what I do."

"Please stop." It wasn't an order. There was a hint of—desperation? He looked miserable.

So he should. She'd been ready to make the best of this marriage, and he was driving her away to Suffolk or somewhere for no clear reason that she could see.

Before she could ask him about his change of heart, Grimsby entered and announced dinner. Sadie wasn't hungry at all.

Chapter 38

Course after course arrived for hours. Although Mrs. Anstruther had outdone herself in the kitchen, everything tasted like mud to Tristan. His senses were in a total jumble.

And there were no safe places to rest his tired eyes. The silverware and glasses and gilt-trimmed plates gleamed too brightly. The table was polished to a mirror shine. The undulating yellow roses on the wallpaper seemed to be climbing up to the ceiling right in front of him. He certainly couldn't focus attention on his wife, who was covered in roses herself.

He could smell her rose perfume from across the table, too. She was not positioned at the end of it as she should be, but at his right. She'd made every attempt to prompt conversation, asking him about his school days and his business and his hobbies. He'd been an utter churl, answering with just the barest number of words, sometimes single syllables.

She had finally given up some minutes ago, and was now pushing a scrap of fig across her dessert plate. He could see her slender hand grasp the fork out of the corner of his eye, which was about as much of her as he dared to look at.

She'd had no reaction to the mention of Suffolk. Perhaps he should have been more specific and said Newmarket. Maybe even named names.

Dermot Reid.

Might as well get it over with. She seemed impervious to his hints.

"Do you enjoy riding, Sadie?"

She lay her fork down. "I used to. But I haven't ridden in years. Papa got rid of our horses. They were too expensive. I—I miss it."

Horses were not all she missed, he reckoned. "Do you follow the racing circuit?" He fixed his eyes on her now. She was pale, the two faint dabs of rouge on her cheeks visible.

She shook her head, the silk rosebuds in it quivering. "Not at all. I am no gambler. Not after watching my father fling his money away."

"You haven't been to Newmarket lately?"

"Of course not! I've been here for the past thirty-odd days, as you know, getting cured of my afflictions and addictions. At least gambling is not one of them. Meets there are in May and July, are they not?"

So, she knew that much. "October, as well."

"Are you proposing we go there together next month?" Sadie sounded almost eager.

That was all he needed, to be paraded in front of her lover. "No. I, like you, am not a gambler. I'm much too dull."

She smiled, not one of her full-force ones, but lovely just the same. "Oh, I wouldn't say you were dull. Just—careful. Respectable."

He'd tried to be, but look at the mess he was in. Like Peter, Peter, pumpkin-eater, he had a wife but couldn't keep her. A desirable wife.

Who desired another.

"I thought you might like to go. Alone. You could look at properties."

"You seem determined to get rid of me, and stick me in Suffolk to boot. I thought you said I'd have a choice as to where I'd live."

This was getting tiresome. "I assumed you'd want to live there."

"Why?"

He rose. "Let's not play games, Sadie."

She stood too, and dropped her napkin on her plate. "I assure you, I'm not the one playing games! And if I am, I've obviously lost the rule book. Oh, wait—you've said there are no rules. I really don't have any idea what's come over you. Yesterday you were so—sympathetic. Kind. Chivalrous, even. You said you'd fight a duel for me. Now you are a beast!"

"Really, your performance is very impressive, but don't bother."

"I'm not performing! I am just being me! I'm so sorry if you hate me."

Oh, Christ. Tears again. He squelched his impulse to take a step toward her. Hardened his heart. "I know, Sadie."

She blinked. "Know what?"

"About Dermot Reid."

Her mouth opened, but no sound came out.

"I don't blame you. But you must see it makes things impossible."

The plate hit him square in the chest, then dropped to the thick carpet. A splash of honey dripped down his waistcoat. "What the devil! I'm trying to be understanding!" He'd done everything so far to make her future easier.

She picked up the fork. Did she plan to stab him with it? "Understanding? Suppose you tell me all about Dermot Reid so *I* can understand." She stabbed the palm of her own hand instead.

He was dying inside, but forged ahead. "He is your, uh, paramour."

Sadie raised a sculpted eyebrow. "He is?"

"You can't deny it." He picked up his napkin and tried to wipe the sticky blob away.

"I certainly can. Let me guess. That ass Roddy told you. And then my ass of a father told you. It would never occur to you to ask me, now, would it? Heavens, no. Two men—two asses—have got the wrong end of the stick, as usual. Three asses, if you add Dermot, that lying sack of excrement. Four asses, counting you. I suppose my father told you he bought him off to preserve the tatters of my nonexistent virtue? No matter how many times I told him—oh!" She threw the fork at the wall with such force it stuck in the paper-covered plaster. "I hate you all!"

"What was I to think?"

Sadie sat back down in her chair with a whoosh. "Oh, I don't know. That they're asses? That they've never had my best interests at heart? It's probably my fault. After all, I was—*am*—a born liar. No wonder my father didn't believe me. I was a difficult, headstrong girl. Of course I would sleep with my groom. He paid attention to me. Was *nice* to me. I was fifteen—"

Tristan frowned. "Fifteen?"

"Yes. Did you think all this happened just last month? I haven't seen or heard from Dermot Reid in six years. But don't let that stop you from jumping to conclusions. Why, I might even be pregnant! A very long gestation, mind you, like an elephant or—" She burst into tears.

"I don't care if you're not a virgin," Tristan said, knowing as soon as the words were out of his mouth they were a dreadful mistake. He ducked and the wineglass shattered behind him, but not before the flying liquid splashed against his shirtfront.

She looked at him with loathing, her green eyes hazed with tears. "I am a blasted virgin, not that you're ever going to find out. But then again, I could fake it, couldn't I? I understand you can get a bladder of pig's blood or something equally disgusting and smear it on the bedsheets. I might not even be intact anyway after all the *riding* I did with Dermot. I'm not to be trusted, correct? Roddy told you I was a whore and you believed him!"

"I never thought that! Women are not whores simply because they enjoy carnal relations with men."

"Good! Because I haven't enjoyed anything!"

"Ah, now who's lying?" Sadie could not have been more responsive. But perhaps it was not judicious to bring that up at this juncture.

"Get out!"

"I'm not leaving until we get this settled." Or she killed him with tableware.

"Oh, it's settled. We have both made a horrible mistake. I, for thinking you might be better than the rest of your gender, more fool me, and you for getting saddled with a woman you believe the worst of. You didn't even *ask*. Try to talk to me."

"It was so embarrassing. By the way, I sacrificed my principles and would have let you live with your lover." Oh, God. The letter. He'd deal with that tomorrow.

"That's not a question. That's a statement. And poor you, such noble— and misplaced—generosity. You are just too good for this world, Tristan Sykes. No wonder your wife—" Her lips snapped shut.

"Don't." His tone even scared himself.

"I won't. Not to worry, there will be no honesty between us. No *anything*. But I'll tell you one thing—I am not moving to bloody Suffolk!" She swept the rest of her place setting off the table.

Chapter 39

She had been childish. Lost her terrible temper. So much for her night of seduction. The dining room resembled a battle scene.

Unfortunately, Tristan was still alive, redolent of wine and honey like a character from the Psalms.

The servants, no matter how well trained, were probably right outside the doors, listening to every word. Sadie didn't care. They should know that their master was an idiot. How could she have fallen in l—

Oh. God. No. She'd fancied herself in love once, with Dermot Reid, of all people. And that's how she came to be sitting amidst broken china and crystal in the middle of Nowhere, Gloucestershire, sent here for her many sins. It was ironic that the *one* sin she hadn't committed had caused her over half a decade of problems.

She'd been fifteen then. Practically a child, although she was already taller than most men at that age. Awkward as a spotted giraffe, with just as many freckles. She had been easy prey for an ambitious young man who'd abused her trust and lied to her father. Yes, Dermot had stolen kisses. Many of them. Groped her. Sadie might have gone further, because she was so, so needy. Lonely. It was rather miraculous that she'd exercised the good sense she really didn't have and drew a wobbly line.

But Dermot, thwarted, had gone to her father with her foolish letters and his own twisted version of the affair.

Sadie had had six years of regrets. There had been times when she wished she'd tossed her virginity away, for she was being punished anyway. It was so unfair that a man could consort and cavort with as many women as he could get his hands on, but a woman had no such option.

"You can't stay here," Tristan said, making her remember he was still standing there like a great towering handsome lump and they were still fighting.

"I'm not leaving." When she was calmer, she might think of a place to go, but she wasn't calm yet.

"No, I mean *here*. The servants need to clean this mess up and go to bed at a decent hour."

Sadie's cheeks grew warm. It had been thoughtless to vent her spleen on forks and plates, and expect someone else to tidy up. "I'll take care of it."

Tristan's wooly eyebrow rose. "You?"

"I can wield a broom as well as the next person." To prove it, she got up and started picking up shards of glass with exaggerated fervor.

Oops.

She must have hissed, for Tristan was at her side in an instant with his dirty napkin.

"Now see what you've done. You're bleeding onto the Aubusson."

He *would* care more about the rug. "It's nothing."

"Nothing? You probably need stitches." He grabbed her hand and tried to wrap the napkin around it.

"Where did you get your medical degree?" Sadie snapped. "And get that filthy thing away from me!"

"You need carbolic. A bandage. Watch your hand—you'll drip on your dress."

She could buy another dress now that she had access to her funds. A dozen dresses. Although she did like this one, even if it was four kinds of pink.

Tristan left her and opened the sideboard drawer. He came back with a clean lace-edged, embroidered linen napkin, which Sadie pressed on her wound to stanch the bleeding.

"We'll get Mrs. Anstruther. She'll know what to do," Tristan said, throwing open the dining room doors.

Grimsby, a footman and a maid nearly fell into the room. "Fetch Mrs. Anstruther and her medical kit. We will be up in Lady Sarah's suite."

"*We* will not."

"Oh, yes we will. What if you faint on the way up the stairs?"

"Over a drop of blood? Don't be silly!"

"Stranger things have happened. Don't fight me on this."

"I will fight you on anything I choose!" Sadie cried.

Tristan's response to this statement was to sweep her and her napkin into his arms and mount the stairs.

"I have feet!"

"Be quiet."

She was jostled about like a sack of potatoes, and despite her halfhearted attempts to clout him on his ear with her good hand, he refused to put her down even when they reached her room.

Both Hannah and Audrey were there, and their efforts were distressingly evident. Candles burned, a sheer nightgown lay across the foot of the bed, and actual rose petals had been scattered among the pillows and sheets. A bottle of wine and two glasses rested on the bedside table. Sadie wanted to curl up and die.

Tristan didn't seem to notice the preparations. "Where the devil is Mrs. Anstruther?"

Both maids rushed out. Sadie would have too, if he'd only put her down. Tristan was cradling her with competence, as if she didn't weigh more than a kitten. She had to admit it was nice to be cosseted in a strong man's arms, no matter how stupid he was.

"Let go of me at once!"

"Stop squirming. I will not be responsible if I happen to drop you. You are as slippery as an eel."

"How you flatter me," Sadie said through gritted teeth. Eels had fangs, didn't they? Would she have success biting him? His chin was close.

"I don't want to flatter you. In fact, I'd like to spank that ruffled bustle right off your charming derriere. You have been torturing me for days. Trousers! I ask you! I'm only human. Do you never think of the consequences of your actions? You may be accustomed to Marchmain Castle serfs cleaning up after you, but the servants at Sykes House will not be treated so shabbily."

"There are no serfs! There are barely any servants at all."

"You probably drove them away with your nonsense."

How unfair he was being! He knew nothing of the straightened circumstances she'd lived with for too long.

She decided to take a different tack, and stilled her body. "*Please* put me down, Tristan. What will Mrs. Anstruther think?"

"She'll think I've finally come to my senses and taken control of my wife."

"Control?" Sadie, quite literally, saw red as she watched her bloody hand connect with Tristan Sykes's firm jaw.

"Yow!" They tumbled backward over a table to the floor. Sadie was unable to continue her assault as her arms were now trapped under Tristan's heavy body. He had somehow managed to slither and maneuver himself on top of her as they fell. Who was the real eel?

"Should I come back later?" Mrs. Anstruther stood at the door, a basket under her arm. Sadie could see she was trying very hard not to laugh.

"Not at all," Tristan replied, as if he spoke from the floor regularly. "Lady Sarah has need of your nursing skills. She has cut her hand. There may still be a sliver of glass in the wound."

"If you will just, um, release her, Mr. Tristan, I'll take a look."

"In a moment."

Sadie looked up at Tristan's flushed face. He shifted, and then she knew why he was not leaping straight up. She had felt that hardness before. Seen it with her own eyes.

He was aroused. Even after she'd screamed at him and threw things and hit him. She wiggled her hips and watched the agony flash in his eyes.

This more or less proved her supposition that men were pigs, yet she was glad she had an effect on her husband. Maybe the rose petals wouldn't go to waste after all.

If she decided she wasn't furious with him.

"I'm sorry," she whispered. "I shouldn't have hit you. I—I promise to never do it again."

"You're probably crossing your fingers behind your back," he said, gruff.

"I am not. If you will just raise yourself a little, I'll roll out. While Mrs. Anstruther attends to me, you may compose yourself."

"I have a feeling I'm never going to be composed again."

Chapter 40

He might as well jump from the roof now. He would spare himself the next forty—or, if he was unlucky, fifty—years with his pugilist bride.

Tristan was standing on shifting ground. Quicksand. Of course he wasn't standing on anything at present. He was still lying on the carpet trying to figure out how he could scuttle away in his tenting trousers without attracting any undue attention from his father's housekeeper.

He waited until Sadie was seated in a chair near the fire, a branch of candles on the table. Mrs. Anstruther was bent over, examining Sadie's cut. This was his chance. If he could only get up, he could go to the Red House and get out of his stained and rumpled clothing. Lock all the doors. Ask Anstruther to handcuff him to the bed to keep him out of harm's way.

Everything he thought he'd known about Sadie was proving to be wrong. Except she had an impressive right hook, just as the dossier claimed. The left was allegedly its equal as well.

"You were very foolish to try to pick up broken glass with your bare hands," Mrs. Anstruther admonished.

"I'm sorry," Sadie said meekly. That was two apologies in two minutes, some sort of record, he was sure. "I was ashamed. I've let my emotions get the better of me twice today. I didn't mean to make more work for you and the staff."

"That's what we're here for. Hold still. Yes, I see a splinter of glass. Mr. Tristan, could you hold Lady Sarah's hand still while I remove it?"

"He doesn't have to. I won't move."

"Best to be safe. I think a stitch or two is in order, too."

"Surely not."

"Don't argue, my lady. Injuries to the hand are tricky. So hard to heal.

You wouldn't want to lose the use of it through infection. Mr. Tristan, are you all right down there?"

He would be if someone shot him and put him out of his misery. "Just a moment, Mrs. Anstruther. I need to wash."

Tristan escaped into Sadie's bathroom and ran cold water, liberally splashing it all over, willing his erection to deflate. He caught sight of himself in the mirror, his curly hair on end, his wine-stained tie ruined, his waistcoat a sticky mess between the blood and honey. He removed his jacket and stripped himself of the dirty clothes and immediately felt better.

Sober too. He'd barely touched any of the wine at dinner. Tristan wished now that he'd indulged, for his conscience was stabbing at him with knitting needles. He'd been judgmental. So quick to mix up the past with the present. Sadie wasn't Linnet, and he wasn't the innocent young man he used to be.

Tristan knew there were two sides to every story, sometimes three. And now Sadie might never forgive him for being, as she said, an ass. He should have known that the duke and Charlton were unreliable storytellers. He'd had the presence of mind to dislike both of them on sight—why had he listened to them?

He emerged from the bathroom in a more sedate state, even if he was in his shirtsleeves. He was going to do better in the future. He had to.

"There you are. Please hold Lady Sarah's palm open. I've got my tweezers ready." Mrs. Anstruther dabbed up a glob of blood.

Sadie's eyes were shut. Tristan had the opportunity to examine her eyelashes, copper tipped with gold. They were mercifully still—he'd seen the damage they could do as she batted them about at unsuspecting victims. One incisor nipped at her plump lower lip. She was in more pain than she would admit, stubborn wench.

"There." Mrs. Anstruther returned the napkin to act as a temporary bandage. Tristan was shocked at the size of the glass removed from Sadie's palm. "You're doing well, my lady. Very brave. Mr. Tristan, this next bit will be a little more difficult, but I know I can depend on you."

Mrs. Anstruther sat on a chair to thread a needle. Tristan continued to hold Sadie's hand, smoothing his fingers over hers, keeping the napkin in place.

"Drat. My spectacles are downstairs, and I really should have them for this if we don't want a scar. How silly I was to come up without them. I'll only be a moment."

The housekeeper left them alone. Sadie attempted to pull her hand away but Tristan was too fast for her and held tight. "It will be all right."

"Of course it will be all right. It's not as if I've been shot," Sadie grumbled.

"I expect you'd like to be the one who did the shooting."

"How bloodthirsty you must think I am! You don't think much of my character."

"That's where you are wrong. I've come to—admire you. Greatly." Much against his will, he might add, but stopped himself from saying so. He was not as much of an idiot as prideful, insufferable Mr. Darcy.

Sadie rolled her eyes. "Don't bother to try to cozen me. An hour ago you thought I was a—"

Tristan put a finger to her mouth. "I didn't. You misunderstood everything. I was trying to make you happy."

"Happy!"

"To reunite you with Whatever-his-name-is. And I find I'm quite glad that you have lost interest in the fellow. That means there's a chance for me. Even if I'm an ass."

Sadie's lips twitched. "You are."

"I cannot argue. I am groveling for your good opinion. I would be on my knees, but I've spent most of my day in that position, and I'm not as young as I used to be." He gave her hand a gentle squeeze.

"Ouch."

"Forgive me."

"All right. But don't squeeze my hand again."

"I don't mean about the squeezing. About me being an ass."

Sadie flicked her eyelashes, the minx. "You are sure to be an ass again."

"Undoubtedly. I've had a lot of practice." What if he'd been more understanding with Linnet? He'd been full of wounded pride and outrage back then. She'd been so young, flirtatious, and he'd driven her into the arms of other men with his cold disapproval.

Tristan couldn't do anything about his marital history—that story had been told, with its unhappy ending. He'd been unyielding in what he perceived as his own virtue. In his urge to be always good, always reasonable, always responsible, he'd been a dull dog for far too long.

"What are you proposing, Tristan?"

"That we start fresh. Let's pretend I haven't been a *consummate* ass, and that you never lost your temper. We are two people getting to know one another."

"What's the catch?"

Let me take you to bed.

"There is no catch."

Sadie's eyes narrowed. "There's always a catch."

"I will trust you. I want you to trust me. Do you think you can?"

She was spared of answering, as Mrs. Anstruther hurried into the room. Sadie shut her eyes again as the housekeeper cleaned the cut and made three neat stitches in the soft flesh of her palm. She then wrapped Sadie's hand in a swath gauze and cotton fit for an Egyptian mummy.

"You'll have to use your left hand only for a few days. I'm sure Mr. Tristan will help you with anything you need tonight."

"A good thing I'm left-handed so I can at least feed myself. What about Hannah and Audrey?" Sadie asked.

"I've sent them to bed, Lady Sarah. I hope I did right. They were, um, tired, and it's very late."

Did this mean Tristan would get to undress his wife?

If she'd let him.

Sadie exchanged an odd look with Mrs. Anstruther, then nodded. "I suppose that will have to do. Thank you for your assistance, Mrs. Anstruther. You've been very kind."

"Pish. You are the mistress of the house and deserve all consideration. Good night, my dear. Mr. Tristan."

Sadie remained seated before the fire. The silk flowers in her hair were askew, and a long strand of red hair had fallen from its pins. Somehow he liked her better this way, a bit bedraggled from her sinuous trip up the staircase. She'd been far too dazzling at dinner, especially when he'd thought some other man would have the privilege of gazing upon her under the candlelight.

"Are *you* tired?" he asked.

"A bit. I can ring for another maid. Or Mrs. Anstruther, if you feel unequal to helping me."

"I feel very equal." More than equal.

"All right."

She stood, kicked off her shoes, and turned her back to him. A thousand covered buttons—well, a hundred at least—wended their way down her spine. Tristan was methodical, his hands accustomed to delicate tasks. He could graft roses. Wield a compass. Lay brick if necessary. What were mere buttons?

If only his hands wouldn't shake.

Her scent was subtle yet compelling. In fact, the whole room smelled like roses. He would never be able to wander in a garden again without thinking of her.

Her dress loosened and shimmered to the floor in shiny pink waves. He held her good hand while she stepped out of it, clad only in a shift, a corset with its figured cambric cover, starched petticoats, and stockings.

He untied the corset cover to reveal a truly beautiful work of art. At one point in his life, Tristan was fairly adept with corset strings. It seemed a long, long time ago. It might be easier if he attacked the corset problem from the front hooks.

"Turn around. Please." His voice was thick.

She obliged, a pretty blush on her cheeks. "You'd better fetch my nightgown. It's on the bed."

The bed was turned down, and the source of the aroma in the room was solved. Rose petals were sprinkled on the bedlinens. Did Sadie sleep amidst roses every night? No wonder she smelled so delicious. The nightgown lay on the coverlet, practically transparent—he could see the embroidery right through it.

And then he noticed the wine and two glasses on the bedside table. The vases of roses. The flickering candles on all flat surfaces. The room had been set up for seduction—his, he presumed. He stifled his grin, draped the wisp of silk over his arm and set to his very pleasurable task.

Chapter 41

This evening had not quite turned out as she'd hoped. And it was most annoying that she had injured herself, no matter what the apparent benefits were. Tristan was in her room in his shirtsleeves, now unhooking her new corset. It was exquisite, trimmed with black lace and stitching over cream satin. In seconds she would be free of it, and then what?

Her plan to consummate the marriage should be put on hold. If Tristan could imagine that she'd marry him while loving another, then he didn't know her at all. She would never compromise herself in such a way. It was one thing to make a marriage of convenience which had some advantages, quite another to enact a lifelong tragedy.

She realized they didn't truly know each other's character at all, even if it seemed they might be compatible physically. Lust was not enough.

Although it was *something*. Tristan's nearness and his deft touches were doing odd things to her insides. Sadie remembered too well where all that had led before.

She took a step back. "Hand me my nightgown."

"If you're worrying about me seeing your charms, covering up with this won't help. It's designed for revelation." His voice was smoky and rough. "Just stand still."

Sadie felt like a hart at the mercy of the king's men. The last metal hook came free, and Tristan caught the corset before it fell to the floor.

Her shift was as sheer as her nightgown. Her nipples hardened from his gaze.

"Beautiful," he murmured. "Too beautiful for the likes of me. I don't deserve you."

"No, you don't."

"I will endeavor to earn your regard. Even if it takes years."

"I'm very difficult. You know that."

"Yes. You are a challenge. I hope I'm up to it."

Involuntarily, Sadie stole a glance at his trousers. "I'd say you were."

His warm hand cradled her cheek. "I want this to work. Us to work. Do you think there's a chance?"

Now was not the time to lie. "I don't know."

"But you will try?"

Sadie wanted to say yes. But could she break a lifetime habit of sabotaging everything? She wasn't sure she could.

"I will do my best."

"That's all we can hope for. I'm going to untie your petticoat now."

She swallowed. "All right. Do I get to undress you too?"

"If you wish." More smoke and roughness.

Save for her stockings, Sadie was soon nude in the flickering light. Tristan made no effort to cover her with the flimsy night rail. She kept her hands at her sides while Tristan stepped back. His expression gave her reason to believe he liked what he saw very much.

"Your turn." She unbuttoned him one-handed, which took longer but somehow raised the stakes. Untucked. Unbelted. And now Tristan was Adam to her Eve.

"What do we do next?" Sadie asked.

"Surprise me."

"What do you mean?"

"Do as you please. Isn't that what you've always wanted?"

Was it? She wasn't sure how to proceed. Did she kiss him? Touch him? Lie back on the bed and close her eyes and wait for *him* to surprise *her*?

"W-would you like some wine?"

"I would not. But I'll be happy to pour you a glass." Tristan moved to the bedside table.

Dutch courage. Any of the champagne and wine she'd had earlier at dinner had fizzled right out of her system after their argument. But she found when Tristan gave her the glass she couldn't lift it to her lips.

She set it on the mantel. "I am out of ideas."

He raised a brow? "Really? You? I would think that your diabolical mind was chock-full of ways to drive a man mad."

"I have retired from man-maddening."

"Not if you continue to stand in front of me as you are. I may have to check into one of Puddling's programs myself."

"Is there a program to discourage lust?"

"I don't think it would work in my case, even if there is one. No amount of gruel and healthy walks would diminish my current state."

He really was most impressively erect. How curious men were, their thought so obvious upon their bodies, while women's secrets were safe within.

"Are we really going to do this?" Sadie asked, her voice unsteady.

"I think we should. We've done everything but. We *are* married." He extended a hand and she took it. He led her to the bed, which was both miles away and too close.

He untangled the roses from her bun. "I want to brush your hair. Have wanted to for days."

Sadie nodded, sitting down at the edge of the bed. He gave her the bunch of silk roses to hold, which was a welcome distraction for her nervous hands, while he fetched the hairbrush from the dressing table. With meticulous precision, he pulled out every pin that kept her heavy hair up.

"To think you tried to pass as a man." He gentled through her tangles, and Sadie closed her eyes. This was a far different sensation from when any of her maids had performed the same service.

"I didn't. I just enjoyed wearing trousers."

"You may wear them at home, only for me."

"We'll see." She didn't feel like fighting over it at the moment. She was happy to be bare, her skin rippling with anticipation. She might not ever put clothes on again.

Tristan put the brush down and tipped her backward on the mattress. He kissed her injured hand and placed it at her side. "I will be careful. Of every part of you."

"Thank you."

He left her to extinguish all the candles, and Sadie felt a stab of disappointment. It would have been interesting to watch Tristan's face as they had conjugal relations. She would like to see her own. Perhaps a mirror over a bed would solve that problem.

She must be very wicked to even think of such a thing. But something was uncoiling inside her, making her hot and cold and wanting. She would like a hundred mirrors and a thousand candles. She'd have to make do with the firelight.

The bed dipped as Tristan lay beside her. He began by using just one fingertip to draw lines on her body, some straight, some squiggles, all making her squirm a little. She wanted more than one finger, and bumped her hip into his.

"Patience."

"I'm not known for it. I feel very strange, Tristan."

"Good." His mouth replaced his finger and she lost herself to all coherent thought. She clutched at him, forgetting the cut on her hand, and cried out at the sudden pain.

"Lie still. Let me do all the work."

All right. She could try. But when he moved lower to kiss her as he had before, lying still proved difficult indeed.

Chapter 42

Tristan didn't think he'd ever get tired of the taste of her. Her reaction to his every touch. Even her stubbornness was becoming endearing. Lady Sarah Marchmain was his wife, and all was right with the world.

Well, more or less. There was another letter he'd have to write tomorrow, and building plans to go over, but honestly, he couldn't think of such trivialities right now. Real life outside this room could wait. His wife had invited him into her bed and he was going to make good use of his time and tongue.

It wasn't long before she was thrashing beneath him, his mouth filled with her essence. He brought her to release several more times—he'd lost count. But if he didn't enter her very shortly, counting to infinity would not stop him from spilling onto the bedclothes.

Tristan didn't want to hurt her. He hadn't ever taken a virgin before in his life—he knew now that though Linnet had been very young on their wedding night, she'd been wild and heedless before it.

Damn. He didn't want to think of his first wife at a time like this—she had no power over him anymore. It was time he woke up from his self-imposed sexual slumber. He'd been celibate for years; he'd paid the price of his youthful folly. The glory and the guilt, all of it. He'd been given a second chance and he wasn't going to waste it.

He wished he'd left some candles burning, but hadn't wanted Sadie embarrassed or shy. Really, what had he been thinking? She was not in the least shy. Really somewhat brazen. Remember those trousers! He could watch her walk around in them until he was stone cold dead.

Plenty of life in him now. He kissed his way back up her body all the way to her lovely lips. She welcomed him with a hungry kiss, her good hand stroking the length of his back. This was good between them. Too damn good.

But they deserved it, didn't they? Tristan believed his life was about to turn a corner.

He rose up on one arm and grasped his swollen cock with the other, feeling his way in the dark. Sadie angled up toward him, and he rubbed against her, coating himself with her wetness. *So* damn good.

He slid back and forth until she was as frantic for him to enter her as he was. In one slow thrust, he was surrounded by liquid heat. She was tight. Perfect. He wouldn't last long, but it was just as well. Their first time need not be a marathon. There were many nights ahead.

"All right?" he asked, almost breathless.

"Yes."

"You're sure?"

"*Please.*"

He strove to do what she needed, inserting his hand between them as his cock smoothed in and out. He drove ever deeper with each thrust, reveling in her response. She toppled into the timeless dance, hissing his name, rising to meet him. Tristan lost himself to exquisite, elusive sensation. No, not lost. He was found. Home.

He rubbed her clitoris until the hisses were helpless shouts as she bucked beneath him. He poured his heart into her as she clutched at him and cried out. Had it ever been like this before with anyone?

He thought not.

He collapsed and rolled her on top of him, where her hammering heart knocked against his. He kissed her damp brow, brushed away the tangled length of her beautiful hair. He wanted to say something, but his words were glued together in clumps behind his tingling lips.

She was quiet, too. So quiet for Sadie, who enjoyed having the final say. He held her tight, trying to catch his breath. Organize his thoughts. What next? He was afraid to ask her how she felt. Tristan knew she had climaxed several times, but that was purely physical. What was in her head at this moment?

Her bandaged hand lay on his shoulder, the rest of her soft and hot against him. He'd neglected her breasts, and made up for that now, causing her to shiver as he gently circled a nipple.

"You must stop," she whimpered.

He did so instantly. "Why? Are you hurt?"

"I can't stand...*feeling* so much."

He tucked her closer. "Good feeling or bad feeling?"

"You should know the answer. Oh, *Tristan.* I never imagined such—"
She waved her white bandaged hand between them.

"Neither did I." It had never been quite like this.

"Really?"

There was a great deal of doubt in her voice. He kissed her forehead.
"Really. You may find that extraordinary, but it's true."

"But you are old—" Sadie stopped, realizing the insult of her words.

He was only nine years older, but in terms of experience, he held some
cards she had yet to see. "Ancient," Tristan agreed. "Thirty. Decrepit. You
have aged me since we first met, too, what with house fires and all the
associated follies of the last few days. You believed you had been stuck
with a man past his prime, didn't you?"

"I didn't mean old. Perhaps old-headed," she conceded, not making
her accusation much more palatable. He had been a stuffy stick with her
for much of their acquaintance; no wonder she'd thought him dull.

Tristan lay back against the pillows. "Well, someone had to be the
voice of reason here. You know my responsibilities."

"Am I one of them now?"

Careful, Tris.

"You are much more important than a mere responsibility. Yes, I want
to take care of you. But I want you to take care of me, too."

"Like the oxen you talked about."

Tristan laughed. "Exactly. Let's be kind to each other and see where
the journey leads."

"Friends."

Much more than that, he hoped. Was it possible? He'd been on his own
path alone for so long, depending only upon himself.

He gave her shoulder a squeeze. "Friends."

Sadie snuggled into him. "I have never had a male friend before. Come
to think of it, female friends are few and far between, too. Marchmain
Castle is isolated, you know. And I wasn't allowed to go to school."

"Miss Mac," Tristan recalled.

"*She* was not a friend of mine. She spied for my father."

"I'm sure he was concerned for you," he said, thinking no such thing.

"Not in the way he should have been. And the year I came out—the
one season I had—was not...fun."

"How so?"

"I was too tall. Too everything. I didn't take."

"They were idiots, all of them."

"You wouldn't have liked me either. I made sure of that."

Tristan played with a long strand of her hair. "Why were you so set against marriage? I would think you would have seen it as an escape from your father. Didn't you want to have your own household?"

"He made it clear he would pick my husband according to *his* needs. Debts. Consequence. And the candidates were not at all to my liking." Sadie sighed. "I was engaged before Roddy, you know. *Twice* before. I am a scandal."

Tristan had read her report thoroughly and knew exactly how she'd gotten unengaged from the hapless men her father conned. "I forbid you to get engaged to anyone else."

He could see her smile in the waning firelight. "That sounds reasonable."

"I am the voice of reason, as we've established. Are you tired, Sadie?"

She nodded. "A little."

"Shall I leave you, or would you like me to stay?"

She was silent for a long stretch. "I don't know. I'm not accustomed to sleeping next to anyone."

"We've managed it before in the same bed."

"But one of those nights I was shackled, if you recall."

Oh, yes. He recalled. An image of her naked and bound before him was tempting beyond belief, but it was early days yet. Tristan had a feeling he'd have to do a whole lot of persuading to get her to agree to such a scenario. She was strong-willed, but Tristan didn't want to break her, just gently bend her into a semblance of compliance.

He'd have his work cut out for him.

Chapter 43

The giggling woke her. Sadie opened her eyes to see Audrey and Hannah at the doorway. They were both blushing profusely, one equipped with a breakfast tray and the other fireplace cleaning tools. She lurched up, clutching the covers to her bare breasts.

"Good morning, Lady Sarah. Do you want us to come back later?" one of the twins asked, averting her face. Sadie's eyes were clogged with sandmen, and her head ached a little. At one point in the evening, she and Tristan had woken, coupled again, and drunk most of the wine in the bedside bottle afterward as they talked. Or, to be fair, *she* had done the drinking and the talking. Tristan had proved to be a good listener, and an even better lover.

"Yes," came the rumble beside her. Goodness, Tristan was still in her bed. Still naked. Still beautiful.

Sadie was famished. "Leave the tray. My husband will see to the fire." My husband! Two very odd words she thought she'd never say. She lay back against the pillows and shut her eyes to the shaft of daylight which fell through the gap in the curtains. Then one of the girls pulled the curtains open, and she was blinded right through her eyelids.

"Very good, my lady. Ring if you need anything." There was a rattle of china and scuttle of feet, and the door snicked closed.

"Who turned on the sun?" Tristan groaned.

Sadie cracked an eye open. "Shall I pour you some tea?" There was only one cup on the tray, but she was willing to share.

He sat up and stretched, his curly hair adorably disordered. "I prefer coffee in the morning."

Something to learn about him. As she had done most of the soul-bearing in the wee hours, she had the feeling he knew most of her secrets, while he was still somewhat of a mystery.

"I can ring for some."

"No. I have other plans to start the day." He waggled one of his formidable brows and patted the space between them. "Unless you are sore. I've been a bit of a beast."

Sadie covered her mouth. She needed to brush her teeth and make use of the bathroom before she thought of kissing or anything else. "I'm not—"

"I understand. Slip away and make yourself presentable. I will not pounce just yet. Toss me that roll before you go, will you? I won't eat it all."

Sadie pulled on a robe and left him getting crumbs in her bed. The mirror over the sink told her she suffered from an inadequate amount of sleep and too much wine. Her hair was knotted every which way. She made a halfhearted attempt to braid it, but soon gave up. She dealt with the business of freshening up, splashed water on her face and pinched her cheeks.

Tristan showed none of the ill effects of a sleepless night. His tan face broke into a devilish smile as she reentered the room, and her heart squeezed. Would he smile like that at her every morning? She might never leave her bedroom.

He held out the half-eaten roll in the palm of his hand. "I may have taken an extra bite."

She wasn't hungry anymore. Not for a roll anyway. But did people have carnal relations in broad daylight, with the sounds of a waking house all around them?

It seems they did. Tristan drew her down on the bed and ravished her mouth. He must have snuck into the bathroom while she was sleeping, for he tasted of tooth powder and smelled of her own rosewater. It confused her senses to be totally surrounded by roses. There were still a few rose petals trapped in the bedclothes, more underfoot.

"Mm. I could kiss you all day," Tristan said, un-belting her wrapper and skimming his fingertips over her skin.

"Don't you have work to do?"

"My work is right here, learning to be a husband. How am I doing so far?"

"Why, Mr. Sykes, are you fishing for compliments?"

"Of course, Mrs. Sykes. A man wants to know that he's ruined his woman for any others."

"Consider me ruined. Ooh, that tickles!"

They stopped talking and reverted to kissing. Tristan continued to tickle and tease until Sadie took charge. Tentative, she touched Tristan's heavy cock. She must have held it properly, for Tristan twitched in a very gratifying manner and his kiss became wilder.

His member was so soft, yet so very hard. And large. It was difficult to imagine that it could enter her so effortlessly and cause her such exhilaration. She stroked him with increasing vigor until he shuddered and clawed her shoulder.

She was making him lose control. How delightful to know she had the same influence on him as he had on her. Things between them were beginning to get very interesting until a sharp knock on the door interrupted them.

"Fucking hell." Sadie was not sure which of them had spoken. She grabbed her discarded robe as Tristan wrestled with the sheets. When they had both calmed themselves to some degree, she said, "Come."

A sheepish Grimsby stood at the door, twisting his gloved hands. He looked everywhere but at the two substantially naked people on the bed. "I am so sorry to disturb you, but there is an altercation in the kitchen."

Tristan's eyebrows snapped together. "An altercation?"

"I cannot seem to stop it, sir, and I assure you, I've tried. No one can. There is some property damage, too."

"What in blazes are you talking about, Grimsby?"

"Mr. and Mrs. Anstruther are having a disagreement."

Anstruther? Sadie knew he never spoke to his wife. The two of them reminded her of the old nursery rhyme—"Jack Sprat could eat no fat, his wife could eat no lean." Two more physically different people could not be imagined.

"We'll be down in a minute, Mr. Grimsby," Sadie said. "Stay out of the line of fire."

As soon as the butler left, she burst into laughter.

Tristan was foraging around the floor for last night's clothes, still semi-erect. "This isn't funny, Sadie. Kitchens have knives."

"Oh, pooh. They aren't going to kill each other."

"This is my fault. I told Anstruther to speak to her."

"And so he should," Sadie replied, pulling on a modest nightgown one-handed and covering it with her robe. "Do you know what happened between them?"

"Anstruther thinks Mrs. Anstruther is stepping out on him."

Now Sadie roared.

"Just because they are not perfect physical specimens doesn't mean they aren't entitled to love," Tristan snapped.

"Oh! I didn't mean to laugh about that. I know there's a lid for every pot. Everyone deserves happiness. Anstruther's just so—bloodless. He *hates* women. Or maybe it's just me."

"He doesn't hate you. And once he must have cared for Mrs. Anstruther, or he wouldn't be so upset with her. Where's my other shoe?"

"Never mind shoes. Time is of the essence before she throws him into the soup."

They raced down the staircase in their jumbled and shoeless state. The clatter of thrown pots was clear from the hall as they charged toward the kitchen. A cluster of maids and footmen stood in the hall in a combination of fear and gossipy interest.

"Jezebel!"

"Stand still like a man so I can hit you!"

Tristan took Sadie's arm. "Stay here."

"I certainly will not!"

"You might get hurt, Sadie. See reason."

"You can't have all the fun." A crash of china gave Sadie a pause. No. She was temporary mistress of the house, and she couldn't have the servants fighting and breaking things. She shoved past Tristan and caught a flying wooden spoon with her good hand.

"What is the meaning of this?" How often had she heard her father use those words? She sounded just like him—there *was* a benefit in being a duke's daughter.

The slate kitchen floor was littered with an array of cooking equipment and shattered crockery. Mrs. Anstruther's face resembled a boiled beet, and Mr. Anstruther was glaring at her, his lantern jaw mulish.

"I—I beg your pardon, Lady Sarah. I'll clean the mess up at once."

"Never mind that. What did Mr. Anstruther do to provoke you so?"

"This isn't *my* fault," the man muttered.

"Oh? And whose fault is it? Bad enough you stopped speaking to me for no cause—but then, you never had much good to say anyhow. To think you believed I was carrying on with Frank Stanchfield! I should gut you like a fish." The housekeeper eyed a block of knives, and Sadie hustled in front of it.

"The grocer? But he's married," Sadie said. Although who knew what really went on in villages such as this.

"Ask her how she got the food bills down!"

"By negotiating, you nitwit. With *Bertha* Stanchfield. I traded some of our kitchen garden produce to her for their personal use. I didn't think your father would mind, Mr. Tristan, since it saved the household money in the end. Bertha loves her fresh vegetables. And she's too busy at the store to make her own jam and grow her own herbs."

"I saw you with him! You gave him a love letter!"

"It was a packet of sage. Honestly," she huffed in disgust.

"He kissed you!"

"On the cheek, Harold. I've known Frank all my life, and Bertha's my best friend. I can't believe you could think so little of me. You could have asked what I was doing. You jumped to conclusions and we've wasted two years."

"I think there's a lesson to be learned here," Tristan murmured into Sadie's ear.

"For *you*."

"I will never accuse you of consorting with Frank Stanchfield. The man is terrified of you anyway."

"As he should be." She turned and looked into Tristan's amused blue eyes. "I will honor my vows. You needn't ever worry."

A ripple of emotion crossed his face. "As will I." He clapped his hands, interrupting the silent standoff between the Anstruthers. If looks could kill.

"You two need to settle your differences like adults. The rest of you, please go about your business and leave the Anstruthers alone to deal with the consequences of their temper."

And stupidity, Sadie thought, but she didn't say it. Two years of not speaking! There was too much pride all the way around.

"I shall resign, Mr. Tristan," Anstruther said.

"The hell you will. Now, go kiss your wife and make up. Grimsby, I hope we can persuade you to come with us when we build our own house. It won't be quite on the same scale as Sykes House, but you won't be ashamed to work for us."

"We're building a house?" Sadie asked.

"I *am* an architect. We can't stay here forever. I bought a piece of land on the other side of the village near the stream some years ago. I can show you some preliminary plans I've fiddled with over the years. You'll have input, of course."

A house of her own. It was almost too much to hope for.

Chapter 44

Tristan looked up from the ledger at the rap on the doorframe. "David!" He closed the book and pushed it aside. Accounting for the Puddling Rehabilitation Foundation could wait until another day.

David Warren entered the library with a case under his arm. "I told your butler not to announce me. How is married life treating you this time around?"

Tristan leaned back in the chair and gave his friend a rueful smile. "I don't want to jinx anything."

"That sounds hopeful."

"I think it may be. Lady Sarah is not what I expected."

"And you always expect the worst as I recall."

"You read the newspapers." And there had been much worse in her dossier. Unlike Tristan, David Warren didn't live within the confines of Puddling-on-the-Wold, so was not privy to all of Sadie's purported history.

Tristan had read every word, and had been annoyed when he first met her. Called her a madwoman. Didn't trust her an inch. And now—

He felt differently.

"Here's hoping I read nothing scurrilous again." David set the leather case on the desk. "I've brought your wedding photographs."

What a day *that* had been. "How did they turn out?"

"Judge for yourself." He pulled out a sheaf of photographs and spread them across the mahogany desk, and Tristan's blinked.

There was no denying his wife was regal, magnificent in her diamonds and lace, yet she appeared miserable. He looked little better. These pictures perfectly captured the inauspicious beginning of their new life. All that was missing was a *carte de visite* of Sadie with her handcuffs on.

It was common for photographic subjects to have serious expressions on their faces, but the new Mr. and Mrs. Sykes looked *doomed.*

"I think—you should burn them. We can tell Sadie they didn't come out."

David shook his head. "And cast aspersions on my talent? I suppose we could retake them."

"I'm afraid the wedding dress has been cut to ribbons." Noting the confusion on David's face, he shrugged. "It's a long, strange story. I don't want my great-grandchildren to wonder what the hell was wrong with us. We look like we're headed off to our executions."

Great-grandchildren? For that to happen, he and Sadie would have to become parents.

The idea wasn't really so terrible.

"Some might say that's what marriage is anyway—certain death. I intend to avoid it for as long as I can."

"It has its charms."

"I'll have to take your word for it. Where is your bride?"

"I'm not sure. We don't live in each other's pockets, you know." This morning he told Sadie he had work for the Foundation to do, but that wasn't quite all. His letters had been sent, and that should be the end of his ill-conceived notion on how to make his new wife happy.

Could *he* make her happy? Tristan once had as sour a view on marriage as his friend David.

"So, what do you want me to do with them?"

Tristan gathered the photographs up and shoved them in a desk drawer. "Nothing right now. Let me think on it."

"Suit yourself. Are you not going to offer me a drink?"

"David, it's not even noon," Tristan laughed.

"Well, lunch, then. Or a late breakfast. I'm not particular. I've come all this way."

Tristan realized he was very much looking forward to a private luncheon with his wife.

"And I thank you for it. If you'd given me notice, I might have rearranged my schedule." He patted the ledger. "Village business."

"When is your dear papa returning? I cannot believe you let him stick you with all this tedium."

"It hasn't been so bad." It led him to Sadie, for one thing. "But I don't know. I haven't heard from him lately." The letter he sent this morning should tickle the old man. He was now the father-in-law of a duke's daughter. Not too shabby.

"I don't see how you can stand it. Well, if you won't feed me, I'm off. Going down to London on the train tomorrow for a week. May I bring you back anything? A dozen hats? An actress? A dancer?"

"No thank you. I don't relish the idea of getting clobbered by my wife." And he couldn't imagine being attracted to anyone else right at the moment.

Would that feeling last? He hoped so.

After David left, Tristan went back to his columns of numbers. It was almost time for the yearly payout to all the residents of Puddling. Sharing the profits of the Foundation guaranteed a nice Christmas for the villagers, and this year's investments had been solid. Families were financially secure here, so different from other towns affected by the depressed wool market.

Another rap. This time it wasn't his friend.

Wait. Did they not agree to be friends?

"May I come in?" Sadie asked, sounding a little unsure of herself.

"Of course! I was just about to seek you out."

"What did David want? I saw him on the drive when I came back from my walk."

Sadie was attempting to follow some of the Puddling Rehabilitation Rules. She drew the line at the bland food, however. And so far, the Reverend Fitzmartin had not visited.

"Just to tell me he's on his way to London."

"He didn't bring the photographs?"

They had agreed to tell each other the truth. Tristan opened the drawer. "You're not going to like them."

She came around to his side of the desk. "Oh, dear."

"Not album-worthy?"

Sadie picked one up and squinted. "I do look very grand, though. Grim, but grand."

"It was a peculiar day."

"Do you think we can do it again?"

"I beg your pardon?"

"Get married again. In the village church. With me in a proper dress this time. And no Roddy or my father to bungle things."

"No fainting organists." To his surprise, he liked the idea.

"No absent-minded vicars who leave out half the service. Or handcuffs."

Tristan pulled Sadie down into his lap. "I don't know what the church's position is regarding duplicate ceremonies."

"It can be a public renewal of our vows. And we can have a reception afterwards in the garden while the weather is still good."

"It's bound to rain again."

"Inside then. When was the last time Puddling had a party?"

Tristan noted the flush on her cheeks and sparkle in her eyes. "All right. If this is what you wish, consult with Mrs. Anstruther. She'll need a few weeks' notice, I imagine."

"Thank you!" She kissed him with considerable enthusiasm, making him forget they were due at lunch in the dining room in a few minutes.

Sadie had told him she'd never wanted to get married, and now she wanted to twice. Well, he supposed the first time didn't really count. His heart was touched that she wished to declare her good intentions in front of the entire village.

"If you don't stop showing your gratitude, I will not be responsible for my actions," he gasped. He was perilously close to throwing her on top of the desk and having his way with her as it was.

"Be irresponsible after lunch. Please."

He was determined to be a dutiful husband, wasn't he?

Chapter 45

The first of October brought sunshine and a bright blue sky. Tristan had left after breakfast to go into the village on Foundation business. Sadie's empty day stretched before her. She had made her lists and ordered her clothes for the wedding. Every detail had been attended to, and she was free.

It was strange to be mistress of Sykes House, even if it was on a temporary basis. Her father-in-law could come home from France at any time, and she knew Tristan did not want to live under the same roof as the man. She couldn't wait for their very own house to be built.

She didn't feel entitled to make any changes here, and in truth, everything ran splendidly under Mrs. Anstruther's and Grimsby's care. The housekeeper consulted her about menus, but as she knew Tristan's tastes better than Sadie did, her input was unnecessary.

Sadie *wanted* her husband to be pleased. This was a first for her— she'd never given much thought to anyone's wishes but her own, thwarted though they had usually been. She'd spent a great deal of her time coming up with creative ideas to annoy people, especially her father, but there was no need of that now. She didn't want to hurt Tristan; he'd been hurt enough.

David Warren had made that plain. Her brief chance encounter with him had answered questions she didn't know she was asking.

Linnet was not really a lost love after all. Warren had told her not to fear her ghost, but Tristan's pride. And Sadie had taken him seriously when he'd implored her to show more restraint than Tristan's first wife had.

Threatened her, really, in his perfectly charming way. And she was glad of it.

Restraint, a word that had seldom been applied to her. But it was time to leave behind all her silly tricks. So what was she to do with her morning until Tristan returned?

The garden and all its individual "rooms" beckoned. They were in their last flush of bounty, and quite glorious with their gold and russet leaves and seed pods. She might sketch, although she was no great artist. If she set her eye and hand to it, however, she could give Tristan a wedding present that reflected his own skill. Immortalize the last breath of beauty.

The white garden had been stripped of its flowers for her first wedding, but there were other attractive spots. Armed with colored drawing pencils and a pad she had found in the library, she ambled down the hedge-lined hill to the flat acreage below. A light wool shawl over her green dress was enough to keep the breezes at bay. And despite the perfection of her new hats, they remained in their boxes in her dressing room.

The warmth felt delicious on her head. It was too late to worry about her freckles—they had resisted all treatment and were part of who she was. Tristan had seemed fascinated by them as he traced an invisible path between them over her body last night, leading directly to her core. This getting to know each other business was proving to be successful, especially in bed.

For the first time in her life, Sadie felt the hope of happiness.

She stumbled a little at the realization. It was too soon to think their problems were behind them, but they were retreating some. There was a spark between them that could be encouraged to flame and brighten their future. And a proper wedding would help them move forward.

Sadie walked through the garden until she came to the rectangular pool filled with water lilies at its center. All the paths of the garden converged here, and there was a clear view of Sykes House up on the hill. A shiny darting fish caught her eye. She hoped someone was tending to the koi at Stonecrop Cottage's pond, and watering the scraggly ferns in the conservatory that was always on the verge of dying.

She set her things down on the ornate iron bench and lifted her face to the sun. She looked forward to sitting here next year, watching the palette change around her from month to month. Knowing Tristan even as little as she did, she was sure he planned for perpetual color throughout the seasons. He was detail-oriented, a noticing sort of man. He would know at once when she prevaricated.

Truth-telling would take some getting used to.

She began her drawing with the marble statue of Flora that guarded the pool. It had been months since she'd picked up a pencil, and it showed in her first effort. The lily pads were easier. A monarch butterfly landed on one long enough for her to capture it on paper.

Sadie felt as if she was seeing everything for the first time—the many shades of green and gold, the puffy clouds reflected in the water, the nearby bank of humble asters. She was peaceful, so absorbed in her efforts that she didn't hear the footfalls behind her.

She jumped at the hand on her shoulder, spilling the pages to the grass.

"Missed me, did you?"

Sadie turned and was speechless. Unless she was dreaming—nightmaring, more like—Dermot Reid was in the garden. He was taller and wirier than she remembered, his face weathered, his once-fair hair darker beneath a checked cap. He sported a luxuriant sandy mustache and muttonchops, which Sadie found somewhat ridiculous.

He was all grown up. Well dressed. He appeared prosperous, with a flashing diamond pinkie ring and a thick gold watch chain dangling from his pocket.

She felt *nothing*.

"I see you didn't expect me. Your man told me not to come after all, but I couldn't let this chance go by."

"What?"

"Your new husband. He seems a little mixed up to me. First he wants me to have you, then he changes his mind. I thought I'd come to see what you have to say."

She heard the individual words, but none of them strung together made sense. "I don't understand."

"The letters." He pulled two crumpled envelopes out of his jacket pocket and handed them to her. "You didn't know? The fellow was anxious to see you settled."

Sadie put her pencil down. The writing was in Tristan's hand—she recognized it from the sweet notes he'd left for her this week. Neat and bold, just like he was.

He had written to Dermot? Why?

She found out soon enough from the first letter—idiot Tristan would not stand in the way of their long-standing affection. He sounded like a deranged White Knight who had got the business end of the lance to his head one too many times. She might laugh at the absurdity of Tristan's chivalry if she wasn't so bloody angry. Bad enough he'd believed the lies. How *dare* he give her away and not fight for her?

And she wasn't his to give to begin with.

The second letter was less convoluted. A mistake had been made, etcetera. Evidently, he'd enclosed a check too for Dermot's trouble, which had probably financed the trip from Suffolk to Gloucestershire and this suit of obviously new clothes.

"Why did you come?"

"Not even a smile, not to mention a kiss. You don't seem happy to see me," Dermot admonished. "May I sit down?"

The bench felt too small all of a sudden. "You can't stay."

"I was invited! Before I got uninvited. I can always say the second letter never reached me. You're looking swell, Lady Sadie. Bang up to the elephant."

Sadie shivered. Lady Sadie. He was the only one besides her mother who'd ever called her that.

"There's no reason for you to be here. I'm married. My husband was misinformed about our history. *Ancient* history."

"Now the other one, the viscount—what was his name, your ex-fiancé—Charlton? He believed me right enough when I told him we were still sweethearts. Got some money off him for my discretion. No reason why I can't do the same with Mr. Sykes. A comedown for you, pet, from a viscount to a plain mister. Your da must not be best pleased. Though I reckon from the size of that house up on the hill that your husband is filthy rich."

"It is his father's house," Sadie said. There was probably no chance in discouraging Dermot from another blackmail scheme, but she had to try.

"Then I'll talk to *his* da."

She leaped off the bench. "He's in Paris. Why are you doing this, Dermot?"

"For the money, my girl. I've done well for myself, as you can see, but a man can never have enough. I'm a trainer now, come up in the world. You know my way with horses. This year's Grand National—I had two horses in the running. Conflict of interest." He chuckled. "Rotten weather though, too much snow. Unusual for March. Seaman won it, but next year, who knows?"

"If you're doing so well, you needn't resort to lying and bribery."

Dermot raised a sandy eyebrow. "I can't help it if your men don't trust you, Sadie. That's at your door. I read the gossip rags. You're a star. People are interested in you and are willing to pay top dollar for details. What you do and who you do it with. You've sold a lot of papers in your time."

The implication was clear—he would go to the newspapers if he wasn't paid off.

She would murder him before she gave him any of her money. But how? Could she toss him in the pool? Stab him with her drawing pencils? Her fingers itched.

"I don't have any money to give you."

He snorted. "There's another of your lies right there. You're married now and must have access to your mam's inheritance. See, I remember. We talked about running away all those years ago, didn't we? And if you won't give me any long-tailed banknotes, I bet I can persuade your husband to."

"Fine. He won't give you any either. He doesn't care what becomes of me. After all, he was ready to send me away to you after one day of marriage." Sadie was gratified to see the brief look of uncertainty on Dermot's narrow face.

He recovered his smugness too quickly. "We'll just see about that, won't we? How about a kiss and a cuddle for old times' sake, my dear? You always used to like my kisses and doing the bear."

"That was before I knew—" Sadie shut her mouth. It wouldn't do to praise Tristan to Dermot when she was making the case that her husband didn't like her and wouldn't pay a penny for her continued presence.

"Knew what?"

"That I prefer women!" Sadie said wildly.

Dermot grinned. "I don't mind two women in my bed. But maybe I could change your mind back to the straight and narrow."

Oh, God. Why had she said such a stupid thing? If it was meant to deter Dermot, it hadn't worked.

"I lied. About liking women. I don't." She buried her head in her hands. "I don't like being touched by anyone. That's why Tristan doesn't want me. I—I—there's something the matter with me." She sobbed for good measure, hoping to engender some sympathy. If he was still capable of it.

"Then you really have changed. You were a clingy thing when I knew you."

She had been, more fool she.

"And I knew you were lying," he added. "Your lower lip twists a bit when you do. You haven't changed in that respect."

Her lip twisted? Really? She'd have to look in a mirror for the tell. "Of course I've changed. So have you." And not for the better. The boy she'd thought she loved had turned into a sly, self-serving boor.

Or had he always been that way? She'd been so naïve she'd been too blind to see who he really was as he'd urged her to ever more daring acts of impropriety.

Fifteen. So foolish. She was six years older now. Probably as much of a fool, for she loved her husband. Although if he were handy, she'd toss him in the pool, too.

Dermot flopped down on the bench and squinted against the sun. "Well, we can soon get this settled between us. I presume that's Sykes scurrying down the hill right now."

Sadie turned. Here came Tristan, hopefully to get her out of the sticky jam he'd gotten them in.

And stay dry in the process.

Chapter 46

As soon as he'd come home for lunch, he'd been informed by Grimsby that "a person" had come seeking him out. It was clear from the way the butler said those two words that he did not approve of the visitor. He'd refused the man entrance, but not before taking his calling card. "Dermot Daniel Reid" was printed on the cheap stock along with the name of his training stable at Newmarket.

Tristan shut his eyes briefly and pocketed the card. He should never, ever have written to the man in his misguided attempt to try to make Sadie happy. Now the fellow had been on his doorstep.

"Did he say when he would return?"

"He's still on the premises. In the stables, I believe. He said you were interested in a filly he had. I told him to speak to Faraday."

Bloody hell. *A filly.* Tristan yearned to smash something.

"Where is Lady Sarah?"

"In the garden, Mr. Tristan."

Tristan went through the drawing room French doors that led to the terrace and path below. He stood, surveying the sweep of the acreage. Even wearing green, Sadie was easy to spot, as she was in the heart of it.

And so was a man in a loud plaid Norfolk jacket and matching pants.

Bloody, *bloody* hell.

He wanted to run. It took everything in his power of self-control not to.

His eyes never left them as he worked his way through the garden. Sadie was backing away, the white bandage standing out as her hands fluttered. Reid dropped onto the bench as if he owned the whole estate, his legs splayed out in relaxation. Tristan knew at once when the man saw him coming—even at a distance he could see the cocky tilt of Reid's smile.

Sadie glanced behind her, and he waved. She didn't wave back.

Not a good sign. But then this whole debacle was his entirely fault. Why should she be pleased with him? Blackmailers were never satisfied. Reid had tricked Islesford and Charlton into giving him money, and now he was here for more.

Unless he was under the delusion that Sadie still cared for him. Tristan was sure—well, mostly sure—that Sadie was falling in love with her own husband. All the signs were there.

And they were reciprocated.

Bloody, bloody, *bloody* hell. He couldn't fool himself any longer; he loved his wife, though she drove him insane a good deal of the time, and was bound to continue to do so.

He picked up his pace. "Sadie, my dear, who is our guest?" He dropped a kiss of possession on her cheek, though she was as stiff and white as the marble statuary.

Reid remained seated. Still not a gentleman despite his gaudy but expensive clothes.

"This is Dermot Reid. I told you about him."

"Ah. The groom who was kind to my wife when she was a child."

Reid guffawed. "Is that what she told you? There was a little more to it than that, if you know what I mean." The man leered, and Tristan noticed Sadie's good fist clench.

"The Duke of Islesford and Viscount Charlton may have believed your fairy tales, but they are both men of inferior intellect. I understand you are here to try to sell me a—horse? You surely haven't come here to try your luck at bribing me too."

"I see why you don't want to go to bed with him, Sadie. He's a cold fish, ain't he?"

Tristan shot her a look, but she didn't meet his eyes. In fact, she was talking to the statue of Flora, facing away from both Reid and him. "I told him we have a marriage of convenience, and that you care nothing for me, Tristan. I'm sorry."

What game was she playing?

Ah, trying to save him from being bled by this leech.

"Even if you don't want her, you can't have your wife's reputation dragged through the mud," Reid said.

"It won't be the first time," Tristan said tightly. "Didn't you do your research? My first wife cuckolded me at every opportunity. I survived that, and I can survive anything you can dish out." As he said it, he knew it was true. He could live through anything as long as Sadie was beside him.

"I don't believe you. Your first letter—you can't tell me you don't feel something for the tottie."

A red haze swam before him. No, giving into rage would not be helpful—that was Sadie's method, and look where it had landed her. True, she'd wound up in his bed, thank God, but many miserable years had preceded it for her.

"She is my wife, at least in name. But I doubt we'll have children, so there's no worry about besmirching the family escutcheon. You know, I'm just the son of a country baronet. We are nothing in society, buried in this backwater. Why should anyone care what happened or didn't happen years ago? Sadie was, I repeat, just a child. You might have been horsewhipped. Or jailed. You still might be."

Reid rose from the bench. He looked strong and sinewy, and for just a second Tristan wondered who would win an altercation should he lose his tenuous temper. "Are you saying you won't pay me off?"

"I guess I am. I cannot see the advantage of giving you anything. You'd just be back for more next month. In fact, if you want to take Sadie with you, as I originally offered, I would not stand in your way. I warn you—she's expensive to keep. And somewhat unbalanced." Pray to God she understood what he was doing.

"You think you've got one over on me, don't you?" Reid shouted.

"I think nothing of the kind. I'm only telling the truth as I see it."

Reid spat at Tristan's feet. "Pah! You nobs wouldn't know the truth if it bit you on the arse. I wish you joy of the slut. Does she still have that freckle that looks like a crescent moon on her left breast?"

Don't do anything stupid now, his inner voice warned him. It was a struggle to comply.

"I wouldn't know. You'll find your own way out, I hope?"

He watched as Reid headed toward the stable block. After an interminable silence, Tristan cleared his throat.

"I don't know where to begin."

Sadie gave up her inspection of Flora. "You were brilliant. It's as if you read my mind. I love you. Does my mouth look funny?"

He hadn't expected that. "I beg your pardon?"

"Does my lower lip twitch when I say it?" She came closer. "Look carefully. I love you."

Her mouth looked perfect. Kissable. "I see nothing irregular. Do you mean it?"

"I suppose I must. I'm very angry with you, though."

"As you should be. I'm so sorry, Sadie. I told him not to come, but he must not have gotten the letter."

"The second letter."

Tristan felt his face go hot. "Yes."

"You gave me away. To *him*." She said it with contempt.

"No. It wasn't like that. I thought—well, you know what I thought. I was a monumental idiot. We were forced to marry, and I thought you deserved to be with someone you love."

"I love *you*." She held a finger to her lower lip as she said it. "Curious. How very odd. It must be true. What a pickle."

"Why is that?"

"Well, as you said, we were forced to marry. And now I love you, and you cannot possibly love me back."

"Why can't I?"

"I'm expensive to keep. And unstable."

"Oh, my darling, dearest girl." Tristan put his arms around her. "Everything I said to that wretched man was a lie. Except about Linnet."

Sadie hugged him tighter. "I knew. Your friend David Warren told me. I'm so very sorry, Tristan."

"It's not something I brag about." Or talked about. He *must* love Sadie if he'd confessed to Reid.

"But it's over. And nothing like that will ever happen to you again. I'll be the best wife I can possibly be, even if you don't love me." She was so sincere. So lovable.

"Of course I love you. And we'll have a dozen children if we're so blessed."

She looked up at him in alarm. "That number is unacceptable."

"Fine. You decide."

"You're not going to ask how he knows about the crescent-moon freckle?"

"I am not. It looks more like a flying bird anyway. We've discussed it before as I recall."

He had to kiss her, so he did. When he thought they might fall to the grass and lose their collective minds before God and all his garden creatures, he stopped kissing her, painful as that was to do. "Why do you think I didn't want you here? I knew the moment I saw you howling on the Stanchfields' floor that my fate was sealed. It was Lady Maribel all over again."

Epilogue

The second wedding ceremony went more smoothly than the first, but Dr. Oakley came prepared with his medical bag just in case. This time St. Jude's was crammed to the rafters with every living soul in the Puddling environs, and a few strangers, too, who were curious about the wild duke's daughter who had married Sir Bertram's sober son.

Sadie didn't feel quite so wild anymore, and they must be disappointed if they thought they'd rub elbows with the Duke of Islesford. A flattered Ham Ross and his dog Moll, wearing a scratchy new suit and a pink ribbon respectively, gave the bride away. There was no sign of the duke at all, not even a telegram to be read wishing his daughter happiness. Of course, he'd been present for the first debacle. And the fact that Sadie hadn't invited him for the second ceremony might have had something to do with his absence. Tristan had struck a deal with her father, who was now on a generous Sykes-funded allowance, to make himself scarce for a year or two. Should his behavior result in any negative attention, those funds would promptly dry up. So far, the duke was in grudging compliance.

Lady Sarah Sykes knew she was a vision in a long-sleeved cream silk gown, with a dashing green velvet hat perched on her red curls and emerald drops in her ears. The earrings had been sent from Paris by her new father-in-law as a wedding gift. Sadie used every opportunity to nod her head, the emeralds sparkling in the bright October sunlight.

Mr. Fitzmartin was far more prepared this time around. He clutched the prayer book in both hands and wore new spectacles that Dr. Oakley had prescribed for him for the occasion. Mrs. Fitzmartin, serving as the matron of honor, had turned her organ duties over to the brand new resident of Stonecrop Cottage, Nicola Mayfield, who played very well considering she didn't speak one word. Sadie wondered if she would be able to help the young woman now that she was an official Puddling Person, but first she had to go on her honeymoon.

Mr. Fitzmartin managed to get through the service this time with no hiccups, and the congregation shifted uneasily while Sadie and Tristan kissed at the altar for an unconscionably long and delicious time. Then everyone was invited to go up the narrow lane from the church to a reception at Sykes House.

The newlyweds led the crowd, walking through the gate up the grassy track arm in arm. A marquee had been set up in the garden, with long tables under it. Mrs. Anstruther had recommended serving the local cider, and barrels of the stuff were everywhere. Braziers were lit against the fall chill. With the pumpkins and gourds decorating the tables, it looked more like a Harvest Home than a wedding lunch, but that was all right. Ham had been proud to supply the pumpkins, and Sadie had pledged to leave them undisturbed.

Sadie and Tristan stood for what seemed like hours greeting all the guests. Some faces were unfamiliar, but she recognized her nemesis Mrs. Grace at once. The woman had fully recovered from the injuries she sustained at the fire last month, and was muckling onto Dr. Oakley, clutching him rather possessively. True, she was a handsome if horrible woman, but weren't they too old for that sort of nonsense?

Perhaps not. Sadie hoped she'd be muckling onto Tristan in the decades to come.

What an odd place Puddling was, Sadie reflected. There must be magic in the crisp Cotswold air. She certainly felt rehabilitated, and it was all thanks to Tristan. And she had done him good as well. Gone was the distant, rather chilly young man Dr. Oakley had delivered thirty years ago, when he was a young man himself.

"You both look happy," Mrs. Grace said, giving Sadie an awkward kiss on the cheek. "I wasn't sure you'd do for him, but I was wrong."

Sadie decided not to take offence. "Wrong? I don't believe I've ever heard you say such a thing."

"Even I make mistakes. Those Bath buns, for example. I almost burned the cottage down."

"We have to thank you for that," Tristan said, smiling.

"The new kitchen's a joy to work in. You both should come to tea after your wedding trip. I'm sure Miss Mayfield would like the company."

Sadie wasn't sure of any such thing, but she nodded. It was too perfect a day to find fault with anything, even Mrs. Grace.

And then she heard the fiddlers. She turned to Tristan in surprise. "I didn't hire any musicians."

"No, but I did. Didn't you say you liked to dance? I'm not very good, but I expect you'll teach me to shuffle about. I love you enough to make a fool of myself."

Sadie knew, even without touching her lips, that she loved him back.

If you enjoyed *Seducing Mr. Sykes*, be sure not to miss the next book in Maggie Robinson's Cotswold Confidential series

Redeeming Lord Ryder

Keep reading for a special sneak peek!

A Lyrical e-book on sale November 2017.

Chapter 1

From the journal of Mary Nicola Mayfield

December 13, 1882
I have been in Puddling now for two months to the day, and nothing is changed.

Nicola sat back and wiped her pen nib. What more was there to say? Aye. That was the rub. She couldn't say *anything*. Still.

The scar at her hairline was barely noticeable now—her fringe performed its duty admirably. Yes, her collarbone ached when it rained, but that was a minor inconvenience. But she could not speak, no matter how many times she opened her mouth.

The accident had been more than nine months ago. Nicola had recuperated at home with her parents for seven of those months, until they had all been at their wits' end. Her hand had cramped from writing her thoughts and wishes until her family couldn't bear to read them anymore.

Her mother cried constantly; her father was nearly as silent as Nicola was. When a cottage became available in the secret spa Puddling-on-the-Wold, her parents jumped at the chance to send her there.

To get rid of her, really, in the prettiest place imaginable.

The village was known to work miracles on difficult relatives with difficult problems. Nicola wasn't the usual kind of Guest—she didn't imbibe too freely, gamble, break engagements in fruitless rebellion, disrobe in public, flunk out of school, or do any of the naughty things that drove parents to disown their disreputable children, or children to hide their cringe-worthy parents.

She just couldn't talk, and her parents were exasperated.

She knew they loved her—they'd spent a small fortune they didn't really have on specialists. Doctors had poked and prodded at her. Inserted vile tubes down her throat. She'd worried sometimes that her jaw would remain locked open as they gazed into the dark depths of her windpipe. Her tongue had endured sharp needles, her tonsils were removed as a precaution.

More surgery had been discussed; one doctor went so far as to suggest shaving her hair off so her brain could "breathe." Thank heavens her papa had drawn the line there. Nicola was fond of her hair. It was long and gold and her one true beauty.

The rest of her was unremarkable, except, of course, for her lack of speech. Had she different parents, she might be in an asylum now, locked up with people who couldn't make sense. Nicola's wits were perfectly intact, but she was miserably mute, and her parents were desperate to help her.

Not at home in Bath anymore, though, which was just as well. She'd drunk enough of the foul-tasting water there in hopes of a miracle cure. And Richard lived right next door. After he'd broken their engagement, it had only caused her mama to cry harder. Nicola had been suffocated under her parents' concern and despair for her. Even Richard had been ashamed, but as an ambitious young MP, how could he marry a girl who couldn't campaign for him?

No, not a girl. A woman. Nicola was twenty-six, long past her girlhood. She didn't even really mind that Richard had cried off. While she liked him very much and shared his political goals, it had never been a heart-fluttering love match. Marriage to him had seemed a practical arrangement for both their families, and she did so want her own children. It was not enough to be a fond aunt to Frannie's little boys.

Nicola had waited years for Richard to establish himself. But evidently he couldn't wait a few months for her to speak again.

She picked up the pen. *I want to talk. Dr. Oakley seems to think that if I have a positive attitude, my speech will return.*

But how could she be positive? It was almost Christmas, and her parents were going to Scotland to stay with Aunt Augusta, her mother's widowed sister. Frannie, Albert and the boys too. Nicola would be alone in her little cottage with only Mrs. Grace for company.

Her housekeeper had been extraordinarily kind, had coddled her from the moment she was picked up at the Stroud station. It was the first time Nicola had been on a train since the accident, and the Puddling Rehabilitation Foundation governors had suggested she get over her anxiety by making the trip from Bath by rail. Rather like getting back on the horse after a fall, she supposed.

But Nicola had been worse than anxious. Much to the other passengers' disgust, she'd vomited repeatedly, and by the time she'd arrived she was so weak she could barely stand up. She'd been put to bed for a week, only getting up to play the church organ for a local wedding when the vicar begged her to.

Music was her one release, and her father had donated a small piano for Stonecrop Cottage. She played for hours, when she wasn't staring at the blank pages of her journal.

She was meant to write down her thoughts and worries. And then Dr. Oakley or the elderly vicar, Mr. Fitzmartin, would discuss them with her during their daily visits. Sometimes she would pray, the one time she didn't feel self-conscious about being silent.

Nicola snapped the journal shut and tucked it into a pigeonhole in the little desk. She had no further thoughts today, nothing that she hadn't already written for the sixty-one days she'd been present in Puddling.

The parlor was a bit cramped now with the piano, but there was cheerful, a bright fire burning in the hearth. Mrs. Grace had gone home a little early for the day, pleading a headache. She'd left Nicola a chicken pie in the ice box for her supper. Raspberry tarts too—she'd already cadged one as they were cooling. If she wasn't careful, Nicola would return to Bath several stone heavier.

If she returned. She didn't want to be a burden to her parents. Perhaps she could stay here. Not in this cottage, of course; it belonged to the Puddling Rehabilitation Foundation. But she'd come into money of her own—a settlement from the accident. Guilt money. Her papa had written to her when he sent the piano. As a prominent Bath solicitor, he had negotiated hard on her behalf. The amount was enough to purchase her own home and keep her in modest comfort for the rest of her life if she was careful.

And why wouldn't she be careful? Nicola had always been conservative. She'd never been frivolous, only owned two ball gowns that were refurbished on a yearly basis with new lace or ribbons or both. Richard had admired her frugality, for he earned very little in his own law practice and did not stand to inherit a fortune like some members of the House of Commons. Her mama had not been so sanguine, but Nicola simply wasn't much interested in evening clothes.

She didn't need her ball gowns for Puddling. Life was purposefully quiet here, so Guests could recuperate. But now that the steep streets were coated with a dusting of snow and a slick of ice underneath, she could use a new pair of boots.

It was part of her prescribed routine to walk around the village for at least an hour a day, and the exercise was becoming a touch treacherous. She would write to Mama and ask for some better footwear, something suitable for a clumsy mountain goat.

Nicola knew she was treated differently than some of the other Guests had been. Apparently it was forbidden to contact the "Outside World" by mail or telegram or anything else during the course of one's stay here. But letters flowed freely back and forth to Bath, not that she had very much to report.

Nothing ever happened in Puddling. There were five intertwining streets, and Nicola knew every house and shop, all five of them, by now. Everyone had been so welcoming. She was often stopped and given biscuits or balls of yarn or books by the friendly villagers and their children. She wished she could say thank you, but had to make do with her most sincere smiles.

Oh, she was feeling sorry for herself, and that was pointless. She'd go out for a short second walk, not too far. The sun would set over the Cotswold Hills in about an hour, but fresh air would do her good. Bring roses to her cheeks, which the mirror told her were as pale as the moon. Then she'd put her pie in the oven. Eat. Wash her dishes. Get on her knees to pray. Go to bed.

How boring it all was.

Which it was meant to be. Evidently the Puddling governors believed that a strict routine was the key to recovery. No excesses of any kind. Which suited Nicola, as she was not an excessive sort of person.

Although the cottage had a small generator—and all sorts of modern conveniences, for it was the newest and most luxurious of the Guest residences, which wasn't really saying much—she was a little afraid of it. She preferred the golden glow of lamp oil instead of the harsh, erratic electric light. She extinguished the lamp on the desk and banked the fire. Her fur-lined cloak hung on a hook by the front door, and she slid her stockinged feet into her old shoes.

A brisk gust of wind almost knocked her down in the front garden. The koi she'd seen in the autumn were asleep under a skim of ice on their pond, and the bare branches were stark against the graying sky. Would she be here in the spring to see the garden awake? According to Mrs. Grace, most Guests were enrolled in the program for twenty-eight days. Nicola had been here over twice as long, and was no closer to a cure.

Would they let her stay indefinitely? She knew more cottages were being built for additional Guests, having passed the new construction on her walks. She didn't want to take up a valuable spot for someone who truly needed it.

She might be a lost cause. She wasn't sure the routine and all the kindness she'd been shown was helping her whatsoever.

Nicola closed the gate behind her and took the stone steps down to the cobbled lane. Adjusting her hood, she headed away from the heart of the village, toward the bottom of Honeywell Lane. The fitful gurgle of Puddling Stream was audible the closer she got, and frost-covered hills were before her. Sheep foraged for grass through the snow and bleated plaintively—country sights and sounds she didn't experience in busy Bath. It was all very comforting.

Until her foot hit a patch of ice and she slipped, tumbling ignominiously to her bottom.

The pain in her twisted ankle was excruciating, but even though her mouth was open, there was no noise.

Damn.

It was difficult to get purchase to raise herself. She must look comical, rolling about the street like an overfed seal, her gloves and knees sodden. Nicola didn't know whether to smile—since laughter was out of her reach—or cry at her predicament.

Her decision was halted by the rapid footfalls behind her. She turned to warn the runner to be careful, but of course, no words came out.

The gentleman was luckier than she had been. He remained upright and stood over her, a concerned look on his face.

His rather handsome face. Nicola felt herself go hot. No white moon face anymore, she'd wager. She was always betrayed by her blushes.

"Are you all right, miss?"

She nodded violently. A lie. Suddenly shy, she wanted him to go away and leave her alone to wallow in the slush.

"Let me help you up."

She shrugged and he pulled her up by both hands. The weight on her ankle was too much, and she buckled before the man caught her.

"You're *not* all right! Is it your ankle?"

Nicola nodded again.

"Cat got your tongue? Go ahead, be unladylike and scream. I won't mind a bit. And lean on me. I promise I won't hurt you."

Oh, it wasn't that she was afraid of him. It was always so mortifying to have to explain her condition to strangers. She had a little card in her pocket for just such occasions.

But if he was a normal resident of Puddling, he should know all about her, shouldn't he? The entire village was a sort of lovely, lush hospital, and everyone knew everything. There were explicit dossiers on each Guest. Nicola had been permitted to read her own and invited to embellish it with any suggestions she thought might be useful to her improvement.

"I'll help you home." There was no arguing with that statement; she needed the help.

"Where do you live?"

Nicola pointed the way back up Honeywell Lane.

"On this lane? Me, too. Which cottage is yours? I'm in Tulip. A ridiculous name, don't you think?"

Nicola covered her mouth with one damp glove and shook her head very slowly.

His dark eyes narrowed. "Ah. You cannot talk. You're not deaf, are you? Well, I suppose if you are, you won't be hearing me ask the question."

She couldn't help but smile.

"Oh, good. I can natter on, and you can't talk back. A silent woman. Every man's dream, I imagine. Not mine," he said hastily. "I respect women no end. I'm thinking of my late father, who used to lock himself in his study when my mother was on the warpath. Which was often. They fought like cats and dogs. I'm making a fool of myself telling you all the family secrets, aren't I? I'm Jack." He took her hand and shook it with almost excessive vigor.

"You're a Guest too, aren't you, come for the famous cure of whatever ails you?"

Oh, dear. Nicola nodded with reluctance. What was wrong with this fellow? He appeared prosperous, was very good-looking with his neatly trimmed dark beard and sympathetic brown eyes. Was he a drunkard? A womanizer? An opium addict? He was much too old to have had his bad-tempered mother send him here for youthful misbehavior.

Nicola knew some troubled souls signed themselves into the Puddling Rehabilitation Program for rest and relaxation. He might be one of them.

Something about her reserved expression must have given her worries away.

"Don't be concerned. I won't ravish you. That's not my problem at all," he said with a touch of grimness. "Here, let's go back up the hill. Can you walk, or do you want me to carry you?"

She made walking motions with her fingers, but after a wobbly step or two found herself swept up and firmly ensconced in the man's arms.

"No wriggling or writhing, and certainly no punching. When we get to your cottage, I'll drop you onto something soft and comfortable and fetch the old doctor. What's his name? Oakley? I only got here yesterday. I'm not even sure why I came, to tell you the truth. Another one of my hare-brained ideas. Tap my shoulder when we get to your house, all right?"

All Nicola could do was nod. The man was a force of nature.

Maggie Robinson is a former teacher, library clerk, and mother of four who woke up in the middle of the night, absolutely compelled to create the perfect man and use as many adjectives and adverbs as possible doing so. A transplanted New Yorker, she lives with her not-quite-perfect husband in Maine. Her books have been translated into nine languages. Visit her on the web at maggierobinson.net.

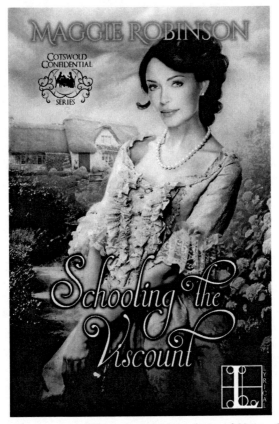

After a harrowing tour of duty abroad, Captain Lord Henry Challoner
fought to keep his memories at bay with two of his preferred vices:
liquor and ladies. But the gin did more harm than good—as did Henry's
romantic entanglements, since he was supposed to be finding a suitable
bride. Next stop: the tiny village of Gloucestershire, where Henry can
finally sober up without distraction or temptation. Or so he thinks...

A simple country schoolteacher, Rachel Everett was never meant
to cross paths with a gentleman such as Henry. What could such a
worldly man ever see in her? As it turns out, everything. Beautiful,
fiercely intelligent Rachel is Henry's dream woman—and wife.
Such a match would be scandalous for his family of course, and
Rachel has no business meddling with a resident at the famed, rather
draconian, Puddling Rehabilitation Foundation. All the better, for
two lost souls with nothing to lose—and oh so very much to gain.

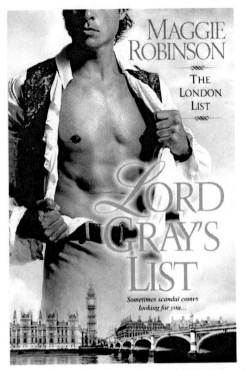

From duchesses to chambermaids, everybody's reading it. Each Tuesday, *The London List* appears, filled with gossip and scandal, offering job postings and matches for the lovelorn—and most enticing of all, telling the tales and selling the wares a more modest publication wouldn't touch...

The creation of Evangeline Ramsey, The London List saved her and her ailing father from destitution. But the paper has given Evie more than financial relief. As its publisher, she lives as a man, dressed in masculine garb, free to pursue and report whatever she likes—especially the latest disgraces besmirching Lord Benton Gray. It's only fair that she hang his dirty laundry, given that it was his youthful ardor that put her off marriage for good...

Lord Gray—Ben—isn't about to stand by while all of London laughs at his peccadilloes week after week. But once he discovers that the publisher is none other than pretty Evie Ramsey with her curls lopped short, his worries turn to desires—and not a one of them fit to print...

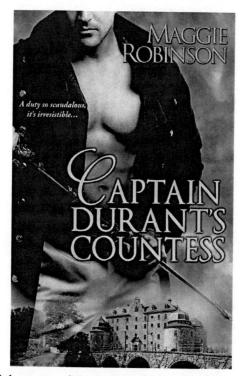

Tucked amid the pages of The London List, *a newspaper that touts the city's scandals, is a vaguely-worded ad for an intriguing job—one that requires a most wickedly uncommon candidate...*

Maris has always been grateful that her marriage to the aging Earl of Kelby saved her from spinsterhood. Though their union has been more peaceful than passionate, she and the earl have spent ten happy years together. But his health is quickly failing, and unless Maris produces an heir, Kelby's conniving nephew will inherit his estate. And if the earl can't get the job done himself, he'll find another man who can...

Captain Reynold Durant is known for both his loyalty to the Crown and an infamous record of ribaldry. Yet despite a financial worry of his own, even he is reluctant to accept Kelby's lascivious assignment—until he meets the beautiful, beguiling Maris. Incited by duty and desire, the captain may be just the man they are looking for. But while he skillfully takes Maris to the heights of ecstasy she has longed for, she teaches him something even more valuable and unexpected...

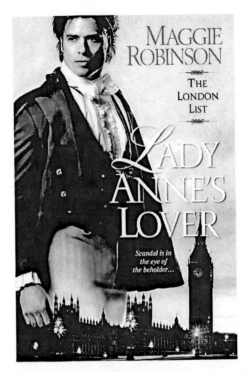

Lady Imaculata Anne Egremont has appeared in the scandalous pages of the London List often enough. The reading public is so bored with her nonsense, she couldn't make news now unless she took a vow of chastity. But behind her naughty hijinks is a terrible fear. It's time the List helped her. With a quick scan through its job postings and a few whacks at her ridiculous name, she's off to keep house for a bachelor veteran as plain Anne Mont.

Major Gareth Ripton-Jones is dangerously young and handsome on the face of it, but after losing his love and his arm in short order, he is also too deep in his cups to notice that his suspiciously young housekeeper is suspiciously terrible at keeping house. Until, that is, her sharp tongue and her burnt coffee penetrate even his misery—and the charm underneath surprises them both. Trust the worst cook in Wales to propose a most unexpected solution to his troubles. . .

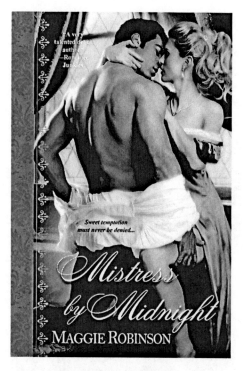

*A very talented
debut author*
—Romance
Junkies

*Sweet temptation
must never be denied...*

*Mistress
by Midnight*

MAGGIE ROBINSON

First comes seduction...

As children, Desmond Ryland, Marquess of Conover, and Laurette Vincent were inseparable. As young adults, their friendship blossomed into love. But then fate intervened, sending them down different paths. Years later, Con still can't forget his beautiful Laurette. Now he's determined to make her his forever. There's just one problem. Laurette keeps refusing his marriage proposals. Throwing honor to the wind, Con decides that the only way Laurette will wed him is if he thoroughly seduces her...

Then comes marriage...

Laurette's pulse still quickens every time she thinks of Con and the scorching passion they once shared. She aches to taste the pleasure Con offers her. But she knows she can't. For so much has happened since they were last lovers. But how long can she resist the consuming desire that demands to be obeyed...?

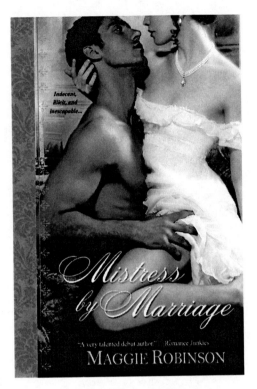

Too late for cold feet...

Baron Edward Christie prided himself on his reputation for even temper-
ament and reserve. That was before he met Caroline Parker. Wedding a
scandalous beauty by special license days after they met did not inspire
respect for his sangfroid. Moving her to a notorious lovebirds' nest
as punishment for her flighty nature was perhaps also a blow. And of
course talk has gotten out of his irresistible clandestine visits. Christie
must put his wife aside—if only he can get her out of his blood first.

Too hot to refuse...

Caroline Parker was prepared to hear the worst: that her husband had
determined to divorce her, spare them both the torture of passion they
can neither tame nor escape. But his plan is wickeder than any she's ever
heard. Life as his wife is suffocating. But she cannot resist becoming her
own husband's mistress...

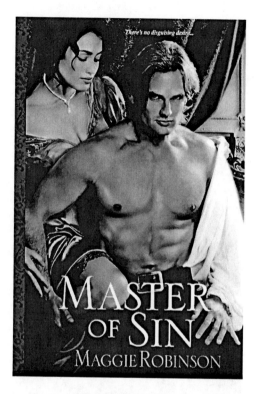

There's no disguising desire...

MASTER OF SIN
MAGGIE ROBINSON

Flying from sin...

Andrew Rossiter has used his gorgeous body and angelic face for all
they're worth—shocking the proper, seducing the willing, and plea-
suring the wealthy. But with a tiny son depending on him for rescue,
suddenly discretion is far more important than desire. He'll have to bury
his past and quench his desires—fast. And he'll have to find somewhere
his deliciously filthy reputation hasn't yet reached...

...into seduction

Miss Gemma Peartree seems like a plain, virginal governess. True, she
has a sharp wit and a sharper tongue, but handsome Mr. Ross wouldn't
notice Gemma herself. Or so she hopes. No matter how many sparks fly
between them, she has too much to hide to catch his eye. But with the
storms of a Scottish winter driving them together, it will be hard enough
to keep her secrets. Keeping her hands to herself might prove entirely
impossible...

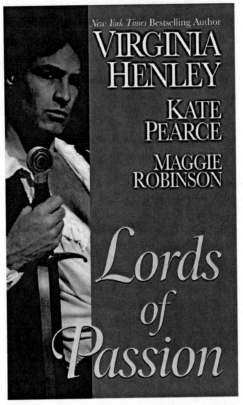

New York Times Bestselling Author
VIRGINIA HENLEY
KATE PEARCE
MAGGIE ROBINSON

Lords of Passion

"Beauty and the Brute" by Virginia Henley

It's been three years since Lady Sarah Caversham set eyes on arrogant Charles Lennox—the husband her father chose for her to settle a gambling debt. Now Charles has returned, unaware that the innocent ingénue he wed is determined to turn their marriage of convenience into a passionate affair...

"How to Seduce a Wife" by Kate Pearce

Louisa March's new husband, Nicholas, is a perfect gentleman in bed—much to her disappointment. She longs for the kind of fevered passion found in romance novels. But when she dares him to seduce her properly, she discovers Nicholas is more than ready to meet her challenge...

"Not Quite a Courtesan" by Maggie Robinson

Sensible bluestocking Prudence Thorn has been too busy keeping her cousin Sophy out of trouble to experience any adventures of her own. But when Sophy begs Prudence's help in saving her marriage, Pru encounters handsome, worldly Darius Shaw. Under Darius's skilled tutelage, Pru learns just how delightful a little scandal can be...

CPSIA information can be obtained
at www.ICGtesting.com
Printed in the USA
LVOW08s1440130617
537962LV00001B/191/P